TWO-HEARTED CROSSING

Also by Toni Morgan

Patrimony
Echoes from a Falling Bridge
Harvest the Wind
Lotus Blossom Unfurling
Queenie's Place

TWO-HEARTED CROSSING

A Novel By

TONI MORGAN

Adelaide Books
New York/ Lisbon

2017

Two-Hearted Crossing
A Novel
By Toni Morgan

Copyright © 2017 By Toni Morgan

Published by Adelaide Books, New York / Lisbon
An imprint of the Istina Group DBA
adelaidebooks.org

Editor-in-Chief
Stevan V. Nikolic

For any information, please address Adelaide Books
at info@adelaidebooks.org

ISBN13: 978-0-9995164-8-5
ISBN10: 0-9995164-8-5

Printed in the United States of America

For my sons, Mike, Rob and Charlie.

Contents

PART ONE
Into This Good Night

Fall 2000

PART ONE

Into This Good Night

Let not mercy and truth forsake thee;
bend them about thy neck;
write them upon the table of thine heart.

From
The Book of Proverbs

Fall 1999

Chapter One
KEN

After a fitful sleep, Ken was relieved to see dawn shredding the last vestiges of night. Outside his bedroom window, a thick glaze of frost covered the ground. He pulled on the clothes he'd worn the day before and shoved his bare feet into an old pair of leather boots. A board creaked as he tiptoed past his mother's door. He stopped to listen, hoping he hadn't awakened her. The hum of the refrigerator came from the kitchen. No other sound. A moment later, he grabbed his windbreaker and stepped onto the porch.

His eyes swept across the fenced-in meadow separating the house from the highway. Every spring his father had traded venison or elk meat for a calf, which they'd fed up there. Marie always tried to make pets of them, no matter how many times he warned her not to, and every fall she cried when he and their father loaded the fattened animal into the back of the truck and drove off with it, heading for the butcher.

On the north side of the house, aluminum pie pans swung on dirty, wet string. A scarecrow, its tattered remains anyway, lay propped against a broken bale of straw. Ken chuckled softly. Both were evidence of the war his mother waged each summer, trying to keep the deer, rabbits, and birds from her garden.

Hands stuffed in his pockets, he walked out to lean against the fence. A trail of dark footprints followed him. Across the valley, wedged beneath a cloud-packed sky, white -crested mountains soared, their flanks blue-black with timber.

He sniffed the air. It would snow soon.

"Ken?" His mother stood in the doorway, wrapped in a faded chenille bathrobe. Her arms were crossed against the cold and she held a steaming cup in her hand. "Coffee's ready."

Later Ken went out to start the truck, careful to avoid getting dirt on the shoes he'd polished to a glossy sheen the night before. He started the engine and let it warm up a few minutes before going back in the house for his mother.

"You look handsome in your Marine uniform," she said as he drove down the lane. At the end of the lane he turned onto the highway.

"Thanks."

After their argument the night before, they were still being cautious with one another.

When they reached the church, Marie and Paul waited in the vestibule. Marie held the baby. It was hard for Ken to think of his little sister as a mother. At eighteen, her face still carried the soft contours of her own childhood. Paul, beside her, stood awkward and silent. His big hands stuck out of the cuffs of his white dress-shirt, so new the creases from when it had been in the store wrapper were visible.

Ken hugged Marie and shook hands with Paul. Marie's eyes and nose were red, but she pulled back the edge of the blanket to show off her son. It was the first time Ken had seen the baby and he wasn't sure what he should say. Paul tugged at his collar, lifting and extending his chin.

Ken glanced around, surprised at the number of people. They'd never been much for attending church—from something his father had once said, he knew the old man had been brought up Catholic, though to his knowledge his father had never attended the Catholic church in town. His mother had taken him and Marie to the local Methodist church a few times, but that had stopped years before. And they'd never participated much in town events—the Fourth of July rodeo was about it.

His mother had grown up in Platt City, though. Her parents had owned the local grocery store. And he and Marie had gone to school there, so he guessed some knew his father well enough they wanted to pay their respects.

He wondered what his father would have thought about being buried Protestant, if it would have mattered to him. At sixty-three had his old man thought he had plenty of time to make his peace with the priests? Maybe he'd made whatever peace he needed to while lying on the ground next to the woodpile, his face crumpled and twisted, or in the ambulance, its siren sounding and lights flashing while the medics worked on him.

The baby stirred and Marie hushed him by stroking his back and whispering to him. Between them, Ken's mother sat with her chin up, gazing at the minister. No tears flowed, but her hands were gripped together in her lap and she twisted her wedding ring around and around her finger.

Ken fought the urge to reach over and take one of her hands, hold it, but he was afraid if he did she would crack, as though the self-control holding her rigid and upright would disintegrate at the touch of another human.

He tried to listen to what the minister was saying, but couldn't stay focused; how could the man say anything relevant about someone he'd probably never met? If he had met his father, maybe he could explain all the dead-end jobs his father had held or jobs he'd quit or walked away from—just so he could go hunting or fishing or whatever the hell he did up there in the mountains.

Across the aisle, Ian McCort, dressed in the uniform that identified him as head forest ranger for the region, fingered the cord on the hat resting on his knee, his eyes closed as though he was remembering something. A woman sat between McCort and Bill Tate, the sheriff. Ken figured she was Tate's wife. McCort's wife had divorced him years before. Or he'd divorced her, since she'd been the one doing the cheating. It had made a stink in the area because McCort was well-known and well-liked, but after she moved away the talk eventually died.

In the pew behind McCort was a Native American woman Ken supposed was from the reservation—though she didn't really look Nez Perce. He couldn't tell her age—maybe forty-five or fifty. Her eyes were red, like she'd been crying. *Who the heck is she and what is she doing at my old man's funeral?* He looked for her when the services were over, but didn't see her.

He held his mother's elbow as they stepped outside the church into the blustery wind. A neighbor, Ben Hartley, came up to them, his mane of thick gray hair blowing around his weather-etched face. Holding his hat in his left hand—the tips of his middle and index fingers missing, the result of a long-ago ranch accident—he extended his right. "If there's anything I can do for you, missus, you tell me. I liked your man."

His mother gave a weak smile. "Thank you." Her softly spoken words were whipped away in a gust of wind that rattled the bare branches of a nearby cottonwood tree.

It was too cold to stand and chat; as soon as the brief ceremony in the cemetery was over, people fled to their waiting cars and trucks. The family, including Paul's father, caravanned back to the house for the meal Ken's mother had prepared the night before. When they reached the house, they found a ham and several covered dishes on the porch.

His mother picked up the ham. "People have been doing this for days. You'll have to take some home with you, Marie. You, too, Frank," she said to Paul's father. "Otherwise it will go to waste."

During the meal Marie kept looking at their father's chair and crying. Paul tried to comfort her, but she wouldn't be. The baby woke up crying, too, until Ken's mother picked him up and held him on her lap. Paul's father tried to keep a conversation going, but eventually gave up when he got no help.

Like the rest of them, Ken pushed his food around on his plate and thought his own thoughts—mainly about how his mother was going to cope. The place always needed something done: firewood chopped; the garden plowed every spring; there was a porch rail that came loose each summer when the wood dried out. He thought about her sitting alone in the evenings, lonely and brooding. His enlistment would be up in a year-and-a-half. He'd planned to re-enlist, to make the Marine Corps a career, but if she wouldn't leave this house he'd have to get out. He'd have to come home and take care of her.

"I don't know why you won't sell," he blurted out, surprising himself, but unable to contain his thoughts.

"We've already talked about this, Ken." His mother's voice was even, though her eyes held a warning gleam.

"He's right, Mom."

Ken had talked to Marie on the phone the night before, a long, whispered conversation after their mother had gone to bed. They'd agreed one-hundred percent their mother should sell.

Marie gripped her mother's hand. "This house is too big for one person. You should sell it and move into town near Paul and me."

"Or use the money to travel." Travel is what Ken would do. Who'd hang around Platt City when there was a chance to get out and see the world? She wasn't even old yet.

"I've told you, both of you, this is my home. I'm not leaving."

By the set of his mother's jaw, Ken knew it was no use talking sense to her, at least not now. Just because his father had built it, she acted as though it was the Taj Mahal or something. It was a house, for Christ's sake, not a fucking monument. Why couldn't she figure that out?

Paul's father pushed back from the table. "I guess it's time for me to head on home." Head cocked to one side, he looked at his son and daughter-in-law.

Marie answered his unspoken question. "We'll stay a little longer."

"Now don't you be worrying about the dishes," Ken's mother said. "I can take care of them in no time."

Marie picked up her dish and silverware. "No, Mom. You go relax; play with your grandson. Paul and Ken will help me."

Later, when Marie, Paul and the baby had gone home and his mother, looking drained, said she was going to bed, Ken took the truck keys from their hook by the door.

The truck's headlights poked down the lane, dipping and bouncing through the ruts. The lights on the dashboard glowed faintly. He cranked up the heater and turned on the defroster. As soon as he pulled onto the highway, the headlights steadied and the engine hummed; his father had always taken good care of machinery. Ken would give him credit for that, anyway.

The sign to the logging road whizzed by and soon he was passing the airport. He made out the shapes of several small private planes parked at the side, those that weren't in hangers, then the bulky shape of the Marrick-Pacific building. A couple of CH-46 helicopters rigged for logging were on the pad next to the building. A security light shone above the door.

The airport was closed to flights after sunset. When he'd been a kid, calling it an airport would have been a real stretch—back then it was just a landing strip and a couple of Quonset huts. There'd been no helicopters, no sleek private jets. Once, before he and Marie were born, Platt City had been a place where ranchers and loggers came for supplies, or people from Boise stopped for gas on their way to Lewiston or Coeur d'Alene. Now, it was a full-fledged resort with boating on the lake in the summer, skiing and snowmobiling in the winter. Big, fancy houses dotted the landscape. Land values were soaring because of rich easterners and Californians buying up whatever became available. He knew his mother could get a good price for her property, small as it was, if she'd just put it on the market.

It wasn't only the town that kept growing. Frank Klein, Paul's father, had said the logging mill was still going strong because of all the new home starts around the country. Ken guessed that if he didn't re-enlist he could always get a job there. Or drive a logging truck—his dad had done that sometimes, though never for long.

He slowed down to thirty-five when he came into town, even though the streets were all but deserted. A few cars in the parking lot in front of the grocery store and a few more outside Rose's Tavern were about it. He found a spot and parked the truck.

The nicer stores, the stores catering to the tourists, were at the other end of Main Street. This part of town, between Third and Sixth, held the old businesses—the barbershop, the dry cleaner, the shoe repair shop, a second-hand clothing store. And Rose's.

It was warm inside the smoke-filled bar, a sharp contrast to the raw weather outside, where Ken's summer-weight uniform had given him little protection. He stopped just inside the door, rubbing his hands together and blowing on them as he looked around. Four people sat smoking and talking in one of the booths. A couple of guys a few years older than him were shooting pool. He recognized them— they'd been seniors and on the high school football team when he'd been a freshman and too small to even think of trying out. A woman stood alone at the bar, talking to the bartender in a low voice.

Ken walked over and asked the bartender what he had on tap.

The bartender looked him over. "Coors, Henry's, or Miller's."

"Give me a Henry's."

The woman stubbed out her cigarette and gave Ken a brief, curious glance before she picked up her drink and ambled across the room to the pool table. She was maybe thirty, thirty-five Ken guessed, and polished to a hard finish. Even he could see her clothes and hair were expensive. What was she doing in Rose's, slumming?

The bartender set the beer in front of him. "First one's on the house, Marine."

"Thanks." Ken picked up the mug and downed a quarter of it.

"Cigarette?" The bartender held out a crumpled pack.

Ken shook his head.

"Don't smoke, huh? Wish I could quit." The bartender pulled himself a glass of beer. "So, you're in the Corps. You wasn't in 'Nam—prob'ly not even a gleam in your old man's eye back then. I drove trucks there, mostly around DaNang. Heard of it? No? You haven't missed much. What a shit-hole. So, you home on leave or what?"

"My father died. I'm home for his funeral."

The bartender mumbled condolences.

Ken stared into his beer. *My father died.* That sounded wrong, like he'd meant to say one thing and something entirely different came out of his mouth. He fingered a bit of foam running down the side of the mug, wondering once again what had made his old man tick. Ken couldn't begin to count the dead-end jobs his father had held or jobs he'd quit or walked away from—just so he could go hunting or fishing. No matter how many times his father took off, leaving his mother to struggle with the bills and everything else around the place, no one was ever supposed to say a bad word about him.

The clinking sound of balls careening off one another and the low mumble of voices fell away. Suddenly Ken was five years old again, standing on the porch next to his mother as the old green pickup truck his father drove swerved around the worst of the ruts as it headed down the lane. His mother held herself so still she didn't seem to be breathing.

The truck appeared to hesitate. Then, in a swirl of dust, it turned right, toward the mountains. Instead of going to work, his father was going hunting. Even at five, Ken understood this was not what fathers were meant to do. They were supposed to go to work and take care of their families.

His mother's shoulders sagged before she turned and stepped back into the kitchen. Ken followed her inside and watched as she crossed to the sink and filled it with soapy water. Marie sat in her highchair, carefully examining each tiny circle of cereal before pushing it into her mouth. When the sink was full his mother began washing the breakfast dishes piled on the counter. She finished a bowl, rinsed it, and put it in the rack to dry. As she reached for another, she scrubbed at her eyes with the back of her wrist. Suddenly she dropped the second bowl, splashing water down the front of her dress. She put her face in both of her hands. Her shoulders shook.

Ken went to her and leaned his forehead against the back of her legs. "It's okay, Mommy. Marie and me will be good."

His mother turned and gathered him close, resting her check against the top of his head. "I know you will, honey. You're the man of this house when Daddy's away."

The image of his weeping mother had remained firmly planted in Ken's memory. As he moved from childhood to teenager, his resentment toward his father grew, creating a wide gulf between them—a gulf frequently charged with bitter words and accusations.

Their final fight had come without warning, moving in as quickly as the lightning-filled summer storms that arrived every August, bringing with them the forest fires his mother dreaded.

They always ate dinner early on Sundays. His father finished and pushed his plate aside. "I'm going fishing tomorrow, up on Elk River." He reached for his coffee. "I don't know how long I'll be gone."

Anger, sudden and full-blown, flooded Ken. "You can't go fishing. What about your job? You don't have any vacation time coming yet. You're just taking off again, aren't you?" His face was rigid with the effort it took to keep from shouting.

His father took a sip of coffee. "Don't worry about it."

His father's implacable calm enraged Ken even more. "Somebody around here has to, because you sure as hell don't. You're never around when we need you. There's never enough money, either. Mom is always having to do without things, worrying about bills, how to get enough food even."

The last part wasn't true, they always had plenty to eat, but by then Ken didn't care.

His father shoved his cup aside. A muscle twitched in his cheek. "You leave your mother out of this."

Ken's chin jutted forward. "I won't leave her out."

Marie remained silent. Her eyes, large and shocked, moved from their father to Ken.

His mother's face drained of color. "Ken, please...please don't do this."

Tears stung Ken's eyes, making him even angrier that his father would see his weakness. He clenched his hands to keep them from trembling and ignored his mother's effort to keep the peace; this had been building for too long.

He drew a deep breath. "She won't tell you how many nights, while you're off playing mountain-man, or whatever it is you do up there, I hear her crying. She won't tell you how people look down their noses at us. The kids at school laugh at Marie's clothes. They laugh at her, for God's sake. Mom won't tell you the truth about any of it. But I will. I don't know why you don't just do us all a favor and stay up there in your goddam mountains. You love them so much, why don't you just stay up there?"

His mother's hand flew to her mouth. "Ken!"

Ken jumped up, knocking the chair over in his haste, and bolted out of the house, his father's shout left hanging in the air behind him. He tore off through the woods behind the house and didn't stop running until, panting and sweat-soaked, he reached the river. Leaning forward, he braced himself with his hands on his knees as he fought to catch his breath.

The riverbank's smooth stones were still warm from the late afternoon sun. When his heart finally slowed and his breathing evened out, he sat and stared over the water, noting a flicker of silver where a trout fed.

He heard the pickup's engine long before it turned off the logging road onto the track leading down to the river. He didn't turn to look as the truck crunched to a halt behind him. Instead, he kept his gaze forward, fixed on the river. The truck door slammed and footsteps sounded in the gravel. He tensed as his father paused and then eased down beside him.

His father was the first to break the silence.

"You surprised me, Ken. I guess saying I'm sorry I haven't been the provider your mother deserves isn't going to change things much. Won't really change things between you and me."

Ken worked to swallow the tension in his throat. "I've got to get out of here. I'm eighteen. I'll be graduating in a couple of months. I'm going to join the Marine Corps."

For a long minute, his father studied him, like he was trying to see underneath Ken's words. "You're sure that's what you want to do? You're not just thinking you'll run off because you're angry?"

The pressure Ken had felt for so long, as well as the lump in his throat, eased a bit. "Yeah, I'm sure. I've been thinking about it a lot lately." Ever since the recruiter had come to school. He needed to get away, wanted to get away—wanted to test himself and prove he had what it took to be a man.

"I won't try to change your mind if you've already decided. I was hoping you'd set yourself on a different track, but each man needs to decide for himself what road he's going to follow. If the Marine Corps is yours, I'll respect it."

Ken nodded, as much to himself as to his father. "It's what I've decided."

The bartender's gravelly voice brought Ken back to the present. "Another beer?"

Ken looked down and discovered his mug was empty. "Sure. Why not?"

It was close to three a.m. before he turned off the headlights and drove slowly down the lane. He stumbled over the rug in front of the kitchen door. "Shh," he whispered to no one and reached down to pull off his left shoe and then his right, nearly tipping himself onto the floor in the process.

When he got to his room, he fell back on the bed and was asleep in seconds, the woman's perfume still clinging to him. He barely resurfaced when the door opened and his mother came in. He felt the weight of the quilt being spread across him, then heard her retreating footsteps and the sound of his door closing, then nothing.

Winter 2000

Chapter Two
MARIE

It was still dark when Marie got up to feed the baby. When he'd gotten his fill and she was able to put him down, it was time to fix Paul's breakfast.

"Paul….Cereal and toast, or bacon and eggs?"

"Cereal."

Water ran in the bathroom. She pictured him standing in front of the mirror, shaving, a towel wrapped around his thin waist. During the first months of their marriage, when she couldn't bear to be separated from him even for a minute, she'd sat on the edge of the tub every morning, watching him pull the razor through the lather on his cheeks. He didn't use an electric razor. He shaved the old-fashioned way, like her father.

"Why don't I fix bacon and eggs? I'll make extra bacon and pack you a bacon, onion and peanut butter sandwich for lunch." His lunchtime favorite had astonished her the first time he told her about it. Out of curiosity she'd tried one herself, but couldn't get past the first bite. It wasn't that it was disgusting—it even smelled kind of good—it was just so foreign to her. Like Japanese or Greek food, she supposed it was something you had to acquire a taste for. Hearing no response from the bathroom, she pulled the frying pan out of the oven, the only place to store it in their miniscule kitchen.

Paul walked out of the bathroom, pulling on his shirt with the company logo embroidered on the left, over his heart. They lived in a garage apartment with one bedroom and what their landlord called a great room, which was just a fancy name for a room that served every other purpose—living room, dining room and kitchen—none well. The kitchen portion was an all-in-one unit: refrigerator, sink, and stove with a cupboard hanging on the wall above it.

Paul carried his plate to the table in the corner of the room. He pushed aside the stack of junk mail and set his plate down on the table's brown Formica top. Marie was sure the table, like the apartment, was a relic of the seventies.

"So, what are you doing today?"

"The usual, I guess. Laundry. Shop for dinner. I wish the refrigerator was bigger and I didn't have to shop so often. Don't worry," she said as he looked up, a forkful of egg poised in mid-air. "I'm not complaining. I know we'll have a bigger house some day with a bigger refrigerator." She smiled her assurance of their rosy future. "And I'm going to write a letter to Ken. Did you need me to do something?"

She felt a little guilty sending him off to work every day while she got to stay home with the baby. But what kind of work could she do? And who would watch Henry Reed? Not her mother—she thought her mother would probably be willing, but they'd need to buy a second vehicle, then it would cost so much money in gas taking him back and forth, not to mention time, there'd be little benefit. On the other hand, it might give her mother something to do, something to look forward to every day.

Paul crossed to the sink with his plate and rinsed it. He walked back to Marie. "I don't need anything." He leaned down and kissed her. "Time to go. I'll see you this evening."

"Love you. Don't forget your lunch."

January 23, 2000
Platt City

Dear Ken,

Paul has left for work and my little lamb is still asleep, so I thought this would be a good time to write you. You didn't tell me how you like his name. I'm sure glad Dad got to see his namesake and to hold him. I'll never forget the look on his face the first time I put Henry Reed into his arms. It's so hard to believe Dad's gone and we won't ever see him again. I know he used to go away a lot when we were growing up, but I always knew he'd be back in a week or two. Not anymore.

I went out to see Mom yesterday. She's doing okay, I guess. I wish our place was big enough for her to live with us, but it's not, and she wouldn't come anyway. But I worry about her living alone, especially when we get a heavy snowstorm. What if she needs something or there's an emergency and the phone lines are out? I tried to talk to her about it, but she just said not to worry so much. Also, what is she going to live on? I doubt they saved much. With the kind of jobs Dad held, who knows how much he paid into Social Security. Probably not much, so I doubt she can count on a lot from them. Actually, I don't know how they figure it—if it's based on how much you pay into it or what. But it's worth a try. I'm going with her to the Social Security office next week. She didn't want to go, but I insisted. We were going to go this week, but she begged off. I'm not sure what her deal is. But like I told her, even though it may not be much, it's bound to help. I'll let you know what we find out.

How is life in the Marine Corps since you got back? I didn't get the chance to talk to you about it when you were here. Do you like Southern California? I suppose you go swimming in the ocean a lot. That must be fun—unless you worry about sharks. Do you?

Are you going to re-enlist when your time is up? I think Paul envies you. Sometimes I think he wishes he weren't married and a father. When we were in high school, he always planned on being an engineer, maybe move to Seattle after college and work for Boeing. I guess working in a lumberyard in Platt City isn't exactly what he expected for himself. Well, me either, for that matter—you know I always planned to become a kindergarten teacher. But how could either of us wish away our precious little Henry Reed?

Did you see that woman at the funeral—the Native American one? Do you know who she is? I asked Mom about her, but she said she had no idea. I haven't seen her since that day. It seems kind of weird that she would have come to the funeral and then not talked to anybody, don't you think?

Well, my son will soon be awake and demanding my attention, so I'll close now. Take care of yourself and write soon.

Love, Marie

She read the letter over, pausing at the reference to their father. It was so hard to think he would never be back—to realize he hadn't just gone fishing or hunting. At first, she'd cried all the time—to the point Paul had thrown up his hands, no longer even trying to make her feel better. She'd begun to think she might be going crazy or maybe having a delayed case of postpartum depression.

Her mother finally told her she would be sorry if she didn't get a hold on her emotions. "You're not doing the baby any good like this. Nor your marriage, either."

Marie shook her head. "But I can't help it."

Her mother had gripped Marie's shoulders and stared into her watering eyes. "Yes, you can help it if you try. And you know how much your father would hate to see you like this."

On the way home from her mother's house, Marie had considered those words. Her mother was right about one thing—her father had hated it when Marie moped. She was probably right about the other part, too, about needing to consider Henry Reed and Paul. More tears had welled up at the thought of the husband and baby she'd been neglecting. She'd sniffed and wiped the tears away with the back of her hand. She would try.

For the next month, whenever she'd begun to feel sad, she forced herself to think of the happy times she'd spent with her father, like going out to hunt for mushrooms or simply going for a walk in the woods—there wasn't a tree, bush, or bird he couldn't identify or tell a story about. She concentrated on how much she had to be thankful for—her son and husband, their good health. She willed the unhappy feelings to pass. Over time, just as her mother had predicted, things did get better.

She sighed and finished reading the letter, folded it, and put it in an envelope then went to get Henry Reed from his crib.

The air was clear and cold, the stars just beginning to fade in the early morning sky, when Marie stopped to pick up her mother, who was ready, but still protesting. "I don't know why we're doing this—I don't expect anything," she said when she squeezed into the truck next to Henry Reed's car seat and closed the door. Henry Reed reached for his grandmother's purse.

"But you don't know, Mom," said Marie, shifting into gear.

"It's such a long way—almost to Lewiston. I think it's going to be a giant waste of time."

Marie tried to make light of her mother's complaints. "We have nothing else to do today."

Her mother frowned.

It was obvious there was more to this than her mother was letting on. Marie stopped before turning onto the highway and gave her mother a long, puzzled look. Her mother's strawberry-blonde hair and the blue eyes of her Danish ancestors had dimmed a little in the last few years. A touch of gray had appeared at her temples, and though her eyes were still the color of a deep lake in summer, they looked tired. Lines were etched below them. "Mom...what is it you're afraid of?"

Her mother frowned and shook her head. "Nothing. I just don't like other people knowing our business. I don't want some government person thinking badly of your father because he didn't make a lot of money."

Marie's shoulders relaxed. "Oh, Mom. For heaven's sake. It's their job to help people." She reached across Henry Reed and patted her mother's hand, still gripped on the handles of her purse. "That's what they get paid for—not to judge folks."

"I don't care. I still don't like it."

The roads were nasty; they'd been plowed and sanded, but remained icy and dangerous in spots. Much of the time Marie kept the truck in four-wheel drive. After her initial protest, her mother said little. Marie didn't know if she was still upset about where they were going or if her driving was making her mother nervous.

The wait, when they finally arrived at the Social Security office, seemed endless.

"It's a quarter after ten and our appointment was for nine-thirty," Marie told the woman at the receptionist counter.

Bouncing Henry Reed on her hip, she was tired from the drive and she felt a mess. Her clean blouse was wrinkled and pulled from the waistband of her slacks on one side. Her hair was coming down from the clips she'd fastened in it that morning.

"We had to leave home at six-thirty this morning to make it here on time, but we made it. I don't understand why we're being kept waiting so long." Henry Reed grabbed at a pen held to the high desk by a chain. Marie jiggled her keys to distract him.

"We have people out sick today," the receptionist told her, barely lifting her eyes from her computer screen. "I don't know how long it will be before your caseworker can see you. If you want, I can reschedule you for another day."

The tone of her voice made it plain the woman had made this offer many times in the past, and was indifferent to whatever Marie decided. ~

Marie shifted Henry Reed to her other arm. "We'll wait. We've already invested several hours." She went back and sat down beside her mother.

"What did she say?"

"She said we could reschedule for another day."

"I think she's right." Her mother started to gather their things. "We should come back another time."

"Oh, Mom. It would be the same thing on another day. Besides, we've waited this long…it would be silly to leave now."

Her mother settled back in her seat. "I was just thinking of Henry Reed. He's probably had enough."

"He'll be fine. I'll go out to the truck and get another bottle."

Fifteen minutes later Henry Reed was sucking on his bottle with total concentration. A woman stepped out from a door to the left of the receptionist.

"Ellen Morris?"

"Maris," said Marie and Ellen together.

"Maris," the woman repeated. "Come this way please."

Marie stood. "I'll come, too, if that's okay." Her mother flashed her a look Marie couldn't read. She hesitated.

"That's fine," the woman said. Marie followed without

waiting for her mother's approval. "I'm Cynthia Bell," the woman said, holding the door open for them. "Sorry to keep you waiting. One of the other caseworkers is out sick. I've been swamped."

There had been no one else in the waiting room, but Marie refrained from pointing that out as she followed the woman down the hall past several closed doors. At her side, her mother gripped the handles of her purse so tightly her knuckles were white. "Mom? Are you okay?"

"I'm fine." The words were clipped and stiff—not like her mother at all.

At the end of the hall, the woman ushered them into an office. In the center of the room was a gray metal desk with a tall chair behind it, the maroon upholstery on its arms beginning to fray. She pointed to the two chairs in front of her desk and invited them to have a seat. Sunlight poured in through a tall window.

"Should I close the blinds?"

Marie judged the woman to be in her mid-forties, although her hair was gray and she had a network of fine lines around her eyes and at the corners of her mouth. Marie thought the lines might be from spending time in the sun.

"We're fine," Marie said, adjusting the blanket around the baby so the sunlight wouldn't be on his face. Even though there wasn't much warmth to it, the sunlight was welcome after so many gray, cloudy days.

As she and her mother waited, Cynthia Bell shuffled a few papers in the stack on her desk. Finally, she looked at Ellen. "I'm sorry to hear of the death of your husband, Mrs.

Maris. Was it sudden or had he been ill for some time?"
Marie noticed the woman's hands were large, and her nails
were cut straight across. As she spoke she fingered a rubber
band around her wrist.

"It was very sudden." Her mother looked down and
fidgeted with her hands, twisting her ring before raising her
eyes to the woman's face. "He was almost never sick, and it
was over in just a few hours. I'm thankful for that, at least.
For him."

Cynthia Bell's eyes dropped. She nodded. "Too often
final illnesses drag out for months, even years, exhausting
any cash reserves. Very hard on family members, too. I'm
glad you were spared that." She took a pad of paper from
her desk drawer and picked up a pencil. "Now then," she
said, tipping her head toward Marie. "I believe your
daughter told me on the phone that your husband was born
in Canada."

"That's right." Defiance filled her mother's voice,
surprising Marie. "He was from eastern Canada. Quebec."

"Do you know if or where he applied for U.S. Citizenship?"

"No, I don't. Sorry." Her mother sounded so unhelp-
ful, Marie shot her a questioning look.

"I've been trying to locate his file on our system, but, I
can't come up with anything."

Marie frowned. "What do you mean?"

"I mean he doesn't appear to have been a U.S. citizen.
And I don't find that he was ever issued a Social Security
number."

Marie's frowned deepened. This made no sense. "He

lived in Idaho almost thirty years. How could he own property, work here, if he wasn't a citizen?

"Citizenship isn't required to have a Social Security number or work here, Mrs. Maris. Or to own property, for that matter." The woman addressed Marie's mother, ignoring the fact that it was Marie who'd asked the question. "But I'm not finding any documentation. I'd like to get a list of the places where he worked. They should have checked his identification. I need to know what number they used to pay Social Security taxes and his state and federal income taxes."

"Don't worry, Mom. We'll straighten this out. It's probably a computer glitch or something," Marie said when she saw the worried look on her mother's face.

Cynthia Bell looked up from her notes, frowned, but didn't contradict, although a few minutes later she gave them something new to worry about on the long drive back to Platt City. Marie hoped it wasn't on purpose.

"You might want to check the deed to your property when you get home, Mrs. Maris. Make sure your name is on it and the taxes have been paid."

Platt City
March 8, 2000

Dear Ken:

Mom said you have orders to engineers' school in North Carolina. When will you go there? Wow, from one ocean to another. You're sure getting to see the country. And she said you think you'll be going to the Mediterranean when you get out of school. Will you be going to the Middle East, too? Or is that the same thing? I don't trust that Saddam Hussein, even though we did beat him. He could start something again, so you take care of yourself.

I went to see Mom again this morning. It's the weirdest thing. Every time I see her, she's making bread. She says she's trying different recipes. I don't know what she plans to do with it. Her freezer is full of bread. She gave me six loaves! For making Paul's lunch, she said. I had to give most of it away— our freezer is miniscule. I don't know if it's a compulsion, or what. Do you think I should talk to a doctor? Paul says we should just let her find her own way for a while. He says I'm always trying to fix things that would fix themselves if I'd just leave them alone long enough.

Speaking of Paul, he got a promotion to assistant yard manager last week. We went out to The Cabin on the Corner to celebrate. It was the first time we've been out together, just the two of us, since Henry Reed was born. Our landlord watched him. She said he was good as gold, slept all the time we were gone. We didn't stay out late, though, because I was worried he might wake up and be frightened when I wasn't there. But we had such a nice time. It almost felt like a date. You know, it's so easy to get caught up in being a mother sometimes I forget I'm a wife, too. And I forget what a good person Paul is. I know he's kind of shy and awkward around the family and doesn't talk much, but he is so responsible. I'm afraid sometimes I take advantage of it.

The extra money he'll be getting with his promotion will sure come in handy. And wouldn't you know, the day after they told him about it, the muffler went out on the truck! At least now we'll have the money to pay for the repairs.

We've been having some very nice weather. I think spring may not be far off. Actually, we've had a pretty mild winter. I'm glad, seeing as how Mom is alone out there.

There's nothing new to report on the Social Security issue. Like I told you before, we did find the deed to the property. I'm still amazed it's in Mom's name only. We checked on the taxes and found out they'd been paid every year. I've contacted a few of the places where Dad worked, but that has been one dead-end after another. Either they've lost the records, don't keep records, or they've said it was so long ago they've thrown the records out. What it boils down to, I think, is that Mom won't get anything from Social Security.

And so far as I can find out, Dad was not a U.S. citizen, either. That just blows me away! I thought that Cynthia Bell person was crazy, but now I don't know. The weird thing is Mom won't talk about it. Every time I bring it up, she tells me to forget it. It's like she thinks I'm prying or something when I'm only trying to help. Well, I'm not going to forget it. I'm going to keep working on it. I'll keep you posted.

Write soon.

Love, Marie

P.S. You'll never guess who I saw yesterday—the strange woman from Dad's funeral. She was just coming out of Morrison's when I was going in. I thought for a minute she was going to stop and talk to me, but then a friend of mine came out of the store and said hello and the woman went on. I noticed, though, that she had a University of Idaho parking sticker on the bumper of her car. Next time I see her, I'm going to stop her and find out who she is. I can't figure out how Dad would have known her.

Marie talked with Paul about the web of innuendo and half-truths she kept running into when trying to find out about her father's Social Security number and tax information, but he didn't take her concerns seriously.

"I don't know why you're worrying about this, Marie," he said one night as they were getting ready for bed. "I mean the problem, as I see it, is to figure out how your mother is going to take care of herself, not what your dad was up to." He rolled up the jeans he'd just taken off and shot them like a basketball toward the laundry basket. "Bullseye," he said before walking into the bathroom.

Marie followed him and sat down on the closed toilet seat, watching as he turned the water on and squeezed toothpaste onto his brush.

"You told me yourself you didn't think there would be much to the Social Security thing with your dad's work history," Paul said around the toothbrush.

"I know that." She was frustrated Paul couldn't see what was bugging her—he wasn't usually so blind. "The thing is, I thought I knew my father."

Chapter Three

ELLEN

After the initial shock of Henry's death passed, a kind of numbness set in—Ellen thought she would die, too. She wanted to die. She looked down a tunnel of empty days, and grief filled her eyes and mouth, drowning her in a dark brown melancholy. She'd sit in the rocking chair Henry had favored, the ticking of the grandfather clock she'd inherited from her parents, loud in the silence of the room, keeping its own record of time.

For months, she sensed Henry's warm body, his broad shoulders nearby, heard his soft chuckle. At odd moments, she'd look up and expect to see him walk into the room. Or she would think of something she wanted to tell him and turn to where she imagined him to be, only to find the space empty.

His presence seemed to be imprinted into the house itself, even into the very air, to the point where his scent—that of the woods, the smoke of campfires and soap—lingered and she'd involuntarily sniff, her nostrils flaring, in an effort to capture his being once more.

At night, she lay in the bed, the smell of him embedded in the pillow next to hers, and stared into the void above her head. Each time she heard the distant sound of a truck, she'd hold her breath, her heart racing as it drew closer. And each time she'd let out her breath and force her body to relax as the truck passed her lane and the sound of its engine faded.

Sometimes she'd sleep—mostly in brief snatches. When she awoke, everything seemed normal and for a minute or two she was happy. Then reality would come crashing back. It got so that she resented those brief moments of happiness—the subsequent feelings of loss were even more overwhelming, like she'd been tossed into a quagmire of grief and hopelessness, unable to find solid footing. Some nights she didn't sleep at all.

Day or night, baking bread somehow soothed her. Maybe it was the routine of it, or maybe it was the kneading, combined with the earthy scent of the yeast, that calmed her, allowed the muscles in her shoulders and chest to loosen and relax, like the dough when she turned it onto the floured board. She supposed it didn't matter, so long as it worked.

On an overcast afternoon in March, four months after Henry's death, Ellen drove toward town. A powerful feeling came over her that Henry sat beside her, watching her, about to tell her something important. Her nostrils quivered at the thought of his scent, his warmth. She started to smile and turn to him, but then knew that if she looked, he wouldn't be there. She kept her eyes fixed on the road ahead and began to weep.

When she got to Platt City the tears still welled in her eyes and slid down her cheeks. She tried to staunch the flow with the sleeve of her jacket, but instead smeared mucous from her running nose across her cheeks and over her mouth and chin.

She turned off the highway and drove down the road to Marie's apartment. The tears wouldn't stop. Without slowing, she drove past the apartment, turned at the corner and drove the ten miles back home.

For several hours, she sat in Henry's rocking chair in the corner of the living room, her hands folded in her lap. The phone rang. She didn't move. A few minutes later, it rang again. Marie. She let it ring. When night fell, she went to bed. After a while, she drifted into a light sleep.

Henry swam away from shore. The water was still and calm. At first, she thought it must be Platt Lake on a summer morning. It wasn't. Willow trees were spread along the bank where she stood, and some reeds, but because of a rising mist she could make out nothing on the other side. The air was as still and calm as the water. The only sounds were Henry's arms dipping in and out. He swam farther and farther away from her. Finally, the mist swallowed him.

Then his voice whispered in her ear. "It's okay, Ellen. I made it across. You can rest now."

Ellen awoke to banging on the kitchen door. She wanted to sink back into the peaceful oblivion of sleep, but she knew it was Marie. "Just a minute," she called to her daughter as she struggled to sit up and throw the bedcovers aside.

As soon as the door opened, Marie rushed through, Henry Reed on her hip. "My God, Mom. What happened to you yesterday? I thought you were coming by so we could go shopping together." She clutched Ellen's arm with her free hand. "I called and called, but you didn't answer." Marie's eyes were both concerned and accusing. "I wanted to drive out last night, when Paul got home from work, but he said you would call if something was wrong."

"I'm sorry. Yesterday was a bad one. I went to bed early." Ellen didn't tell her daughter that she'd driven into town and she didn't tell her about the dream. "Paul's right, though. You're not to worry so much about me. I'm going to be all right. I slept well last night."

Marie peered at her. After a moment, her face softened. "You do look more rested." She pulled out a kitchen table chair and collapsed onto it. "I've been so worried about you, Mom, being out here alone and all. I wish you'd think again about selling this house and moving into town."

Henry Reed reached for a salt shaker on the table. Marie took a plastic bag from her purse and gave him a cracker. He grabbed it and aimed it for his mouth.

Ellen pretended she hadn't heard Marie's words. She sat in the chair next to her daughter and held out her arms to her grandson. He lunged toward her, almost breaking Marie's hold on him before Ellen could pull him onto her lap. She bounced him on her knee and he squealed with delight. "Isn't it funny how babies can be happy so long as they have someone to feed them and hug them, even when tragedy is all around?"

Marie hugged her mother, Henry Reed squeezed between them. "I'm so sorry Dad's gone and you're all alone now." Her voice, hoarse with emotion, broke. The baby squirmed and Marie sat back in her chair. She sniffed and rubbed her eyes with the back of her hand. "Mom, seriously, won't you just think about moving into town?"

Ellen used the corner of a napkin to wipe gooey crumbs from her grandson's check. "Your father built this house, started it the year after we met, after he bought the land from Mr. Hartley. He worked for Mr. Hartley when he first came here, you know." She glanced up to see Marie nod. "Did him some sort of special favor, and in return Mr. Hartley sold him the land cheap."

Marie got up and filled the dented coffeepot with water then scooped ground coffee into its metal basket. "I've heard about that, but never what Dad did for him." She put the pot on the burner. "I don't suppose this bit was all that useful to Mr. Harley."

Ellen gave her grandson another cracker from the bag on the table. "You're right. It's such a small parcel—by his standards anyway—not even thirty acres and most of it woods, so no good for grazing. Cut off from the rest of his ranch by the highway, too." Even though Marie would have heard the story a dozen times, for Ellen, telling it brought those years back, brought Henry back. "Whenever I wasn't in school or working in the store, I'd ride my bike out, sometimes with a picnic lunch in the basket on my handlebars. I'd spread a blanket on the ground, usually under that tall fir next to the fence by the lane—you know the one."

She paused, a smile playing across her lips, remembering how she'd felt seeing Henry on a ladder, the sunlight dappling his tanned, muscled shoulders as he pounded nails, building their home, their future. "I'd always include a big wedge of cake or pie Mom or I had baked. Henry had a sweet tooth. How about you, little one—will you have a sweet tooth like your grandpa?" She looked down at her grandson, but he'd fallen asleep, his thumb plugged into his mouth, the gooey remains of the cracker clutched in his fist. She smiled and stroked his cheek.

"He must be getting heavy, Mom. Let me put him on your bed."

"No, no. He's fine. He feels good here."

"Okay, if you're sure. Ready for coffee?"

"Please. Let me just shift him over a little. I don't want to spill any on him. Ahh, thanks." She closed her eyes, savoring the rich chicory flavor. "There's nothing to compare with that first sip of fresh coffee in the morning, is there?"

Marie chuckled. "You sound like a commercial." She filled a cup for herself and sat again. "So, what was it like then, Mom? Did you have any other neighbors beside Mr. Hartley?"

"The Weitzels and the Sterns, but no one else between here and town. The Sterns weren't very friendly—even then Mrs. Stern showed signs of mental illness. Marta Weitzel is twenty years older than me, which made her seem ancient, but I'd often visit her and she taught me a lot." Ellen leaned back in her chair, remembering the girlish confidences and the laughter she had shared with the older woman, now reduced to living in 'seniors only' apartment in town. "She's alone now her husband's gone. They had no children, you know."

"She always had something nice to say whenever I saw her."

Ellen nodded. "She was very good to me. I didn't know much about being a wife or living in the country. And in the beginning, this house wasn't much." The baby stretched and opened one eye then closed it and went back to sleep. "The kitchen and front room were all one at first, but Henry built two bedrooms right away. He said no child of his was going to sleep on a cot in the parlor, like he'd had to do."

Marie squeezed her mother's hand. "Dad was a complicated person, wasn't he? I mean he'd go off on his own, fishing or hunting or whatever, and I know Ken hated that—he thought Dad didn't care enough about us. And yet, I always knew if I needed him, he'd be there." She patted her pocket then got up and walked over to the box of tissues on the counter. "Maybe not with money," she said before dabbing her eyes and blowing her nose, "but with thoughtfulness and good advice. I don't know where he learned so much."

"Your grandparents didn't approve of him." Ellen's stomach clenched as she said the words—words she'd never spoken aloud before. She hadn't even wanted to think it, it seemed so disloyal. She forced herself to relax.

Marie's brows furrowed. "They didn't? Why?"

"They liked him they said, but they thought he was too old for me and they didn't know anything about his people. He never talked about his past—just said he grew up in the city and was glad to be out of it. He so loved the country. Remember how he'd sit on the porch to watch the sun go down or a storm come across the mountains?"

"Yes, and when I was little, how I'd sit on his lap when a storm was blowing in and we'd watch for the lightning flashes so we could count until we heard thunder. I'd put my hands over my ears and Dad would hold me tighter, the louder it got."

Ellen closed her eyes, tears pricking at the memory her daughter conjured. "Before we met, I'd occasionally see him around town. My friends and I used to giggle and talk about how good looking he was. Your father was very handsome when he was young, with that black hair and those dark eyes and dimples." She opened her eyes and looked at Marie, who smiled and nodded. Unlike Ken, blond and blue-eyed, taking after her side of the family, Marie was the image of her father. "He wasn't much taller than me, but that didn't bother me a bit."

"I'll bet he was embarrassed with all the attention from you and your girlfriends."

"The first time he came into our store to buy supplies, I made sure I was the one to wait on him." It had been unlike her to be so forward—she was generally shy with strangers. Her palms were moist and her heart had pounded when she took a determined step forward and asked what he needed.

"It was a general store and we carried a little of everything. I can even recall what he bought: soap, a comb, some canned goods, a length of rope and an axe handle. He spoke with the cutest accent. Sometimes I'd tease him and try to imitate the way he talked, but I could never get it right. I think his accent faded after a while. Or I just got so used to it, I didn't notice."

"When did you see him after that first time?"

Ellen's cheeks tingled and she gave an embarrassed giggle. "Oh, he came in pretty often after that. He always seemed to make a point of it being after school or on Saturday, when I was there to wait on him." She straightened in her chair. "That was in the winter of my senior year in high school. Mom and Dad wanted me to get my teaching certificate, but after I met Henry, I didn't want to leave Platt City. Until I met Henry, I'd never disagreed with my parents about anything important."

Marie cocked her head to one side. "Did you fight with them?"

"When they couldn't talk me into going away to school, my father tried to keep me in my room until I 'came to my senses' as he put it. But it didn't work."

Her brows raised, Marie leaned forward. "What did you do? Sneak out to meet Dad anyway?"

Ellen shook her head. "Henry never knew. I never told him." Her lips twitched. "But I stopped eating until my father gave in." Even now, after so many years, she could still hear her parents' whispered argument—they must have thought she'd been asleep that warm May evening. "My mother finally convinced my father it was no use. Henry and I eloped three months later."

Marie refilled both their cups with coffee. "Did your parents blame Dad?"

"No, but things were never really good between them. For one thing, my parents wanted him to work in the store. They thought the store would be our future, after they were gone. They were trying to help, I know that. But Henry would have died standing behind a counter, waiting on customers."

Marie stroked her arm. "That must have been hard on you, Mom."

"It was, a bit." Ellen fingered the rim of her coffee mug, her forehead creased, remembering. "There were no loud arguments or anything like that. It wasn't my parents' way to fight, nor Henry's, either. But their unspoken disapproval was loud enough for anyone to hear. I would get so angry with them." Her mouth tightened. "Your father never said an unkind word about them, though. They died right after your second birthday."

"Yes, I know—in a car crash on their way back from Boise."

"I was devastated. More so than would have been normal, I think, because I still blamed them for how they'd treated Henry. But your father was wonderful. I couldn't have asked for better support. He took care of you and Ken when I didn't feel up to managing—for months it seemed. He was so good with you. Gentle and patient."

Marie nodded, smiling. "I don't think Dad ever got hyper, no matter what Ken or I did." Her lips turned up on one side. "And Ken pushed him pretty hard sometimes. I guess I did, too. But Dad never lost his cool."

"After my parents died, there was all the business about the store to see to."

"Did you have to go and run the store? I never heard anything about that."

"No. We closed it. It was practically worthless. I could not believe there was nothing left but bills. All my life my parents worked in that store—six days a week, fifty-two weeks a year. They lived in an apartment right above it—it's where I grew up. The trip to Boise was one of the only vacations I remember them ever taking. And in the end, there was nothing."

Marie cocked her head to one side, frowning. "Why was the business gone?"

Ellen sighed, still saddened by the futility of her parents' lifework. "When Morrison's and the hardware store moved in, people went where they could get a better selection and cheaper prices. Who could blame them?" She took another sip of coffee. "By the time the property was sold and the bills were paid, there was nothing left except some insurance money."

Marie sat back in her chair. "That must have helped."

Ellen shook her head. "Your father insisted on putting it aside for the future. He would never let me touch it, even when I thought it was the only way."

"But Mom, that's wonderful—you have some savings then."

Ellen shrugged. "There was so little to start with…I can't suppose there's all that much now." She wished she had insisted on talking about these things with Henry. Well, not so much about the money, but about other things—his family, for instance. What they were like. She knew almost nothing of his life before they met. It was as if he'd stepped out of his past and closed the door behind him.

Marie's chin pulled back. "You mean you don't know? Don't you get statements?"

Ellen shrugged again. "I never bothered to open them. I just gave them to your father to put away. I guess I'll have to go through that pile of papers one of these days. I've been putting it off."

"I'll help, if you'd like me to." Her daughter shook her head as though she couldn't believe what she'd just heard. "But I can't tell you how much better I feel, knowing you have some money set aside. Even if, like you say, it's not very much, it will at least give you breathing space until you decide what you want to do." She reached over and rested her hand on Ellen's arm once more. "But, Mom, why do you think Dad never applied for U.S. citizenship."

"Maybe it just wasn't that important to him. But one thing I do want, Marie." Ellen covered her daughter's hand with her own. "I'm going to insist."

"What?"

"I want you to stop calling people your father worked for, asking them questions about what's past." She wouldn't let go of Marie's hand when her daughter pulled back.

"Listen to me. Forget what the woman at the Social Security office said. I don't want anything from them."

"But Mom—"

"No. I'm going to be okay." She hoped she sounded more confident than she felt, because she wasn't at all sure how "okay" she was going to be financially. But that was something she'd have to worry about in the future; right now, she just worried about getting through each day. "Let it go, Marie. I'm serious about this." She gave her daughter's hand a squeeze before releasing it. "And no more talk about me moving. This house holds all my best memories."

After the dream, something changed. Ellen found that she didn't want to stay inside. In the meadow in front of the house, crocus had begun to push above ground, short spear-tipped leaves and little green beads that would later turn into flowers. She looked forward to seeing the meadow grasses laced with purple and yellow, as first the crocus and then the daffodils came into bloom.

One morning she went for a walk in the woods near the house, pushing vines and tree limbs out of her way, intent on following a deer trail. Wild carrots and onions grew along the creek, and at the base of several trees were wild geraniums. It was too early for the geraniums to be in flower but soon their rose-pink blossoms would be nodding against a backdrop of dark tree-trunk and their own green foliage.

It had rained in the night and water still sparkled on the new green leaves of the alder and maple trees. It twinkled where it clung along the edges of grass blades and berry vines. Several blackbirds began scolding her in loud, trilling voices; red shoulder patches edged with yellow flashed on the males' wings, distinguishing them from their dark brown mates.

She threw out crusts from the toast she'd eaten for breakfast and had carried in her pocket to feed the squirrels, but still the birds chattered and scolded, flying from tree to tree, branch to branch. She was in their nesting territory. Life was beginning a new cycle.

Chapter Four

KEN

Ken stood in a loose formation of Marines on the tarmac-covered quay, waiting for a signal to begin boarding. Around him, men smoked, joked, or remained quiet, lost in their thoughts. Ken's own thoughts veered away from home and his worries for his mother. He focused instead on the adventure ahead. Italy. Spain. Places he'd only read about. If only this infernal waiting were over and they could get underway.

He toed a slight bulge in the tarmac and recalled how, in typical Marine Corps fashion, they'd been loaded onto buses in North Carolina at three o'clock in the morning for the drive to Norfolk. They'd arrived shortly after noon, but for no reason Ken had been able to discern, they'd been forced to wait for hours in the Embarkation Center before they were released. No one was allowed to leave the base, though, so it was just more hanging around, only in different places—the enlisted club for some, the Chiefs' club for others, or the food pavilion at the Navy Exchange.

He shook his head. It seemed waiting was all he'd done since he signed up. That and sit in one classroom or another.

His eyes slid over the *USS Delivery*, the ship they were waiting to board. It was classified an amphibious assault vessel, which was why it needed a contingent of Marines. When they finally boarded—before too many more hours he hoped—they would leave Norfolk's deep-water port along with eight other ships to begin the seven-day voyage to the Mediterranean Sea. When they got there, the flotilla of ships already there—a float they called it—would rotate back to the States and it would be the job of Ken's float to support and protect U.S. interests in the region for the next six months. That was the plan as it had filtered down to him, anyway.

He straightened his shoulders to ease his muscles, and shifted positions once again. *Come on—let's get this adventure going.*

"Hey, Maris, what do you think those Eyetalian dames will be like? Think they'll be waiting for us with open arms and roses between their teeth?"

Ken glanced at Sharpe, a man who'd lived in his barracks at Camp Lejeune, and whom he'd sometimes gone into town with. "They'll probably be about as welcoming as the ones on Court Street—happy to see you when you take out your wallet."

Sharpe let out a crack of laughter.

"Listen up," shouted the company's first sergeant, a tall, thin man with a hawk-like nose and no discernable sense of humor. According to rumor, the man had been in the Marine Corps since Christ was an Acting Corporal. He wore utilities, the Marine Corps' standard work uniform. They all did. But somehow, on him, they looked cleaner, crisper. "We're going aboard now."

A ragged cheer went up.

Ken stowed his gear, shuddering at where he was expected to sleep for the next six months, and quickly went up on deck. The slight breeze did little to relieve Norfolk's muggy heat. At just past nine o'clock in the morning it was already eighty -seven degrees, the humidity so thick he felt in danger of drowning by breathing. It was only the second of May. What would it be like in July or August?

As the *Delivery* made its way past piers and docks and ship after ship with tall, white numbers painted on their gray hulls, Ken watched containers being swung by cranes into waiting holds. He sympathized with the men and women down in the bellies of the vessels, struggling with the containers of stores needing to be stowed away. A red flag flapped in the thick air over one ship, off some distance from the others, warning that ammunition and explosives were being loaded aboard.

Small boats darted back and forth, in and out, skimming the surface like water bugs.

They slid past a dock where a destroyer lay festooned with men sitting on planks suspended by ropes. Rubber hoses snaked over the sides of the ship and the racket of air compressors riddled the air. A jet screamed overhead, drawing Ken's gaze upward. The jet's contrail formed a stark line across a deep azure sky. Barely visible on the eastern horizon were a few ragged scraps of clouds.

As they left the protection of the harbor and streamed into the Atlantic, the waters were mostly calm. Even so, many Marines, especially those nursing hangovers, immediately complained about feeling queasy as the swells passed under the ship and the deck began to gently lift and roll beneath their feet. By mid-afternoon, the rails were hung with green-clad men, heaving to the fishes what little remained in their stomachs.

"Get away from the railing," a chief petty officer shouted. "You're messing up my ship. You gotta puke, get below to a head."

The sailors, meanwhile, did nothing to disguise their amusement. Had any of the Marines felt strong enough to take a swing, Ken figured fists would have flown. He hadn't needed to resist the temptations of excess now bringing his buddies low, because he hadn't been offered the opportunity; he'd stood duty the night before. But much more rolling would have him running for a rail, too.

Despite the threat of seasickness, Ken's eyes darted from one foreign object or scene to another, trying to take in everything. *A hell of a long way from Idaho.* In the distance were two other ships he assumed were in their float, although they were too far away for him to see the identifying numbers on their sides. When he became familiar with their silhouettes, he'd be able to identify them at a distance without needing to read the numbers on their hulls.

The following morning, Ken was wakened by a disembodied voice from a loudspeaker mounted on the bulkhead. *"Now hear this. Reveille. All hands, reveille."* Bleary-eyed, Ken rolled off his cot.

Still in his skivvies and surrounded by other sleepy Marines, who, like him, carried shaving bags and clean skivvies. He approached the steep, thickly painted ladder to the deck above, where the showers and head were located. He began to climb just as the ship plunged into a trough. It felt he was being flung straight up. He grabbed the rail with his free hand to keep from falling backwards. A moment later, as the ship surged up the side of the trough, his feet felt filled with lead, pulling him down. He made it to the top of the ladder with the ship's next downward plunge. "Christ," he muttered.

A glum and mostly silent line of men inched along the corridor outside the head. When it was finally his turn to enter, Ken needed to step over a body curled in a blanket. The body moved and a hand came out to clutch the blanket tighter. *Poor guy must have spent the night there.*

A row of toilet stalls ran along one side of the compartment. Men were lined three deep waiting their turns to shave in front of the row of sinks bolted to the opposite bulkhead. Steam poured out of an adjacent compartment lined with showerheads. Ken stripped off his skivvies and stood beneath the stinging spray. He didn't start soaping until someone poked him and told him he'd better hurry before they turned the water off.

A half-hour later, dressed and their racks awkwardly made up, Ken and Sharpe started topside to the mess deck.

Sharpe grimaced. "I can smell the powdered eggs from here."

Ken shot him a look. "I thought Navy chow was supposed to be better than Marine Corps chow."

Sharpe shrugged as they emerged from the ladder-well and into the enclosed entrance of the mess deck. "Navy,

Marine Corps—makes no difference; they're all belly-robbers."

Ken pushed open the door and they walked in. Like all mess halls, in Ken's experience, the close air was redolent of grease and fried food. "It doesn't look too crowded. I guess not so many felt like eating this morning." Just as the words left his mouth, the door opened again and five sailors shouldered through.

"Working party," said one as each man stepped in front of Ken and Sharpe and picked up a tray. Before they could protest, three more sailors moved in front of them.

"What's goin' on?" Sharpe started to grab a tray out of one of the sailor's hands.

"Let it go, Sharpe," came a gruff growl. Ken hadn't noticed their detachment leader's approach.

"Why should I, gunny? What the fuck is goin' on with these swabbies? They can't cut in front of us like that."

"Yeah, they can when they're in a working party. Cool off and get some chow if there's any left when they get through the line."

On deck during physical training drill their third day out of Norfolk, Ken noticed dark clouds on the horizon. The waves were choppier than they'd been the day before, and each was capped with a crest of white foam. By noon, the sea had gone from choppy and brisk to violent and pitching. By late afternoon the wind sounded like a freight train roaring down, and the towering swells appeared as high as the mountains back home, ready to unleash an avalanche of dark, foamy water onto the Delivery's decks.

That night Ken woke to a jolt as the bottom of the ship slammed back into the sea. Like an unbroken mustang, the ship bucked and pitched, rolling so far over, first to one side and then the other, Ken had to grab the side of his rack to keep from being thrown out. Above the whoosh-whir of the air conditioning and the thrumming of the engines, he heard loud creaks and moans from deep inside the ship.

They were layered into the troop compartment like sardines in a can, with rows of racks climbing up the bulkheads. The reek of sweat and vomit in their compartment mixed with the smells of saltwater, gear oil and diesel fuel circulating throughout the ship. A green glow from lights along the bottom of the bulkheads and in the passageways created an eerie twilight. From several bunks away came a muttered, "Hail Mary, full of grace…"

Ken was sure the ship would break up and they would all drown—he imagined what it was like down in the Delivery's belly, welds popping, cables separating—but for some reason the thought didn't frightened him. In fact, he felt oddly removed, as though he were not a part of the wildness of the night. His only regret, he wouldn't get to visit Italy and Spain.

In tenth grade, everybody had gotten a different poem to memorize and recite. Ken's was some ancient Scots thing. He remembered part of it now.

O our Scots nobles were right loath
to wet their cork-heeled shoes.
But long afore the play were played,
their hats they swam above them.

He pictured the lords in their fancy clothes and their fine shoes slowly sinking to the bottom of the sea, leaving their broad-brimmed hats bobbing on the surface, long feathers blowing. Then the broad-brimmed hats of his imagination dissolved and were replaced by white sailor hats and green camouflaged utility covers as the ship pitched, bucked, and rolled its way through the night.

Spring 2000

Chapter Five

MARIE

When the doorbell rang, Marie almost didn't answer it. A teething Henry Reed had awakened, crying, every hour or two the entire night. He wouldn't eat his breakfast, not even the strained peaches he usually relished. When she gave him his bottle, he pushed it away after a few swallows, then whined and fussed some more. She'd put him in his playpen and tried to distract him with a toy, but he'd thrown himself down.

At a loss, she'd called her mother, who advised her to wrap a crushed ice cube in a washcloth and let him chew on it. It must have helped. Or the baby aspirin. Or he'd just plain worn himself out, because he'd finally gone sound asleep. She should have cleaned the kitchen and picked up toys while she had the chance. Better yet, taken a shower and shampooed her hair. Instead, she'd vegged out in front of the TV.

Afraid that whoever was out there would ring the doorbell again and awaken her sleeping son, Marie pushed off the couch. She stepped over a wooden train engine and a pair of Paul's shoes, and crossed to the front door. "Just a minute." She pushed back her unwashed hair, her usual bouncy curls flattened and lackluster, drew a breath and opened the door.

The woman wore tailored linen slacks and a white silk blouse that contrasted with her dusky skin. Her shiny black hair was cut just above her shoulders and curved in, emphasizing her high cheekbones and dark, slightly tilted eyes. Silver earrings swung from her earlobes.

Marie stared until the woman said, "May I come in?"

Still not speaking, Marie opened the door wider.

The woman stepped inside and held out her hand. "I'm Pearl Whitebear."

Marie, uncomfortably aware of the stained t-shirt she wore, an old one of Paul's, over a pair of jeans she'd had since high school, hesitated a moment before taking the woman's hand. She frowned to hide her discomfort. "You were at my father's funeral."

The woman cocked her head to one side and looked past Marie's shoulder. "Perhaps we could sit down?"

Marie led the way, stopping to pick up the wooden train and Paul's shoes along the way. As she passed the television set she snapped it off then tossed the toy into an empty laundry basket next to it. She set Paul's shoes down and waved her hand at one end of the maroon couch, trying not to mind how worn it appeared. At least the yellow pillows brightened it up a bit and covered the worn spots on the arms. She sat at the other end of the couch then sprang to her feet. "Can I get you a drink? A Coke or something? Coffee?"

"No thanks."

The woman appeared to be fifteen years older than Marie's mother, maybe even more, but decades older in sophistication. Marie lowered herself to the sofa again. She felt gauche, uncertain what to say. Suspicious, too. *What does she want?*

The woman cleared her throat. "I've wanted to talk to you since the funeral. In fact, I almost did one day in front of Morrison's."

"I saw you."

"I wasn't sure you'd want to talk to me there, on the street."

Marie's stomach clenched, but she lifted her chin and stared at the woman. "Why wouldn't I want to talk to you?" Her voice had a rough-edged quality and was louder than she'd intended. She frowned and lowered her voice. "Look, I don't know you or why you're here, but if you've got something to tell me about my father, then just come out with it."

"I'm sorry. I'm doing this badly. Let me begin at the beginning."

"Okay." Though still wary and one of the yellow pillows clutched protectively to her chest, Marie eased into the corner of the couch and waited for Pearl Whitebear to begin.

"Do you know anything about your father's life before he came to Idaho? Before he came to the United States?"

Platt City

Dear Ken,

You're not going to believe this. I'm still trying to get my head around it. The strange woman from the funeral—her name is Pearl Whitebear. She isn't Nez Perce, like we thought, she's Canadian—what they call a Native People. She knows all

73

about Dad's family in Canada—Montreal to be exact. And here's the part that's going to blow you away—we have a grandfather, along with an aunt, an uncle, and a cousin!

Apparently, there was some trouble back in the sixties and seventies and Dad left Canada for some reason. And get this. She said Dad was a well-known journalist for a French-language newspaper in Montreal. He even made political speeches. Our dad! But then he got involved with some kind of organization with his brother. Have you ever heard of the FLQ? I guess it had to do with having a separate government for Quebec, like they wanted to secede from Canada, which seems kind of hard to imagine. Pearl told me some of the history, but she didn't go into a lot of details, and I couldn't follow it, anyway. If Henry Reed is better tomorrow (he's cutting a tooth) I'll go to the library and look it up on their computer.

Anyway, Pearl doesn't know much about what happened exactly—with Dad, I mean—just that there was an explosion and Marie-Catherine, that's our aunt, was injured and for some reason, Dad felt responsible. Their brother—his name was Marc—was arrested and committed suicide while he was in jail. He had a little boy, but didn't even know it. Isn't that tragic? Marie-Catherine adopted him—the baby—and brought him up on her own, at least until she got married, I guess. I just can't get over it. Here we always thought there was just the two of us, and now we have an aunt, an uncle, a cousin, and a grandfather!

Pearl said Dad never contacted his family and they never knew where he was. Then someone who knew him in Montreal or had seen pictures of him, was in Idaho on vacation last year and saw him in Platt City. That person told our aunt and she asked Pearl to contact Dad—Pearl and our aunt went to college together and have remained friends ever since. Pearl is a professor in forest management at the University of Idaho now and comes to town once or twice a month to consult for Marrick -Pacific.

But, can you believe it? Pearl said Dad was easy to find— he barely changed his name—but she said he didn't want to talk to her. When Pearl told him how much his family wanted to see him or at least talk to him, Dad told her it was too late. Why would he have thought that? I think there's a lot more Pearl didn't tell me. Or doesn't know.

I haven't talked to Mom yet. I told Pearl I would tell her, but I'm not sure how I'll do it. Do you think she'll want to know? Well, she'll have to—we can't keep it a secret forever. But she hasn't been very happy with me just trying to find out about Dad's Social Security. She does seem to be better, though. She's been taking walks and working in the garden and she's had some repair work done at the house. She told me she's thinking about a job, but that's all she'll say about it. I don't know. Maybe I'll wait for a while until I think the time is right.

Pearl gave me Marie-Catherine's phone number. I'm dying to talk to her, but I wanted to tell you first. I won't call until I hear back from you.

At first, when Pearl started telling me all this, I was saying no way. Not my father. In fact, when she first started, I thought she was going to tell me they'd had an affair or something. She straightened me out on that right away, but when she told me about the FLQ and the kinds of things they did, I would almost have rather heard the other. I told her I didn't believe her. I told her there had to be some sort of mistake and that she'd gotten it wrong. Dad wasn't like that. The more she talked to me, though, and the more I thought about it, the more I began to think it might be true. Part of it, anyway. There was something terribly sad about Dad, something he wanted to forget but couldn't—you could see it in his eyes at times.

Your nephew calls—gotta go.

Love,

Marie

P.S. Write back to me as soon as you get this!

P.P.S. I wish I could see your face while you're reading this!

Footsteps sounded on the stairs and the apartment door slammed. Paul. She'd finally showered and washed her hair, but hadn't had time to straighten up. Toys were still scattered around the room and two empty glasses sat on the coffee table. Although she'd put a meatloaf in the oven, she was still cleaning up the kitchen.

"Marie, I know the baby is teething and fussing and all, but this place is a mess."

"I know." She was too excited with her news to take offense. "You're right, Paul. I'm sorry." She brought him a glass of iced tea and picked up the two empty glasses. "Sit down, honey. Have I ever got a story to tell you."

When she finished, Paul remained silent.

Marie frowned. "Well. What do you think? Can you believe it?"

"Are you sure it's not some kind of hoax?"

"That's exactly what I told Ken I thought it might be. Or they were having an affair or something."

"You've talked to Ken?"

"I wrote to him. I can't wait to hear back."

"What about your mom...have you told her yet?"

"No. I'm not so sure she'll want to hear it." Marie bit her lower lip. "It worries me, Paul. I can't withhold it from her—she has a right to know. But what is she going to think? How did Dad keep it a secret all those years?"

Paul sat forward on the sofa, his hands dangling between his knees. "She's bound to feel betrayed."

"I think that's why she hasn't liked me looking into things—she either suspects something, but doesn't want to know, or she knows and doesn't want Ken and me to find out." Marie got up and paced around the room. "I just can't think how I'm going to tell her."

A cry came from the other room. Paul went into the bedroom and came back with Henry Reed balanced on his arm. The baby rubbed sleep from his eyes with one hand and clung to his blanket with the other.

"Hey, bubber." Marie rubbed her son's back as he laid his head on his father's shoulder. She reached up and ran her fingers under his chin, gently tickling him. He hunched his shoulder to keep her hand away, but couldn't hide the smile.

Paul sat down on the couch and the baby leaned against him. Marie sat beside them and let her head fall back, trying to relax. She'd felt giddy all afternoon, like butterflies danced under her skin.

"Maybe you shouldn't tell Ellen anything about this. At least not yet. She has enough on her plate right now."

"I know what you mean. I don't want to hurt her more." She twisted on the cushion to face him again. Agitated, she started pulling at a thread dangling from the button on her shirt. The button dropped into her lap. "Dammit," she said and stuck the button in her pants pocket. She drew a quick breath. "I'm just so angry with Dad right now. Not because of what he did in Canada." She stood and began to pace again. "I have no idea what drove him to get involved with that FLQ organization. Whatever it was, it must have been something compelling, because I know he was a good man. He wouldn't do anything that wasn't morally right. But why didn't he tell anyone about his family? It's so unfair to Mom, to have to find out all of this now."

Paul eyed her. "Well, there we are. Does she really have to find out now? Or ever, for that matter?"

Marie stopped pacing and stared at him. "I can't keep this from her, Paul. She has a right to know. I'd want to know. At least I think I would."

Henry Reed, now fully awake, pushed himself off his father's lap and turned with exaggerated caution to the low table in front of the sofa. He reached for Paul's empty glass.

Marie rushed to him. "No, bubber. You can't have this, but I'll bet you'd like to chew on some more crushed ice." She went to get another washcloth.

Platt City

Dear Ken,

I got your letter this morning. No, I haven't told Mom yet. Paul doesn't think I should tell her at all, but I have to. Don't you agree? We couldn't keep something like this from her. And you're right—Henry Reed needs to know what his roots are. When it comes down to it, so do we. Now that you agree, I'll call Marie-Catherine. After I've talked to her, I'll decide when and how much to tell Mom.

We're all fine here. Henry finally pulled through two more teeth. He was pretty miserable for a few days—and so was I.

I hope you're taking lots of pictures. The gold souk—that sounds so mysterious and exotic. Bahrain. Did you ever in your wildest dreams think you'd see places like Bahrain?

Paul sends his love. Hugs and slobbery kisses from Henry Reed.

> *Love,*
> *Marie*

Summer 2000

Chapter Six

ELLEN

Ellen shook her head from side to side. "No. It isn't true. Your father would never have kept all that from me." Some of her hair fell forward, out of the clip she'd put in that morning. She shoved it behind her ear. Although they sat in her kitchen, surrounded by the familiar and comforting smells of bread dough rising and fresh-brewed coffee, the crazy things Marie was telling her...they made no sense. She shook her head again. "He wouldn't have done that."

"It's complicated, Mom."

When her daughter arrived that morning with dark circles under her eyes, Ellen's first thought was the baby must be cutting another tooth. If only it had been something so simple.

"I've talked to his sister. Her name is Marie-Catherine."

Wonder filled Marie's voice, as though she savored the idea she'd been named for someone she hadn't known existed. Ellen's frown deepened. She hadn't known the woman existed either; Henry had only claimed to like the name when they were choosing one for their infant daughter almost nineteen years ago.

"She told me there were problems in the family and in the country; terrible things happened—bombings and riots, kidnappings and assassinations. I read about it on the computer at the library." Marie's words poured over Ellen, who willed her daughter to stop talking. She didn't. Her voice ran on. "The Prime Minister even had to declare martial law and call in the army. Pearl Whitebear said Dad felt responsible for some of the violence. She said he couldn't get over feeling guilty, even when people said it wasn't his fault. They didn't know where he went or what happened to him until last summer."

Blood pounded in Ellen's ears. She straightened her shoulders, trying to relax the tension creeping up her spine.

Marie finally stopped talking. Eyebrows raised, she waited for Ellen to respond.

Ellen drew a shaky breath and slowly let it out. "Well, there must have been good reason for it, for his not wanting to contact his family."

"Didn't you ever ask Dad about them?"

"Of course, I did." She'd always wanted to know about Henry's life before he came to Platt City, but whenever she'd pressed, he would either withdraw—frequently taking off to his beloved mountains—or they would spend days alternating between arguments and festering silences and then he'd retreat to the mountains. She'd learned to stop asking.

"He didn't tell you about his sister? Marie-Catherine said they were very close."

"I just told you. No. The family must have done something terrible to make him run away and never contact them. Maybe he was ashamed of them. Maybe that's why he never told me about them."

Marie shook her head. "I don't think it was like that, Mom."

"Why don't you think it was like that? Because this Marie-Catherine person said it wasn't?" Ellen's voice rose. "I don't believe whatever it is she's suggesting—killings and bombings, kidnapping people. Your father would never have been involved in such horrible things." A rivulet of sweat rolled down her skin between her breasts. "He was a good man, Marie. I don't want you or anyone else saying bad things about him now that he's gone and can't defend himself." Her lips tightened.

"Mom, I'm not trying to say bad things about Dad." Tears filled Marie's eyes. She reached for Ellen's hand.

Ellen pulled her arm away. She stood and busied herself, putting some things she'd left on the counter the night before into the cupboard. She banged the metal bread pans onto the shelf and closed the cabinet door with enough force to rattle the dishes inside.

"She's invited me to go to Montreal for a visit. Ken wants me to go."

Ellen whirled around. "You and Ken have already talked about this? Before you talked to me?"

"I wrote to him." Marie lifted her chin. "We both want to know more about Dad's past."

"You want? You and Ken want? What about what I want, what your father would have wanted? Isn't it enough he loved you? Why do you need to go prying into things that happened years ago, before you were even born? Leave it alone, Marie." She'd never longed more than she did that moment for the comfort of Henry's arms.

"Mom, I'm sorry."

Appeal sounded in her daughter's voice, and when Ellen

allowed herself to look, she saw the pain on Marie's face—the face that was so much like Henry's.

"You know I loved Dad. But this is important. I think you need to know what drove him. I know Ken and I do. It's our right to know—it's our right to know our relatives, too. And my son has a right."

Marie stood, blinking rapidly, and began gathering her things.

Even though there was truth in what her daughter said, Ellen held her body rigid, not yielding to Marie's hug and kiss on the cheek. Marie picked up the white plastic carrier in which her son, surprisingly, still slept. "I'll call you tonight, Mom."

Ellen stood at the kitchen window, her fist pressed to her lips to keep them from trembling, and watched Marie drive down the lane, her curly black hair visible through the truck's dusty rear window. In retrospect, Ellen knew she was asking the impossible. Once her daughter had hold of an idea, she never let go. She couldn't, wouldn't rest until she knew everything.

She closed her eyes and tried to empty her mind of the questions Marie had raised, but they refused to be set aside. Why hadn't Henry told her he had a family, one that had wept for him, wanted to find him? Why had he kept his past hidden? What had he done? When no answer presented itself, she straightened her shoulders once more, picked up her gardening gloves and went outside.

As she pulled the door closed behind her, the sound of tires on gravel signaled someone driving down the lane. Was Marie coming back to tell her something else she didn't want to hear? No—Ian McCort.

Ian had been stopping by every week or two, since Henry died, which she appreciated, but right now she really wasn't in the mood to chat. She'd have ducked into the house and not answered the door, but he would already have seen her. She waited as he circled around and came to a stop a few feet away. He lowered the window of his white truck, *U.S. Forest Service* emblazoned in green on its door, and leaned an elbow out. A whisper of cool, refrigerated air brushed Ellen's face.

"Just saw Marie," Ian said in the Texas drawl he still spoke with, even after fifteen years in northern Idaho. "Drivin' hell bent for leather."

"Yes," said Ellen, her posture rigid.

Ian studied her face. "Guess you two musta had words."

Ellen nodded; there was no reason to deny it. She wouldn't satisfy his curiosity by telling him what they'd argued about, even though it was bound to get around if Marie went to Montreal as she planned.

"Guess you don't feel like talkin'." He paused, but when she said nothing, he went on. "Well, just drivin' by and thought I'd check in. You let me know if you need anything."

Ellen nodded again, beginning to feel awkward with her anger. There was no point in directing it at Ian, who'd been nothing but thoughtful. "Thank you. I will."

"Okay then, I'll leave you to get on with whatever you're doin'." He put the truck in gear, nodded to her and drove away.

Ellen watched until Ian turned onto the main highway, which shimmered in the heat. She gazed across Hartley's ranch to the ridge of mountains in the distance. A smoky haze blurred their edges. Although it seemed early in the summer for forest fires, it was hot enough and dry enough— not yet noon and already ninety-five degrees.

She turned toward the garden. It would be wiser to wait until the evening, when it was cooler, but she hoped pulling weeds would help vent some of her anger. She didn't know what upset her most—Henry dying and leaving her, learning now about his secret past and the family he'd never shared, or having her children go behind her back.

At least she wasn't going to lose this house.

Ellen had been shocked when she finally opened a statement from the investment company Henry had entrusted with her parent's insurance money. She'd quickly called to make an appointment. Two days later, still in a state of disbelief, she'd sat across the desk from George Baker. His office, located on the east side of Platt City, well away from the motels, resorts, and restaurants, was small but comfortable.

"I don't understand. There was so little to start with. How did it grow to this amount?" Though she knew it wasn't a fortune, it seemed like one to her.

"Your husband made some wise choices for you, Mrs. Maris—choices that were unaffected by the crash in '87. Since then, the stock market has been doing very well, and your husband continued to make good choices. Plus, he added to it on a regular basis. Not a lot, but steady, which is the best way to invest."

He'd showed her how every month Henry had added to the account—sometimes as little as twenty dollars, rarely more than fifty or sixty. Ellen was amazed Henry had managed to eke even such small amounts from their meager income, month in and month out, year after year, with never a word to her. A rush of love and longing swept over her.

"I was very sorry to hear of his passing," Baker said.

Ellen, blinking back tears, struggled to pay attention as he patiently explained how her money was invested.

"You're not rich, Mrs. Maris. Not by any means," he'd finally told her. "But this should give you a cushion. If you're conservative, and I have no doubt you are, you'll be able to live in your house, pay taxes and take care of repairs when they're needed."

When Ellen had left Baker's office, tears of gratitude filled her eyes. She felt she might overflow with love. Although she'd refused to hear any suggestion of moving, once the shock of Henry's death wore off, her waking hours had been plagued with questions of how she'd manage. She'd known it wouldn't be enough to work hard, raise a garden, mend, darn and do without. Also, she wasn't a fool. She had no skills an employer would want and she felt too old to learn about computers or other machines used in an office—not that there were that many offices in Platt City even if she were to learn. But this news, this wonderful gift...it was like Henry was still there somehow, watching out for her.

And then Marie dropped her bombshell.

Chapter Seven

KEN

As usual, the *USS. Delivery* had been forced to anchor half a mile out in the stream because the *USS Coronado* already occupied the space at the Navy pier. Commonly known as the 'White Whale,' the *Coronado* was the fleet command center in the Persian Gulf. It stayed in port most of the time, only going out to sea a day or two once a month.

Ken and Sharpe, finished with their duties for the day, rode a liberty launch over the open water to the pier. Ken nodded toward the tied-off ship and shouted to Sharpe. "Gunny says they have to move it every thirty days—otherwise it's apt to beach itself on coffee grounds."

Sharpe laughed. "Too many chiefs with index fingers in a permanent hook."

What with having so few products to export, Ken was always surprised to find Bahrain's port, adjacent to the Navy pier, bustling with activity. This time was no different. Several oil tankers were anchored out in the stream, waiting their turns to on-load or off-load at the oil refineries. In addition to the oil tankers, there were the usual cargo ships and private yachts carrying flags from Japan, England, Russia, the Netherlands, and the United States, as well as Saudi Arabia, Kuwait and other Arab nations. Some of the yachts were small and sleek, but several were nearly as big as the Delivery, with thick-necked guards posted around them.

At the Navy pier, he and Sharpe climbed aboard a Special Services-run bus that would take them main-side. Because of the heat, they sat in separate seats. Ken leaned out the open window, his chin on his arm, and let the breeze wash over him.

The storm had caused them to be two days late getting on station in the Mediterranean. Then, before anyone could go ashore, the Delivery was directed to detach from the *float* and proceed through the Suez Canal to the Persian Gulf.

Although the Gulf War was long past, tensions still ran high. Rumors had Saddam Hussain ready to break out again. Other rumors had him building a nuclear arsenal, or set to unleash bugs and gas on the West. Maybe all three.

In the two months they'd been in and out of Bahrain, resupplying the minesweepers that served as escorts for oil tankers, the Marines on the Delivery had been put on alert four times. So far, nothing had come of it. Ken was torn. Like his buddies, he was eager for action. On the other hand, he wasn't sure he wanted to be part of a war that seemed to have started decades, maybe even centuries before he was born.

He lifted his chin to get more breeze, but there was little relief from the oppressive heat. Since they'd passed through the Suez, most days the temperature soared above a hundred degrees. This day was no exception. The driver kept the bus's door wide open on the twenty-minute ride, but that didn't help much.

He'd had another letter from Marie. When she'd first told him of Pearl Whitebear's revelations about their father,

Ken was stunned—he'd read her letter twice just to take it all in. But, like Marie, he no longer doubted the truth of what the woman had disclosed. He'd always felt it was odd how the old man revealed so little of his past. His mother was always telling stories about her family's general store and about growing up in Platt City, but he knew nothing of his father's childhood.

The idea of him as a big-shot journalist didn't surprise Ken that much, either. His old man had always had a book within reach, most often a history book, and if you could get him to talk, he knew a lot about a lot of things. He'd kept a journal, too. Even when they went camping his father had scribbled away by the light of the fire before climbing into his sleeping bag at night.

Nor did Ken doubt that his father held deep convictions, even though he'd always kept a lid on them. His emotions, too. Like he was afraid what might happen if he turned those emotions loose. But thinking his father may have been involved with bombings and kidnappings…that was something else. Was it possible? He wanted to say, 'no way,' but why else had his father become such a recluse? Ken figured Whitebear's revelations went a long way to explaining why the old man kept his past such a deep dark secret.

His thoughts shifted to his mother. Her letters were always filled with unimportant things. Like how crocuses had come up in the meadow. How a pair of Goshawks had taken up residence in the fir tree next to the lane. Not about what mattered—like how the hell she was going to live out there by herself. If only she weren't so stubborn, so determined to stay in that damned house. Marie told him their grandparents had left some insurance money, but he doubted it amounted to much.

The bus pulled to a stop near the gate. He and Sharpe got off and went to find a taxi to take them into Manama.

As usual, the narrow streets and alleys of the gold souk teemed with people. This was Ken's third time in Bahrain's capital, but he still wasn't used to so many people living in such a small area. Luckily, he had no trouble being understood. Bahrain had once been a British protectorate and it seemed everyone spoke English: the native Bahrainis; a large and growing population of Portuguese; the Filipinos, who did much of the manual labor; and the Indians, who ran the tailor shops and did some of the manual labor with the Filipinos. But on the streets and in the souks, when the people were talking to one another, Hindi, Arabic, Farsi, Portuguese, and Spanish filled the air like the chattering of exotic birds.

Several slim, olive-skinned men wearing business suits and carrying briefcases, anonymous behind dark glasses, wove in and out of the jumble of people. Each appeared to be hurrying to an important meeting. The streets were too narrow for cars, but a few motor scooters wove in and out. Not bicycles—it was too hot to pedal.

Tourists abounded. He spotted the Americans, no problem—the men stuck out in their colorful Tommy Bahama shirts and slacks, the women in equally colorful sundresses or shorts, sleeveless tops, and painted toenails. There were plenty of Europeans, too. The light-skinned Scandinavians and Germans seemed to suffer more from the heat, even in their sensible, thick-soled sandals. The French and the British kept to themselves. The Italians moved with more comfort, languid, not rushing anything. He had a harder time with the Asian tourists. Sharpe tried to explain some of the differences between Japanese, Chinese, and Korean. "It's all in their eyes, man." Ken didn't think Sharpe knew as much as he pretended. Like them, though, everyone appeared fascinated by the display of wealth in the gold souk.

Ken stopped to peer into a multi-shelved glass show-case. "Hold on a minute." Like all the other showcases dominating each shop lining the Street of Gold Merchants, the bottom and back of each shelf was mirrored and edged with small, twinkling lights, like Christmas-tree fairy lights, multiplying the fifteen or twenty items on each shelf into a multitude of sparkling gold baubles. He scanned each shelf, but didn't see what he wanted.

Sharpe frowned. "That's the third time you've stopped. What're you looking for?"

"I want to get something for my mother," Ken said, a little defiantly.

Sharpe, who rarely said anything about his background or family, grunted.

Between two stalls they discovered a steep-pitched staircase. A sign indicated more gold shops above. Ken led the way, his shoulders nearly touching the walls in the narrow space. At the top of the stairs he halted. Behind him, Sharpe drew in his breath. At least twenty more gold merchants displayed their wares in the same type of mirrored and lighted showcases, but these cases hugged the walls, facing toward the center of the room, making it appear the room was lined with gold. Ken felt like he'd entered Aladdin's cave.

Two men and a woman in airline uniforms stood in the middle of the room, wonder reflected on their faces. Ken figured his own face wore the same stunned expression. Tourists and black-clad women, shopping singly or in pairs, haggled over prices. The odors of musky perfumes and sweating bodies were layered over the ever-present scent of myrrh and frankincense. The whine of two-stroke engines drifted up from the street, joining the babble of rising and falling voices in a cacophony of sound. And everywhere was the astonishing, intoxicating sparkle of gold.

"Jesus," said Sharpe. "Can you believe this shit? It must be worth millions."

Ken could only shake his head.

"I'm gonna start over there," Sharpe said, nodding his head toward the woman in the airline uniform who now gazed into a showcase. "Maybe ask her advice," he added with a wink.

The only jewelry Ken's mother wore was her wedding ring. He wanted to get her a necklace. He wanted it to be special, something she would never have dreamed of owning. He looked through several showcases before moving to one where a Bahraini woman stood talking to the merchant. The woman deftly moved her black robe aside so that it didn't brush against Ken's trouser leg. She murmured something to the merchant, before she moved away.

Ken was puzzled by her seeming hostility, the look in her eyes when her gaze swept over and past him. He frowned, then inwardly shrugged and returned to his quest.

On the bottom shelf, he spotted the necklace he wanted: a finely braided flat chain of white, yellow, and rose-colored gold. Quiet and understated, yet elegant in its simple design, it would suit his mother perfectly.

The merchant wrapped the necklace in tissue paper and put it in a small drawstring bag before handing it to Ken with a slight bow. "You are a good son."

The drawstring bag resting in Ken's pocket and their eyes finally sated with all the gold and brilliance they could handle, Ken and Sharpe left the souk.

"I guess you struck out with the stewardess," Ken said peeling his shirt from between his shoulder-blades. His skin felt pooled in slime. As hot as he was, he didn't know how Muslim women, Ninja women, the Marines called them, could stand being encased in their black robes, only hands and eyes visible.

Sharpe shrugged. "Married."

Ken laughed. "That doesn't usually stop you."

Sharpe shrugged again. "To one of the guys she was with."

"Oh."

They came to a café where a few tables and chairs had been set out on the sidewalk. Sharpe stopped. "My mouth is dry as shit. Let's get something to drink."

They sat at a table partially shaded by a small awning. After the waiter had taken their orders and gone back inside, Ken noticed a little girl watching them. If not for the whiteness of her dress, he wouldn't have seen her in the café's shadowed interior. He waved to her to come out, but she shook her head and moved farther into the shadows. A woman's voice came from inside the building, low and musical, and the little girl disappeared. Moments later she was back, peering around the edge of the door. Ken waved to her again. Again, she shook her head, but this time stood her ground.

"Who are you waving at?" said Sharpe. He turned to look behind him. "Oh, one of those raghead kids." He turned back around. "Man, they're all over and they'll steal you blind. Don't encourage her, man."

Ken scowled. "Don't be paranoid. She's just a kid."

The waiter, a thin, nervous-looking man, brought their Cokes and set them on the table. In addition to the drinks, he set a plate of cashews, pistachios, and dried fruit between them.

Sharpe pushed the plate aside. "We didn't order this."

A thin scar rode above the man's right eyebrow. Although he didn't smile, he dipped his head. "They are for your pleasure. Please enjoy."

Ken nodded in return. "Thank you."

As the waiter re-entered the café, he bent and picked up the little girl. Her arms went around his neck. Ken figured he was her father. He took a long drink of his Coke, its spicy sweetness reminding him of high school and home.

"When you were a kid did you ever dream you'd be someplace like this?"

Sharpe shrugged. "Nope. Can't say I did. Be like dreaming I'd gone to Hell." He chuckled then added, "My old lady would have said that wasn't no dream, but a prediction."

Ken laughed. A minute earlier he'd been disgusted with Sharpe's callousness. He'd often said things Ken hadn't liked, but his self-deprecating humor so far had managed to keep Ken from being angry for long.

He set down his glass, just as two young men ran down the sidewalk toward them. Feet pounding on the pavement, the man in front knocked over a chair as he passed too close to the restaurant and the man behind him had to leap over it. No one followed the two, but the man in back looked over his shoulder as if he expected someone to be in pursuit. Ken lost sight of them when they ducked into an alley.

"What the fuck was that about?" Sharpe said.

Ken, equally puzzled, could only shrug.

The ship's air-conditioning was no match for the Gulf's heat, at least not in the troop compartment. Ken tossed on his bunk for a while before giving up and going topside. As he worked his way toward the fantail in hopes of finding a breeze stirring, a loud popping noise came from a distance, followed by sirens. Soon, the sky over Manama contained a glow Ken was certain had to be a fire, maybe several. For the next three days, they were confined to the ship and then the *Delivery* headed back out to sea.

The sea in the Gulf was smooth as glass, with gentle gray swells like small hills—whenever he was out on deck, Ken could see them one after another, all the way to the horizon. He often thought he'd rather be back in the storm in the mid-Atlantic than in this queasy-making, mono-tonous rocking—or back in port loading supplies in the blistering heat.

Unfortunately, he wasn't in a storm or back in port, or even up on deck. He was cooped up in the compartment the

Marine contingent had been assigned as an office. With nothing else to do after updating manuals all morning, he propped his feet on the gunny's desk—the gunny had gone to shoot the breeze with someone in Admin—and picked up a copy of the *Gulf Daily News* someone had brought aboard before the ship last left Bahrain.

On the front page was a story about 'foreign-backed militants' creating unrest and trying to undermine the power of the Sunni monarchy. *"Shia militants were responsible for two recent bombings of restaurants and hotels,"* the article claimed. *"Their sole motivation is the disruption of tourism."*

As he read, Ken thought of the café where he and Sharpe had stopped for a Coke, the solemn little girl watching them from the shadows and the man who appeared to be her father. He thought again of the two men running past. What had they been up to?

Shaking his head, he dropped the paper to the deck and picked up a month-old copy of *Field & Stream*. On the cover was a picture of two men on a rocky riverbank. One had his finger hooked into the gill of a German brown trout. Both men were grinning. Behind them, the river cascaded into a rocky chute before it ricocheted out of the picture. A thick forest of pine and fir filled the background. Ken thought if he breathed deeply enough he could smell their earthy fragrance. The water would be icy cold snowmelt. God, what he wouldn't give to be there instead of sweltering in this inferno.

He closed his eyes and thought about the last time he and his father had gone fishing—in the Wallowas when Ken was fifteen. They'd traveled the power station road through Hell's Canyon then headed north, where the road twisted back on itself a hundred times or more as it climbed higher and higher into the mountains, threading its way through tall stands of Ponderosa Pine, before it eventually turned to gravel.

"We're here," his father announced and pulled off the road in a swirl of dust, into a small clearing. Ken jumped out of the truck, glad to stretch his cramped legs. The tangy scent of pine filled the air, and the ground, covered with a plush carpet of long brown needles, was spongy underfoot. Fifty feet away, the gurgling, rushing Imnaha River beckoned.

Late in the afternoon, Ken started a fire to fry up the half-dozen fish they'd caught. His father laid a hand on his arm and nodded toward the river. On the opposite bank, a cougar stood on a granite outcrop surveying its surroundings. The majestic head swung their direction. Ken froze, but in a flash the golden cat turned and bounded away, so quickly, Ken wondered if he'd imagined it.

As the moon came up and the night air chilled, he and his father stretched out in their sleeping bags, next to the fire, and talked about Ken's future, the chances of his wrestling team reaching the state finals again, and about girls. That summer Ken had liked a girl named Julie, whose family had moved to Platt City the year before. But living in the country, and especially with him being too young to drive, made dating a town girl difficult. He had visions of other boys calling her, taking her to the movies, hanging out at her house. His father promised to teach him to drive.

Ken picked the magazine off his chest, where it had dropped, and took his feet off the desk. Despite the good feelings they'd shared on that trip, he'd always found an excuse not to go fishing or hunting with his father again. It wasn't until later that he realized his reluctance came from worry that he, too, might succumb to the pull of the mountains. He didn't want that. He wouldn't be like his old man, running off to fish or hunt whenever he felt like it. Someday, when he had a wife and children, he planned to be a full-time husband and father.

Everything appeared to be normal. Ken looked from the liberty launch to the shoreline where the White Whale was once again tied off the pier. Even from this distance, he made out a sedan at the foot of the pier and two Navy officers climbing out of the rear seat; gold braid on the bills of their caps glittered in the sun. They walked down the pier, up the gangway of the *Coronado* and disappeared.

Sharpe was on ship's detail—a rotating assignment low-ranking snuffies like them couldn't avoid—and for several hours would be storing away in the hold the supplies being barged out from shore. No one else was interested in going to town. Even though they'd been told it was better to travel in pairs, Ken was unwilling to wait and headed for Manama on his own. He had no idea what he'd do when he got there.

The taxi dropped him off near the gold souk, but he'd had enough of crowds. He set off to explore.

Barrels of nuts and dates sat in front of stalls filled with kitchen utensils, knives, and leather goods. Each stall specialized in something different. Mostly older women shopped. As he passed, a few merchants called to him, but without conviction, as though they knew Ken had no interest in buying their wares.

Down another alley, white bedding, shirts, and trousers lay draped over windowsills or hung from lines stretched between the white, two and three-story apartment buildings. Separating the buildings were small, enclosed courtyards. Above the walls, the tops of palm trees bloomed. Although the alley was empty of people, he heard the high-pitched, giggling voices of young children, and from somewhere nearby, the tinkling notes of piano scales.

The alley opened onto a wide street. It should have been inviting, but the buildings lining it looked closed and somehow forbidding. Ken felt a stirring of unease when three young men emerged from one of the buildings. Though he didn't understand the words, from the tone and volume of their voices he knew they were arguing. Seemingly without warning, one man pushed another. The third man put himself between the two opponents. Doing so, he faced Ken; their eyes met. The man said something to the other two, who stopped arguing and turned to stare. The intensity of their loathing crashed into Ken like a physical blow—as if, had they been able, they would crush him with their malice.

All three men started toward him. Ken turned and walked away fast, his heart pounding. Three sets of footsteps sounded behind him. Eyes darting left and right, Ken quickened his pace. The footsteps sped up.

In the next block, an old man inside a bookstall looked up, mild curiosity in his nearly opaque eyes. Ken didn't slow. He passed a second stall where plucked chickens, teeming with flies, hung from hooks. He hurried on. His breath came in short, ragged gasps. He shot a quick look over his shoulder. The three men still followed, half a block behind. Were they simply trying to scare him? If so, they were doing a good job.

Just as he was about to give up, take his chances by turning and facing the three, he came to yet another cross-street. Like a long-sought gift, in front of him were twenty or more food stalls with an equal number of housewives, their children in tow, shopping for their family's evening meals. Only in their midst did Ken allow himself to stop and look behind him; the three men had vanished.

He expelled what little breath he had left in a rush of relief. The women pretended to ignore him, but the children stared until he began to feel foolish. Maybe he'd imagined the men's malevolence. No. Their hatred was real; no way did he want to run into them again.

He headed in what he thought was the direction of the gold souk, but kept finding himself in dead-end alleys or alleys that turned back onto the street he'd just left. He couldn't retrace his steps—the three men might be waiting for him. Maybe they'd trap him in one of the alleys. Shit. He should have waited for Sharpe. It was so damned hot. He'd give anything for a cold beer. Not much chance of that, though. Not until he got back to the base—if he ever found his way out of the rabbit-warren of alleys and narrow streets.

Two women came toward him. "Excuse me. Can you tell me how to get back to the Street of Gold Merchants?"

Like the woman at the gold souk, the heavier and older of the two women stared past him, her posture signaling disapproval.

The slim one answered. "You are on the right path." She spoke with a British accent. "You will soon come to a cross-street, turn to the right. Go down two more streets, turn left and you will see the Street of Gold Merchants."

The tension in Ken's shoulders eased. He thanked her and she nodded. As they walked away, the woman's companion spoke in scolding tones.

The sun was high overhead when Ken reached the souk. Still thirsty and now hungry, as well, he headed toward the café where he and Sharpe had gotten Cokes. He searched for the tables and chairs out front, his frown deepening when he got closer and saw only debris scattered across the sidewalk and into the street.

Jesus! For several moments, mouth ajar, Ken gazed at the scab of rubble that had once been the café. He felt nearly numb with shock. Then his mind flashed back to the article in the newspaper about the foreign-backed militants causing trouble for restaurants that served tourists and American military. Could this have been the fire he'd seen from the *Delivery*'s fantail? Had militants done it?

The buildings on either side of the café hadn't escaped damage; walls adjoining the café were tumbled down and charred, exposing the interiors. On the second floor of the building on the left, a mirror reflected sunlight. Below it was a sink, and next to the sink, a toilet, both broken away from the wall; a large hole was in the bowl of the toilet. Nothing moved in either building.

The dark-eyed little girl who had stared at him from the doorway of the café swam in front of his eyes—had she and her parents lived above or behind the café, as so many merchants did in Manama? In his ears was the voice of the little girl's mother, calling to her from inside the café. He pictured the dark-skinned man who'd brought them nuts and fruit to go with their Cokes. For their pleasure.

Chapter Eight

ELLEN

Ellen sat on the end of her bed and stared at the closet door. Should she read them? No. They were Henry's private thoughts…but he'd never said she couldn't and with all the questions swirling around in her head…. No. It wasn't right. She stood, walked to the bedroom door then, her hand on the knob, she stopped. Just one or two. Surely Henry wouldn't mind if she read one or two.

She pulled the large cardboard box that contained his diaries from the back of the closet. Though he'd always kept a journal, writing in them at odd times, her eyes widened at the sheer number. She could see no order to them; it looked as though he'd merely tossed each notebook into the box when he'd finished it. Her hand hovered over the pile before she picked one.

Jan 7—when I think of Maman, she is sitting at the table shelling peas into a bowl and listening to Father Joseph on the radio. I don't remember her ever buying something pretty for herself, but every week, even when Papa was out on strike, Father Joseph got his donation. How I hated him. And each time I passed one of Montreal's countless cathedrals I thought of the painfully swollen knuckles of Maman's worn hands and I hated him even more—along with all the other priests and nuns who worked to keep us poor in our places even as they professed to be saving our souls.

Ellen frowned. Henry had never told her he felt like that. She hesitated, but only a moment, before flipping to another page.

Aug. 11—told Ken I'd teach him to drive. Maybe it will help.

Ellen smiled at the memory those few words evoked. For days it seemed, Ken drove the truck up and down the lane, Henry at his side, before Henry finally let him drive on the road. She'd stewed. Ken didn't have his learner's permit, much less a driver's license. Henry reminded her that most ranch kids started driving trucks and tractors when they were eleven or twelve. She'd still worried, but Ken had become a good, conscientious driver. It was Marie who'd gotten a speeding ticket and had to be grounded. She sighed and put the notebook back in the box, digging deeper in the pile for a second one.

Nov 5—the old man woke me up with one of his fits again last night. His daughter says he relives fighting from trenches in the Great War (oxymoron?). Don't know how much longer I can take not sleeping.

Who was the 'old man?' She traced the words on the page. This obviously happened before he'd come to Platt City, but when? And where had he been—still in Canada? She closed the notebook and returned it to the box.

She sat on the edge of the bed with her hands clenched in her lap. Why did you keep so many secrets, my love? And what will our daughter learn in Montreal? Once again, Ellen sighed—something she seemed to do whenever she thought of Marie and her plan to spend time with Henry's family.

After a few minutes, she put the lid back on the box; she couldn't rid herself of the feeling she was prying. She didn't put the box back in the closet.

The following day Ellen called George Baker. "Do I have enough money to buy a new oven? A big one?" When he asked her why she wanted a commercial-sized oven she told him her plan.

He cautioned against her idea, saying he doubted it would produce much income. "Not only might you lose money, Ellen, it sounds like a lot of work."

"I need to do something. Without something to do, I'll go crazy."

There were three restaurants on Ellen's list. Each had a busy lunch and dinner trade. They served the tourists who year-round flocked to Platt City in the summer for boating and water sports, and in the winter for skiing and snowmobiling. The parking lot of the first restaurant was nearly empty, but that was probably why she'd been given an appointment with the executive chef at four o'clock in the afternoon. "It's the best time to speak to him," the woman who'd made the appointment said.

Ellen found a bit of shade under a tall maple tree and parked. She didn't allow herself to stop or think—she'd done enough of that already. Here goes. She reached for the basket lined with dishtowels and filled with bread and rolls she'd baked that morning, opened the truck door and hopped out.

She frowned as her eyes adjusted to the restaurant's dimly lit interior. A young man, a boy really, spread a white tablecloth diagonally over a red one and smoothed out the wrinkles. He started toward the next table, more white cloths over his arm. Ellen cleared her throat.

He looked up. "We're not serving right now. Sorry."

"I have an appointment to see Mr. Richards."

"I'll see if he's free." He hung the tablecloths over the back of a chair, then disappeared through a door at the end of the room.

Ellen remained by the cash register near the entrance. All the way into town, she'd mentally rehearsed what she would say. She went over it again.

"Mr. Richards will be right out. You can have a seat if you want."

"Thank you," said Ellen, but the young man had already gone back to his tablecloths. She pulled out a chair from the nearest table, sat and watched him spread several more of the starched white squares.

"Mrs. Maris. I'm Steve Richards. Thanks for waiting. I had a vendor on the phone."

He was younger than she'd expected—not more than thirty-five. She started to stand.

"Don't get up. So, what have you brought for me?" He pulled out the chair next to her and sat, then snapped his fingers in the direction of the young man. "Peter, go get me a bread knife."

Without waiting for either Peter or Ellen to reply, he picked a loaf from the basket, ran his palm over the skin of it and brought it to his nose. He broke off a corner and tasted. "Good flavor. What do you make besides the white?" A few breadcrumbs clung to the whiskers of his blond moustache.

"Whole wheat, rye, dill—just about everything," said Ellen. "I've brought loaves of Russian rye and dill—they're favorites with my family—and two loaves of unleavened breads."

Peter returned and put a long, serrated knife on the table. "Can I have a piece?"

Richards sliced the loaf in the middle, then cut off a slice and gave it to the young man.

"The texture's even. No big holes in the center. The taste is good. I like it." Richards leaned back in his chair. "So, why do you want to sweat all day baking bread for people you don't know and won't ever see?"

Ellen hesitated. She hadn't been prepared for this kind of question. "Well, I like to bake bread. It's very satisfying to me." She decided to be honest. "And I need to earn money."

"Baking for your family isn't anything like baking for hundreds of people every week. Sometimes you aren't going to feel like it. Like now, when it's hot as hell outside, who wants to work in a sweltering kitchen? At least here we have air-conditioning. Have you got air-conditioning?"

"No."

"Have you had your kitchen inspected? Is your oven large enough for the amount of baking you're proposing to do?"

When Ellen returned to the truck, she felt as empty as the basket she placed on the passenger seat before climbing behind the wheel. She took a deep breath and gathered her thoughts. He hadn't said yes, but he hadn't said no, either. She would keep the appointment she'd made for the following afternoon and for the afternoon after that. Then she would know what to do.

She ended up with a thirty-day trial to furnish bread and rolls to the first restaurant she approached. Steve Richards said he talked it over with the owner and they felt offering their guests some interesting and home-baked specialty breads would be a nice touch.

"We'll give it a month and see how it goes," he'd said.

Ellen thought she could take on another restaurant as well, but decided it was wiser to start small. By the second day she was grateful for that decision.

Nothing went as planned. The market in town ran out of whole wheat flour. They placed an order for more, but before it came in she had to drive to stores in Driggers and Martinsville.

"You must be baking for a school or something," said a woman standing beside her in the checkout line, her eyes on all the bags in Ellen's cart.

"I've started a new business baking bread for restaurants," Ellen said. "But I'm having trouble getting enough flour."

"You'd do better to drive down to Boise or up to Lewiston to one of those warehouse stores or co-ops," the woman said. "If you have a resale license, you can buy wholesale."

Chef Richards had told Ellen she'd need to get a resale license and where to apply for one, so she had that. "But, don't you have to belong to an organization?"

"I don't think so, but even if they did require it, as a small business owner, you'd be eligible."

Ellen stood a little taller when she heard those words. *A small business owner.* The sound of it pleased her.

She reached into the refrigerator for milk one morning and her heart jumped into overdrive. The carton wasn't as cold as it should have been. What was wrong? Would she need to buy a new refrigerator? She didn't think she could swing that and a new oven. Maybe Paul would know what to do. Thank God it was her son-in-law's day off.

"I'll see if Dad can help," Paul said.

Although Paul's father was retired, according to Marie, Frank kept himself busy in his garage tinkering with gadgets. Within an hour, Ellen heard their footsteps on the porch. She hurried to let them in.

One day Paul would look exactly like his father. He had the same loose-limbed walk, shoulders slightly rounded and long arms swinging at his sides. They both were slow in their speech, and both found humor in odd things. She knew Paul had an interest in engineering and expected that, too, had come from his father.

"Looks like the thermostat, Ellen," Frank said after he and Paul pulled the refrigerator away from the wall and tested some wires with a meter from Frank's toolbox.

"What does that mean? Will I have to buy a new refrigerator?" She bit her lip.

"No. Not to worry. We'll just bypass it for now and I'll order the part for you. It will take a week to ten days. Until then it should run okay, though some things, like lettuce, may freeze. At least nothing will spoil."

"Thank goodness." Ellen quickly turned so they wouldn't see the tears of relief in her eyes. She set another pot of coffee to brew and put cinnamon rolls on a plate while Frank and Paul returned to work on the refrigerator.

When they left, each carried a brown grocery bag with a half-dozen cinnamon rolls inside.

"I'll enjoy these, Ellen. Thanks."

"Thank you, Frank. And you, too, Paul. You're both lifesavers. I don't know what I would have done without you."

"Any time, Ellen."

Although Virginia and Frank were older than her— they'd been closer to her parents' ages—Ellen had always known them. When Virginia became pregnant with Paul, the whole town rejoiced for them. "You just know some people will be wonderful parents," Ellen had overheard her mother tell her father. "What a blessing it is that Virginia and Frank are finally going to have their chance."

Mama was right. Virginia had devoted herself to Paul, teaching him to read long before other children his age. Ellen remembered Frank playing catch with his son when Paul was barely able to throw, and later it was funny to watch Paul trailing behind his father—even then their gaits and posture matching. When Paul started school, Virginia and Frank attended every parent-teacher meeting and, until she'd gotten too sick from the cancer, Virginia always volunteered at school.

Amazingly, Paul hadn't been spoiled. He'd been a good student and he was a hard worker. Ellen had no complaints about her son-in-law. She knew he adored Marie—had adored her since they were in eighth grade. And his affection was returned in equal measure. She was just sorry that his and Marie's love for each other had interfered with their plans for college.

Ellen didn't regret her own decision at eighteen, when she fell in love with Henry and refused to listen to her parent's arguments that she should finish her education before getting married, but she couldn't help thinking how different her life would be now had she followed her parents' wishes.

Between driving to town to deliver her bread, rushing down grocery aisles to pick up supplies and the hours she spent in the kitchen or in her garden, Ellen didn't have time or energy to dwell on what Marie might find out in Montreal when she eventually went. Instead, she fell into bed every night by eight, and was asleep in minutes. She couldn't even stay awake long enough to worry about her business or if the restaurant would continue to order her bread. Mr. Richards told her they were getting compliments on what she provided, but he hadn't said they would go past the thirty-day trial period.

She was proud of one thing, though: she'd discovered the rhythm she needed in the kitchen. After trial and error, she'd found the most efficient ways to measure and stage. And she was thankful every day for the size of her kitchen and the large island she'd explained to Henry she needed for canning. It was perfect for kneading and for setting fresh-baked loaves to cool. A large fan by an open window kept the air in the room circulating, though she couldn't help but look forward to cooler weather. Maybe someday she could afford an air-conditioner, but for now the fan would do. Besides, with the window open, she could hear the birds.

Frank came out to install the new thermostat in the refrigerator. While he was working, Ellen told him she was looking for a commercial oven. "I went to an appliance store in Lewiston the other day, but the prices." She shook her head. "If only they didn't cost so much."

"You might want to think of getting a used one," Frank said.

"How could I find one?"

"You could ask at the restaurant. They'd be able to tell you. Restaurants are always going out of business—their equipment has to go somewhere."

Ellen's eyes widened. "You're right, Frank. Why didn't I think of that?" She grinned. "I bet I could get a commercial mixer the same way."

"We'll probably need to do extra wiring for the oven, though. I've been looking around, and some of these old wires needs replacing. Paul and I can do it."

"I'm so thankful for you two, Frank. I don't know what I'd do without you."

"Hell, Ellen, you're family."

Chapter Nine

MARIE

Henry Reed astride her hip, his diaper bag and her purse slung over her shoulder, Marie bit back an oath and blew hair from her eyes as she kicked her two suitcases forward on the hard tile floor. Paul had carried the suitcases into the terminal, given her a brief peck on the cheek and left, unyielding in his disapproval of her going to Montreal. They'd argued about it for the last three weeks.

"It isn't going to cost us anything, Paul. She sent me more than enough for a roundtrip ticket. This is important to me."

Paul, normally reasonable, didn't budge. "Why? You didn't even know these people existed a few months ago—now they're all you can think about. Jeez, Marie. Your mother doesn't want you to go. I don't want you to go. Your father wouldn't have approved—you know that's true, or he wouldn't have kept his past a secret. So why do you have to go somewhere you've never been to see someone you don't know, just to pry into something that may hurt you in the end?"

She tried to explain it one more time. "You have aunts, uncles, and cousins, Paul. You've been around them your whole life. Even though you're an only child, you're part of a big family. You don't know how much I envied the closeness you all shared." From the doubtful look on his face, she knew he wasn't getting it. She gave an exasperated sigh. "I don't hold it against you. I just wish you'd understand how important it is to me to find out more about these people. My people."

But he couldn't or wouldn't understand. Neither had her mother.

"I don't want you to go," Ellen had said the day before.

"Mom, the plans are made. She's expecting me; I have the tickets in my purse."

"That doesn't matter. You can call her right now. Pick up that phone and call her—tell her you've changed your mind."

"But I haven't. It's not right for you and Paul to ask me to."

Her mother gripped her arm. "Marie, listen to me. Listen." Her voice nearly crackled with intensity. "Your father must have had a good reason for not sharing his past with us. Can't you trust that he knew best? What you find out in Montreal can hurt you. It will. I know it will."

"Mom." Marie didn't know what to say. She'd never seen her mother so agitated. She covered the hand on her arm with her own. "I know Dad was a good man. You don't have to worry that I'll find out something about his past and decide to hate him." She hugged her mother then drew back. "Stop worrying. I'm a big girl. Besides, you have your new business to keep you busy—you won't have time to worry about me."

Marie wasn't sure how she felt about her mother's bread-making business, which seemed like a lot more work than anything else, but she knew her mother's concern was for her well-being. As was Paul's. But why wouldn't they understand she could take care of herself? She was frustrated with the role they both seemed to have given her. She wasn't a headstrong brat, always needing to have her own way. At least she didn't think she was.

A hand tapped her shoulder. The man behind her nodded to the ticket counter. "You're next," he said.

Heart pounding, Marie searched the crowd at the top of the ramp, straining to see around the off-loaded passengers in front of her. Henry Reed twisted in her arms, gray eyes enormous in his flushed face as he looked around at the unfamiliar sights. She hiked her purse and the diaper bag farther up on her shoulder. What if something had come up, an accident or something, and her aunt hadn't made it to the airport? *Calm down. You have the address and phone number and money in your purse.* But what if her aunt had changed her mind? Maybe her aunt's husband thought the same as Paul.

Then she saw her. She didn't need the *'Marie Klein'* sign in the woman's hand to know it was Marie-Catherine. Marie briefly closed her eyes, took a deep breath, and walked toward her aunt, whose arms were spread in greeting.

"Welcome to Montreal, *chérie.*" A broad smile lit her aunt's face. It was like looking in a mirror—a funny sort of mirror that faded the skin, drooped one eyelid, added a scattering of gray to the cap of curls and showed almost thirty more years of living.

Marie couldn't resist the infectious greeting or the welcome hug. The tension slipped from her shoulders like a heavy coat dropping to the floor. "Thank you. Thank you for inviting me. This is my son, Henry Reed."

"Such a handsome little fellow." Marie-Catherine reached for him, but Henry Reed dug his face into Marie's neck, clinging to her. Her aunt shrugged away the slight. "No worries. He will soon get to know us."

Several minutes later, Marie stared out the taxi window—it was all so different from the ranchland and mountains of home. And nothing like Boise, Lewiston or Spokane, the only other cities she'd ever been in. Her aunt reeled off explanations of what they passed. Marie only half-listened. The driver wove in and out of traffic, zipping around slower cars, speeding up and slamming on the brakes then pressing on the gas pedal once again. Car horns blared. Marie held Henry Reed to her chest. He squirmed and pushed away. She wished her aunt would tell the man to be more careful, but her aunt seemed unaware of his erratic driving.

"Montreal hosted the world fair in 1967. It was held there." Marie followed the pointing finger to an island in the river they drove alongside—the St. Lawrence River, dark and lumbering rather than swift and cascading. "Expo '67 they called it. I was a teenager then." She lapsed into rapid French then back into English. "It was so exciting, *chérie*. You would not believe how many people came here to celebrate—from all over the world. Montreal went wild."

While her aunt described and extolled the virtues of Montreal, questions formed in Marie's mind: Did my father visit Expo 67? Did he drive down this street? Was Montreal like it is now—so busy, so full of traffic and people? What did he do when he wasn't in school or working? Where did he go? And the biggest question of all—why did he keep it a secret? Despite the cars and trucks whizzing by, horns blaring, the many pedestrians on the sidewalks, the sunlight glinting off the river, Montreal felt like a place of mystery, where she'd need to stop frequently and remind herself to breathe.

The taxi finally slowed and turned onto a residential street.

"We're almost home." Marie-Catherine dug her wallet out of her purse, extracted some bills and handed them to the driver when he came to a stop in front of a narrow, two-story brick house with a covered porch across its front.

Getting Henry Reed, their luggage, and the diaper bag out of the cab and into the house left the three of them breathless. In the living room, a game show flickered on a television set in the corner. It wasn't until he began struggling to his feet that Marie saw the old man in the dark green, upholstered chair that nearly swallowed his small frame.

"Papa," said Marie-Catherine, a smile in her voice. "They're here. It's Henri's daughter, Marie, with your great-grandson"

The old man came to stand in front of Marie. He peered at her from under bushy, gray eyebrows, his brown eyes looking at once alert and fading. They bore into hers, searching, before a slow smile spread across his face and folded his grizzled cheeks into rows of deep creases.

"She looks like your maman, my Anne-Marie," the old man said in heavily accented English. "When she was a girl."

"Oui," Marie's aunt said. "Like the picture on your nightstand." She turned to Marie. "Did you understand? He says you look like my mother, your grandmother."

Her aunt handed Marie a rinsed bowl. "We lived near here, your father and I and Emile, before this area was what they call 'gentrified.' Cheap as it was then, we still had to scrape to get by—Henri worked for the newspaper then, while I worked and attended university classes at night. Also, as you can understand, we must juggle our time, since his hours were often erratic."

Marie couldn't get used to the funny way her aunt pronounced her father's name—'Ahnree' instead of plain Henry, as her mother and people in Idaho called him…had called him. 'Ahnree' made him sound like a different person, a foreign-sounding different person.

"We must juggle so that, between us, we could take care of Emile," Marie-Catherine said.

"What about your parents? Couldn't they help?" They were cleaning up from dinner, her aunt washing, Marie drying. René, Marie-Catherine's husband, graded papers in the living room.

Her grandfather had already gone to bed, but not before he'd fed Henry Reed his bedtime bottle. From his position on his great-grandfather's lap, Henry Reed had gazed up at the old man, studied him for a while then, grinning around the nipple in his mouth, reached for the old man's nose. The joy that spread across her grandfather's face had made Marie's eyes sting with unshed tears.

"I wish that had been possible," said Marie-Catherine, rinsing a glass and putting it in the rack. "But *Maman* couldn't bring herself to accept Emile. Henri said it was because she was hurting so much from all that Marc had done—she was so shamed she closed her heart to her grandson. She would not even admit he was her grandson."

"That's terrible," Marie said, grateful once again of the support her parents had given her when she'd confessed she was pregnant, before she and Paul married.

"Don't think too badly of her, *chérie*," said Marie-Catherine. "Things were different then and she was very religious—Marc committing suicide was a terrible sin in her mind. Then to have had a child out of wedlock…well, let us say it took her a while to become accustomed to the idea."

Marie finished wiping a plate and put it on the stack in the cupboard before reaching for another. Marie-Catherine had hinted at some of the things Marc had done—some of those things Pearl Whitebear had already told her about—but Marie didn't think this was the time to question her aunt about them. "Did my grandmother eventually accept Marc's baby?"

"Oh, yes. Came a time and the two of them were inseparable. By the time he was a toddler, she doted on him."

"Good. I hope I meet him soon," Marie said. "It's still hard to believe I have a cousin."

"He'll be here for dinner tomorrow," said Marie-Catherine. "He never stays away for long. And he's anxious to meet you."

"What does he do, this cousin of mine? Is he a professor, too?"

Her aunt gave a warm chuckle. "No. He's a musician, *chérie*. He works at night and sleeps during the day, so we see him at odd hours."

"I've tried to figure out how old he is," said Marie.

"Nearly thirty."

"So old? Is he married? Does he have children?" Did she have even more family to find out about?

"No and no," said her aunt, laughing. "He is too busy butterflying from blossom to blossom."

Marie chuckled at the image her aunt invoked. Although they'd just met, in ways she felt as though she'd always known this woman who was her father's sister. But that begged the question of why she hadn't met her aunt before, why her father had kept his past buried for so many years—refused to acknowledge it even when the past had sought him out, begged him to reconcile. Pearl Whitebear had said the family hadn't known he'd felt so desperate, so riddled with guilt and remorse. He hadn't confided in anyone, just left without a word.

"Your father disappearing like he did, broke Papa's heart," Marie-Catherine said, as if somehow reading Marie's mind. "Henri was his favorite. He was so proud of him—his education, his becoming an important journalist, the stand he took for Quebec separatism. And when he went to work for René Lévesque and the Parti Québécois—well, Papa was just over the moon, he was so proud."

"René Lévesque and the Parti Québécois? What is that?"

Her aunt placed another dish in the rack for Marie to dry. "René Lévesque was the hero of the Quebec separatist movement and an early leader of the Parti Québécois, which supported it. The Parti finally came to power in the mid-seventies." She pulled the sink plug and let the soapy water drain away before turning to Marie. "Unfortunately, your father wasn't here to see it—he'd already left by then."

Henry Reed's gentle, snuffling breathing reached Marie from across the room, where he slept in the portable crib her aunt had borrowed from a neighbor. It was so strange to think that in a house just three streets away, her father had lived for a time with Marie-Catherine and a newborn Emile, the son of their dead brother.

Harder to imagine was why her father had felt so guilty. From everything she'd heard so far, the guilt belonged to his brother—Marc was the one who built bombs for the FLQ. Why should her father have felt responsible for the things his brother had done? Then she thought about how she'd feel if Ken did something so terrible. *I guess we are our brothers' keepers.*

Henry Reed whimpered in his sleep. He squirmed for a moment before settling again. Marie looked at the clock on the nightstand and saw it was after midnight; she'd been up since five, Idaho time. She rolled over and tried to empty her mind, but three images kept intruding: her mother, standing in the doorway of her house, disapproval written on her face, Paul walking away from her at the airport, and her father, turning his back on his family, a family that included a baby for whom he was partially responsible.

Chapter Ten

KEN

The image of the burned-out café haunted Ken. On the surface, Bahrain looked industrious, the people happy, but beneath the surface, anger glowed like hot coals, waiting to ignite the whole area in flames. It was on the faces of the three young men who'd followed him. It was in the pile of rubble where a family once lived and worked. It was even in the eyes of the woman at the gold souk who'd looked through him as if he weren't there.

His gunny took a sip of coffee that must have been stone cold by the look he gave it. "What's up with you, Maris? You been moping for days. Heat getting to you?"

The Delivery rolled slightly as a wave passed beneath it.

"No more than usual," said Ken, marking a page in a manual where another update needed to be inserted. The fan on the gunny's desk fluttered the pages. "I just wonder about the people here and about what's going to happen."

"The people here—you mean the sailors and Marines on board ship?"

"No, I mean the people here in the Middle East. The people in Bahrain, especially. I just wonder what's going to happen to them if this area goes up in smoke."

"Don't worry about it," said the gunny, lighting a cigarette from the stub of his last one. "They've been fighting their tribal wars for more years than we can count." He exhaled smoke. "It's the way they must like it."

Ken couldn't accept that, and he couldn't stop thinking about the little girl he and Sharpe had seen. He wondered if she or her parents had made it through whatever had struck the café. The next time they were back in port he'd ask around. Someone must know.

It took more than a few questions of neighbors and neighboring shopkeepers. Most shook their heads and turned away or closed the door in his face. Almost ready to give up, he approached one old man on the sidewalk near the site of the bombed café. The old man, accompanied by his grandson, was willing to talk.

"Big explosion." He threw his arms wide. "Terrible. Everything in my daughter's house rattles or falls from shelves. Later, we hear man on motorbike throw bomb through door of café."

Ken listened intently, trying to understand the words the man struggled to form.

"Fire everywhere." The boy looked up at his grandfather's face then took his hand. The old man's lips tightened and tears formed in his eyes, but he didn't trouble to wipe them away. "Café was good place. Many people go-ed to her in evening. It not hot then. They drink teas, talks and listen to music. She was good place," he repeated. His voice trembled as he spoke, but he drew a breath and went on. "After, smoke and broken glass all around. Blood, peoples everywhere."

The old man's face was a mirror to his emotions. His words may have been hard for Ken to decipher, but in them he heard the people screaming, saw them running blindly, blood streaming down their faces, or lying on the ground, twisted into grotesque shapes.

"Who would do it?" His voice shook at the horror he so vividly imagined. "Who would throw a bomb into a group of innocent people?"

"No one takes *credit*," said the old man. He spat on the ground. "They know they go too far."

Ken shook his head. "But why? And who?"

The old man shrugged, but behind the wrinkled face and the almond-shaped eyes peering at him from beneath folds of skin, Ken saw he had the answer. He just wasn't willing to say it—not to an American Marine anyway.

"The owners...were they hurt? The little girl?" He braced himself to hear the answer. How could anyone have survived that inferno?

"They dead," said the old man, his voice devoid of inflection. "Little girl go-ed to bed, above café, in back. She not killed, alhamdulillah, but she bad hurt. They take her in ambulance to hospital."

When the *Delivery* returned to port the following week, Ken went to the Red Cross office, located in a building near the Navy Exchange. He spoke to a middle-aged, portly woman sitting behind a desk. Her thin hair was pinned in a loose knot on top of her head. Despite the noisy air-conditioner in the window, the small room was muggy and smelled of tuna fish—the remains of a sandwich were on a wilted-looking napkin. The woman's face glistened with perspiration.

"I want to locate someone in Manama," Ken said after he'd told the woman his name.

"I don't know if I can help you with that, corporal," she said. "Why do you need to find this person?" Her voice was reedy and thin as her hair. She sounded and looked tired.

Ken explained what had happened and said he figured the little girl might still be in the hospital.

"How terrible." Concern filled the woman's watery blue eyes. A dusting of beige face powder glazed her collar, almost concealing a smudge of pink lipstick. "But why do you want to find her?"

Ken wasn't sure why he'd become so obsessed with the little girl, of finding her and making sure she was okay. Maybe he felt partially responsible, having stopped at the café with Sharpe that day. Or maybe just by being in Bahrain. He knew that didn't make a lot of sense, so he told a lie. "Well, ma'am, my sister isn't much older than she is. I thought my mother might send some things Marie's outgrown."

"That's very admirable, corporal," the woman said, her tone all but dismissing his feeble excuse. "But the Red Crescent—that's the equivalent of the Red Cross here in Bahrain—they'll take care of her, I'm sure. And they don't take kindly to outside interference." She glanced down at some papers on her desk and Ken understood she was refusing to help.

"I'd still like to see her for myself, ma'am," said Ken. Unlike Marie, he didn't often dig in his heels. The fact he was doing it now surprised him. "If you'll tell me how to get hold of someone at Red Crescent, I'll see if they can help me."

The woman gave Ken a startled look. "Now listen to me, corporal. You need to stay out of this." An unexpected toughness sounded in her voice. "What goes on in Bahrain politics isn't our business. You go on back to your ship and forget it. That's my advice to you."

Ken stood. "Thank you, ma'am, I'll keep your advice in mind." With that, he turned and let himself out of the room. "Like hell I will," he muttered as he strode down the hall and outside, into the broiling heat. He glared back at the sun through squinted eyes before heading toward the gate and an idling taxi.

In contrast to the ancient souks and neighborhoods, the heart of Manama's business district looked as though it could have been in any big city. International oil and shipping companies had offices there, along with investment banks and insurance companies. The taxi driver let him out in front of a multi-storied building. A blast of refrigerated air met him the moment he opened the heavy glass door. A uniformed guard, seated behind a tall desk in the middle of the lobby, looked Ken over with piercing black eyes when Ken asked directions to the Red Crescent office. After several phone calls, the man sent him to the third floor.

A young man seated behind a computer in the reception area spoke with a slight lisp. "Is Mr. Kamel expecting you?" A faded line on his upper lip traced the surgical repair of a cleft palate.

"No," said Ken. "But it's important I see him."

"He has meetings this afternoon. I can make an appointment for you next week."

"I won't be in Bahrain that long," Ken said, trying to keep his frustration from showing. "And I'm not sure when

I'll be back." He hoped he wasn't going to get the royal run
-around.

"I will let him know you're here and perhaps he can fit
you in," said the young man. "It could be a long wait."

Ken sat and picked up a magazine extolling the
booming economy of Bahrain. Between articles, he glanced
at the clock on the wall behind the young man. Twenty
minutes passed, then thirty, then forty-five. Ken put the
magazine down and was looking around for something else
to read when the young man stood.

"Mr. Kamel will see you now," he said and opened a
door for Ken to go through.

The furnishings were much plusher than the Red Cross
office on the base, where a metal desk wedged under a
window and two upright chairs filled the meager space. This
office was thickly carpeted and in addition to a wide
mahogany desk big enough to land a helicopter on, there
were several well-upholstered chairs and a black leather sofa
against one wall. A glass-topped table arranged with a silver
coffee service and several delicate-looking coffee cups and
saucers stood in front of the sofa.

The man behind the desk wore a neat business suit on
his slender frame. He stood as Ken approached. "You wished
to see me?" His polite voice gave away nothing.

"Yes," said Ken, his eyes assessing everything in the
room, including Kamel.

"And you are?"

"Corporal Kenneth Maris, United States Marine Corps,
sir. I'm here to ask your help in locating someone."

Ken repeated his story, telling how he and a friend
had stopped at the café and how he'd seen the little girl, and

then how he'd discovered the café had been hit by a terrorist bomb. "I just want to see her, sir, to know she's being taken care of."

"I don't understand why you involve yourself in this," Kamel said. "Why do you care so much about this child? From what you say, you never spoke to her. You don't even know her name." His eyes narrowed, his brows drew into a scowl. "I must tell you that in Bahrain we don't allow relationships with a man your age and a child."

Ken's face flamed as he realized what Kamel was suggesting. "Of course not. I haven't got anything like that in mind. I wouldn't do anything like that. She's a kid, for God's sake."

"Then what?" said Kamel, appearing unimpressed by Ken's heated denial.

"Jesus Christ, man. I told you." Angry frustration ready to explode from his mouth, Ken forgot what he'd learned about language in the culture classes he and his shipmates had been forced to take. That is, until he saw the look of distaste on Kamel's face. He took a deep breath, apologized, and tried to explain once more.

"I just want to see her and make sure she's okay. Make sure she's being taken care of and has a place to go when she's better. Can't you understand that? I mean isn't that common decency?"

His anger began to surge again. He stood and prepared to leave—no use wasting any more time here. Maybe he could find someone at the Embassy to help. Anger had propelled him from his seat; now he felt the edges of despair seep in.

"What's wrong with you people? First the Red Cross won't do anything, now you. She's a little girl. Can't you feel anything for her? Don't you care?"

Kamel rose to his feet as well. "Sit down, Corporal Maris." He gestured to the chair Ken had just left. "Please, sit down." Ken retook his seat and Kamel followed suit. "It is normally against Red Crescent policy to give out inform-ation to non-family members, but in this case, since you are so concerned, I will try to help you."

It was several weeks, and several trips in and out of port by the Delivery, before Kamel told Ken he'd located the child. "We found the hospital where she was taken, without trouble." He leaned back in one of the plush chairs in his office. "Contrary to what the neighbor told you, she wasn't badly hurt. She was treated for minor burns and abrasions then released the next day. For a while, the trail ended there."

Ken, seated in the chair opposite Kamel, leaned forward. "You mean the hospital just turned her out? She can't be more than six or seven. How could anyone allow that to happen?"

"You have to understand the circumstances," said Kamel, his tone between placating and defensive. "It was chaos. Many people were hurt. At first no one realized the little girl had no family to care for her."

Ken imagined the terror the little girl must have felt: alone, frightened, hurt. Outrage overwhelmed him. Outrage at whatever bureaucratic fuck-up allowed a mere child to be dumped on the streets, and outrage at whoever had constructed and thrown the bomb, knowing it would kill and maim innocent people. It took a few moments before he trusted his voice enough to speak.

"But you've found her. You know where she is."

"Yes," said Kamel. "We found her. Please be assured she wasn't simply thrown into the street. Such a thing would never happen here."

He lifted the coffee cup he'd been holding to his mouth and drank then carefully set the cup on the saucer before continuing.

"Someone noticed her in all the confusion, knew she'd come from the bombing site and was able to elicit the information from a neighbor that her mother had a cousin in Manama. After a little difficulty, they located this cousin. She is with the cousin now, and the cousin's family."

"And is she okay?" asked Ken, examining Kamel's face, trying to gauge whether the man was hiding anything.

"Physically, yes," said Kamel.

"Can I see her?" Ken still didn't understand why he felt so strongly about this child. He only knew he needed to see her himself. Once he saw for himself that she was okay, he'd be satisfied.

"I will ask," said Kamel.

Ken looked through the meager selection of toys in the Navy Exchange. "I don't get it, man," Sharpe said. "Why should you care about some raghead kid? You said she's with some relative or something. Why the fuck do you want to waste your time?"

"I've told you," Ken said, tamping down on a surge of anger. He'd had to do that more often lately, especially with Sharpe. "Because she's a kid. Because her father was decent. Because I want to. If you don't want to get involved, don't worry about it."

He picked up a stuffed bulldog wearing a 'Smokey Bear' hat. At the register, he gave the clerk the bulldog and a bag of candy and dug into his wallet for money to pay for them. "Don't worry about it," he said again when he and Sharpe were outside the building, this time with less irritation in his voice. "Go do whatever you want to do today, and I'll meet you later."

"You sure, man?"

"Yeah, I'm sure."

Thirty minutes later, Ken followed Kamel down a narrow street lined with small shops and houses. Kamel stopped at a house with what looked to Ken like a type of pepper plant in a large pot next to the door. "This is the place?" Kamel nodded, raised his hand, and knocked.

Chapter Eleven

MARIE

Emile had the family mop of dark brown curls and, like their aunt, his eyes twinkled with good humor. He was short, too. Her father had been short. Unlike her father, though, her cousin was soft-looking, his hands smooth and supple, reinforcing the fact that he spent most of his time indoors. Her father's hands had been rough and callused.

"So, cousin, what do you think of your new family?" Emile asked.

Marie passed him a bowl of herbed carrots. "I couldn't be happier about finding all of you and being found," she said, looking around the crowded oval table in the small dining room. "My brother and I always wished we had aunts and uncles and cousins. And now we do."

"And what about Montreal?" Emile asked.

"I haven't seen much of it except for here in the neighborhood and on the ride from the airport. There hasn't been time for much sight-seeing, because tante and I have been talking non-stop."

Marie-Catherine nodded from her place at the head of the table. Behind her was a glass-fronted mahogany cabinet filled with delicate china figurines and inexpensive mement-os. "There is so much to share," she said. "A lifetime of stories to tell—several lifetimes of stories, in fact."

"Have some of this chicken, Marie." Her uncle, René, held the plate for her.

"Thank you." She speared a piece of breast meat.

Emile poured more wine into his glass. "What do you mean by 'several' lifetimes?"

He reached to top up Marie's glass, but she quickly covered the glass with her hand. "No thanks." Wine wasn't something she was accustomed to drinking every night, though she noticed she was the only one to refrain.

"I mean," said Marie-Catherine, "Henri's life before he left Quebec, your father's, mine, our parents. What went on in Montreal and Quebec in the sixties and seventies, your life growing up here, my life with René. It may take me weeks to tell Marie everything about our family. Months, even."

"*You are* going to tell her everything?"

Puzzled by her cousin's tone and the glint in his eyes when he asked the question, Marie's gaze when from Emile to her aunt.

Marie-Catherine cast a slight scowl at her nephew. "Of course I will tell her everything."

Emile nodded and Marie again looked to her aunt, not understanding the undercurrents she sensed between the two.

"Papa, what do you think about having a grand-daughter and a great-grandson?" René said into the tension-filled silence. "Are you pleased?"

"I am delighted with my granddaughter." The old man smiled at Marie. She appreciated the effort he made to speak in English for her benefit. "And as for the little one, who would not be pleased. My question now is, when will Emile give me a great-grandchild?"

Laughter erupted as everyone turned to look at Emile.

Later, as Emile shrugged into his jacket, he asked Marie if she would like to see something of Montreal the next day. He looked to his aunt. "That is, if you don't mind me stealing her away?"

"Of course not. I always have plenty of work to keep me busy."

Marie flushed. "I'm so sorry. I didn't think about your work. I've kept you from it."

"Nonsense, *chéri*. The one thing about writing is that it will always be there and no one hounds you to finish but yourself."

René's eyebrows went up. "You're forgetting your editor."

Marie-Catherine gave her husband a confident smile. "He'll get over it. And he'll get his article on time. The research is done; the writing will be finished soon."

"Have you read any of our aunt's work?" Emile asked Marie.

Marie shook her head. "I haven't. I'm looking forward to it, assuming some of it is in English."

After Emile left and René had said goodnight, Marie-Catherine suggested she and Marie have tea. Henry Reed was upstairs, asleep in the borrowed crib. Marie's grand-father had retired as well. Her aunt led the way back to the kitchen, the most generously-sized room in the house. The dishes had already been washed and put away, but the aroma of chicken and garlic remained. "Sit," her aunt said, pointing to the round, chintz-covered table. Marie took a seat while her aunt filled a kettle and put it on the stove then struck a match and held it to the gas ring as she turned the knob. "What do you know about Canadian history?"

Her aunt's question caught Marie by surprise. "Not much. We studied about the Hudson Bay Company in school and the French fur trappers." She was embarrassed by her ignorance—especially considering her father had been born and raised in Canada. Even if they hadn't studied it in school, she could have made the effort to learn more.

"I don't mean that long ago—although the enmity between English and French Canadians certainly dates back that far. I'm talking about more recent history—the sixties and early seventies to be specific." Her aunt pulled out the chair opposite Marie. "It was a violent time. Not only here in Montreal. Violence was everywhere. Vietnam, the SDS and Black Panthers in the U.S., the Red Army and Red Brigade in Europe, and the IRA in Ireland. All over the world, it seemed, there was anger and turmoil."

The teakettle whistled. Marie-Catherine rose to attend it. She poured hot water over the loose tea leaves in the bottom of the teapot before bringing the pot and two mugs to the table. She filled both mugs and pushed one across the table to Marie.

She must be nearing fifty, Marie thought. But the way she carries herself, the way she dresses—often in faded jeans and a slouchy sweatshirt—people would guess her to be much younger. Younger than Mom. Marie felt instant guilt for what seemed a disloyal thought.

"Here, what happened in this place, what happened in this family—that is what you must understand." Marie's aunt stared into her tea, as though she were trying organize her memories. She took a deep breath and raised her eyes to Marie's. "To see him now, an old man who spends his days watching game shows on the television, you would never believe what it was like growing up in Papa's house. Politics, the abuses of government, workers' rights—those things meant everything to him then. We never sat down to a meal without Papa thundering and thumping about how French-Canadians were being oppressed by the English-speaking establishment."

Marie frowned and took a sip of tea. At home, dinner-table conversations generally centered on school; something her mother had seen on her morning walk; Ken's games; when their father might be coming home. Things like that. Nothing serious like politics or government.

Her aunt went on. "I won't deny the truth of what Papa said. We were oppressed. As your father often stated in his newspaper articles and speeches, French-Canadians made up a pool of cheap labor the Anglophones could use or not, as they saw fit. They were completely free to underpay us—the average French Canadian made just over half what the average English-speaking Canadian earned. They could mistreat us, and have us clubbed by the police and locked in prison when we objected."

Marie had heard of the way blacks had been treated in the United States before the civil rights movement—in Idaho as well as in the south. She knew first-hand how some people back home talked about and treated Hispanics and Asians. Nez Perce, too. Like they were subhuman. Although she hated when people talked like that, what her aunt described was personal. These were her people being mistreated.

"Many people wanted Quebec to separate from the rest of Canada, with French-Canadian leadership—which would seem a given since we are the majority here. But nothing is as simple as it seems. And nothing got better for the workers."

Her aunt's lips tightened. She poured more tea before going on.

"There was a sign at the Montreal airport that read *'WELCOME TO MONTREAL WHERE LABOUR IS CHEAP AND DOCILE.'* The sign was meant to encourage U.S. businesses to invest here, and maybe it worked that way. But it also made French-Canadians very angry."

Marie thought of her father growing up in the conditions her aunt describe and felt as though a stone was lodged in her stomach. How angry and frustrated he must have been. But hopeful, too, or he wouldn't have fought so hard to change things when he got older. With that thought, the weight in her stomach eased somewhat. Then she frowned, more puzzled than ever. What happened to make him give up that fight?

Her aunt's voice broke in on her thoughts. "In the early sixties, a group of politically active people—people who had grown frustrated with the slowness of change—formed a new alliance: the *Front de Liberation du Quebec*—the FLQ. Most were impatient and young. Some were very young, in fact. My brother, Marc—your uncle—joined right away. He was fourteen or fifteen at the time."

Marie's eyes widened. "Couldn't your parents stop him?"

"He kept it from the family, but I think your father knew. Maybe not right away, but later, he knew. They were very close in age, Henri and Marc, and growing up they did everything together—until they were teenagers, that is. They started to pull apart then...but not so far apart Henri wouldn't have known."

Marie stared. They'd only been boys, barely out of grammar school. At that age, sports and girls had been Ken's major interests, just as they'd been for Paul and every other boy she'd known in high school.

"Henri and Marc had the same goal for French-Canadians and Quebec: equality and independence. But they were as different as night and day in how they went about it. Marc quit school and went to work on the docks with Papa."

"But why didn't your parents or his teachers insist he stay in school?"

Her aunt shrugged. "By law, he was free to leave at fourteen. And he was an indifferent student—too impatient to be a man, I suppose. Henri, on the other hand, liked school and he did very well. He also worked part-time at a French-speaking newspaper *Le Journal Quotidien*. He loved it right from the start; journalism and political science became his majors at university and eventually, after he graduated, he returned to the *Le Journal Quotidien*. Right away he became the paper's star reporter." She stopped and picked up the teapot. She poured a little into her cup and studied it. "This looks too strong. Shall I make some more?"

"I'll do it." Marie got up and ran more water into the kettle. "Please, go on."

"While Henri was studying, Marc was learning things, too—mainly, how to build bombs."

Marie drew in her breath and held it. Pearl Whitebear had told her about Marc's bomb-building, but she still had a hard time accepting it.

Her aunt must have sensed her disbelief. "It is true *chérie.* Sadly. As I told you, it was a very violent time. Everywhere there was the anger and hatred." She paused for another moment, as though searching for a way to put what she was about to say into words. "You've heard of Martin Luther King, Jr. and Malcolm X." At Marie's nod, she went on. "Well, as they grew older, that's what Henri and Marc were like. Henri, like Martin Luther King, wanted to negotiate peacefully—change things with votes. Marc, on the other hand, was like a time-bomb, ticking toward an explosion. They say Malcolm X moderated his views after traveling to Mecca. Marc never did. Your father told me once that Marc didn't know the meaning of compromise. 'He won't be happy until English-speaking Canadians are receiving French-Canadian injustice.' He was right, but I didn't believe him at the time."

Marie frowned her puzzlement. "But I thought Dad was in the FLQ, too. I'm sure Pearl Whitebear told me that. Ken and I talked about it in our letters, but neither of us could believe Dad would have been involved in a terrorist organization—and isn't that what the FLQ was?"

"It was, but many of us didn't look at it that way. We said the FLQ only targeted property, not people. We were tired of the injustice. We weren't going to tolerate it any longer." Her aunt frowned. "Marc took me with him to

North Carolina to buy dynamite, guns and ammunition. I was proud—I thought I was finally proving I could do something for the cause. But your father was angry with me...so very angry. He demanded that I stay away from Marc and all of Marc's 'machinations'. I wouldn't. So your father took things into his own hands."

Her aunt traced a tiny vine on the chintz tablecloth. Her fingers shook. She dropped both hands into her lap. "In desperation, I think, Henri convinced his editor to pretend to fire him so that he could join the FLQ. He told his editor he wanted to write an insider story about them, but he really wanted to prove that more could be achieved through civil protest. Many people loved him for it; he did make a difference." She paused and briefly glanced into Marie's eyes before taking a sip of her tea. Her fingers still shook.

Though she tried, Marie couldn't imagine her father, the man who avoided people and had little to say about politics and current events, as the cynosure of so many eyes. Making speeches? Writing articles? Organizing demonstrations? It didn't seem possible. And yet...?

"Even after all he did to protect me, I remained foolish and stubborn," her aunt continued. "It took a good friend getting killed and me losing the sight in my right eye before I understood what your father had known for years: Marc would stop at nothing—not even murder—to get what he wanted. And when he was arrested, he couldn't face it—not the thought of the two people whose lives he took, not because of the grief he caused his family. No. It was the thought of being locked in jail for the rest of his life that he couldn't stand. So he killed himself. I was the last of the family to see him alive."

Resignation flattened her aunt's words, but Marie could detect no anger in them. Perhaps it had burned out. She'd had over thirty years to come to terms.

It was all too new for Marie. Her father had grown up in a city filled with violence, while she'd grown up in the country, surrounded by love, witnessing only nature's violence. How could she hope to understand what had motivated him?

An hour later, her mind churning from all she'd seen and heard, Marie pulled one of Paul's worn sweatshirts over her head. She thought again of the tense moment at the dinner table when Emile had asked their aunt if she planned to tell Marie everything. The look her aunt had given Emile couldn't have been mistaken for anything but a warning. What had Emile meant? Were there more secrets? She crossed the hall to the bathroom to brush her teeth. She stared at her reflection in the mirror. If there were more secrets, what could they be, what could be worse than what she'd already been told?

Emotionally and physically exhausted, she fell into bed. Sleep wouldn't come, however. All day she'd put off thinking about her phone call to Paul that morning. It had left her feeling edgy and slightly adrift. She'd had to drag everything out of him.

"Hi, it's me. Did I wake you?" She pictured him sitting on the side of the bed, hair rumpled from sleep, his shoulder hitched to hold the phone to his ear while he rubbed sleep from his eyes. She had a sudden longing to be sitting beside him.

"No." His voice was flat. "I'm up."

"So early? I thought you'd be sleeping 'til the last minute without me to get you up and fix breakfast." That wasn't really what she thought and she didn't know why she said it.

"No."

She took a deep breath and changed the subject, fighting to keep her voice light. "Everyone here is great. They're all so nice to me and Henry Reed, especially Marie-Catherine. But when they talk about Dad they call him 'Ahnree,' which makes him sound like a different person."

"When are you coming home?"

"You know when, Paul. My return flight is already booked." Emotion welled up in her throat, but she fought it down.

"That's two weeks from now."

"It's what we planned."

"You mean it's what you planned." He paused and she knew he was expecting her to say something. She remained silent. "You're not going to change your mind and come home earlier?" She could hear the anger beneath his words and her own anger rose up to match it.

"No. Why should I do that and why are you even asking me to? This is my family and I want to spend some time with them—you should be happy for me, not crabby and disapproving."

"I'm your family, too, Marie. And so is your mother. You'd better not forget us in your rush to find someone new and exciting." The line went dead.

She bit down on her lower lip to keep it from trembling as she turned her face into her pillow. Oh, Paul, why won't you understand?

As promised, when Emile arrived soon after breakfast the next morning, Marie had Henry Reed's diaper bag packed and was ready to go. He led the way to the bus stop. "It'll be easier than driving."

In Old Montreal, she marveled at the brick and stone buildings lining the cobblestone streets down to the banks of the river. "A hundred years ago these were all warehouses," Emile said, as they wandered through the galleries and gift shops that, along with upscale restaurants and offices, now filled the old buildings.

Later, in Place Jacques-Cartier, stalls of printed T-shirts, sandals, key rings, and balloons ran down the center of the wide pedestrian mall. Marie stopped to watch an artist do a colored chalk rendering of a teenage girl with spiked hair and a diaper pin in her ear, while Henry Reed stared over her shoulder, wide-eyed, at a white-faced mime.

"Are you ready for lunch?" Emile asked.

"Hmm? Oh, yes, I'm starving."

When they were seated in one of the upscale restaurants they'd passed earlier, a waiter handed them tall menus. Strapped into a highchair between them, Henry Reed banged on the tray with a spoon. "Oops," Marie said and took the spoon from his waving hand. Her son squealed his displeasure, but soon found equal fascination in a cracker Marie unwrapped and handed him.

"Where did you learn to be so unflappable?"

"I don't know." Marie smiled. "People back home would be sure to tell you I haven't always been so patient, and I'm still not about most things. But with Henry Reed…

I guess there must be some mystical process that takes place in the delivery room."

Emile said nothing, but turned his attention to the menu. Marie tensed, realizing he must be thinking of his mother abandoning him as an infant. She felt awkward and tactless, but didn't know if she should apologize. He hadn't mentioned his mother—maybe he didn't want to talk about her, especially to someone he didn't know well.

"What looks good to you?"

Marie tense shoulders relaxed. "I hate to say it, but I'd love a hamburger and French fries. Is that on the menu?" The menu was hard to read in the restaurant's dim lighting.

Emile laughed. "Of course. We are a tourist Mecca here. On this street you can get hamburgers, pizza, tacos, enchiladas and just about any other American fast food staple. If that doesn't satisfy, McDonalds is two blocks away."

Marie smiled. "A hamburger will do." When they'd placed their orders, Marie asked Emile what he knew about their fathers. "Where did they live?"

"Across the river in Longueil. I'd take you there, but there's not much to see, just a bunch of warehouses where the house sat—such as it was. A tarpapered shack, really, torn down after *Grand mere* died and Grandpapa came to live with us. I remember it only very little."

The waitress brought Emile's coffee and Marie's coke. Marie gave Henry Reed another cracker, which he promptly crumbled onto his tray before picking up each tiny piece and pushing it into his mouth.

"Do you remember my father?"

Emile shook his head. "He was gone by the time I was old enough to remember anything. As a baby, I lived with him and Marie-Catherine—not far from where she and René live now. He still worked for the newspaper then." The waitress arriving with their food interrupted Emile's recollections—which were nothing Marie didn't already know—and the topic of their fathers was set aside.

After lunch Emile guided them back to the bus stop. "There are lots of other things you need to see, but I want you to meet someone first."

He wouldn't give her any information other than it was a woman she was to meet, an 'old friend' of her father. It annoyed Marie that he wouldn't be more forthcoming. She recalled the tense moment at the dinner table the night before and wondered if the woman they were going to see had anything to do with it.

Eventually she gave up trying to wheedle more details from him and turned her attention to Henry Reed. The swaying of the bus had him nodding against her chest and she smiled at his futile attempts to force his eyes open as sleep slowly stole across his face.

"We get off here," said Emile. "Do you want me to take him?"

"Thanks, I've got him. If I hand him over, he'll wake up, and that wouldn't be fun for any of us." Marie stepped onto the sidewalk and looked at the large, stately homes on the tree-lined street. "Very nice."

Emile took her elbow and guided her to a house midway in the block.

The woman who answered the door was lithe and slender. Long legs made her look as though she could have been a ballet dancer. Her blunt-cut silvery hair didn't quite reach her shoulders. Huge, mascara-ringed eyes stared at Marie from behind large, dark-rimmed glasses. The casual elegance of her clothes made Marie think of Pearl Whitebear.

After a pause, the woman moved back. "Come in." She opened the door wide enough for them to enter and held out her hand. "I'm Claudia." The smile was automatic and didn't reach her eyes.

Marie balanced Henry Reed in one arm and took the proffered hand. "I'm Marie. And this," she pointed with her chin, "is Henry Reed."

Claudia stared at the sleeping baby, an unreadable look on her face, before turning to lead the way down the hall. "I can offer you iced tea, beer or Coca Cola. Come into the kitchen and we'll talk there."

"Oh, but…we shouldn't interrupt your afternoon," Marie said, but the woman had already disappeared through a swinging door at the end of the hall. "Emile, she doesn't want us here," she whispered, quickening her step to keep up with him. "Why did you bring us?"

Emile, ignoring her question, pushed the swinging door open and Marie reluctantly stepped through.

The kitchen was large, with high ceilings and a black and white tile floor. A round glass-topped table surrounded by four white wicker chairs occupied a small windowed bay at one side of the room. A galvanized bucket of hydrangeas, pink and red roses and large white daisies stood on a long black granite countertop next to a sink.

A tall vase the same blue as the hydrangeas was next to the bucket. Claudia crushed the end of a rose stem under running water then slipped it into place in the arrangement. She added another rose and several daisies before she stepped back and gave the whole a critical look. "That will do for this one."

There were several other vases on the counter and plenty more flowers in the bucket. Marie's arrangements were limited to an occasional handful of daffodils or wild iris. "It's beautiful."

Emile pulled out a chair for Marie then slouched into the one next to her. Henry Reed stiffened. He relaxed back into sleep as Marie stroked his cheek and murmured to him, at the same time trying to keep a rein on the tension creeping up her spine.

"Would you like something to drink? As I said, I have beer or iced tea. Or cola if you'd prefer it." Claudia reached for another vase. "You get it Emile."

Emile stood, scraping the chair back. "What will you have, Marie?"

"Nothing, thanks. I'm fine."

"I'll have a glass of iced tea, *chér*," Claudia told Emile. "On the top shelf."

Marie watched Emile move with familiar ease to fill a glass with ice cubes and tea before getting a beer and opening it. She had to wonder how often he'd been there and what his relationship with this seemingly hostile woman might be. Not his girlfriend—she must be thirty years older than him. He looked enquiringly at her, eyebrows raised. "Sure you don't want something?" When she shook her head, he returned to his seat, beer in hand. He said nothing further and Claudia continued to arrange flowers as though she were the only person in the room.

Marie could stand the prolonged silence no longer. "Emile said you knew my father." She threw the words out.

Claudia didn't turn to look at her. "I knew Henri Morais. Whether he was your father, I don't know."

Chapter Twelve

ELLEN

Steve Richards let Ellen know the restaurant was getting rave reviews for her bread and rolls. "The owner is delighted, Ellen. He's eager to carry on our relationship. I'm assuming you're in agreement."

A pleased smile spread across Ellen's face. At the same time, tears stung her eyes. She went home and called the broker Steve—she called him Steve now, not Chef Richards—had introduced her to. The man had shown her pictures of several ovens and told her the pros and cons of each. She ordered the one he'd recommended. Also, a commercial mixer.

The alarm rang, shrill, demanding. Ellen opened one eye and looked at the clock on the nightstand. Four-thirty glowed in red numbers. She moaned and let her head sink deeper into the pillow. After several minutes, minutes in which each toe, each finger, each limb sent messages of reluctance to move from its cozy cocoon, she threw back the covers and swung her legs over the side of the bed. Her feet tapped the floor, searching for slippers. After another full minute, she stood and headed for the bathroom.

Ten-thirty and the yeasty aroma of her first batch of breads and rolls filled the truck's cab. A second batch of dough would be ready to form into loaves by the time she got back. Her twice-daily trips to town to deliver her baked goods to the restaurant had yet to wear thin. Instead, they buoyed her up, made her realize she was capable of anything—a year ago, six months ago, she'd never have thought she'd have her own business, one she'd created with her own skill, her own talent.

Even as she thought this, like a dog worrying a bone, she returned to the question that seemed permanently lodged in the forefront of her mind: what was Marie learning in Montreal, what secrets was she ferreting out? There'd only been a phone call to say she and Henri Reed had arrived safely, but nothing since. It was unlike her daughter, who normally shared everything.

Ellen considered calling—Marie had given her the phone number before she left. But she was afraid Marie-Catherine would answer. She had no desire to talk to the sister whose existence Henry had kept hidden from her for over twenty years—at least not until she understood why he'd done it.

Pastures and fields gave way to a few scattered commercial buildings and soon she drove past the airport, where private planes and corporate jets shared space with planes used by the Forest Service and the Air National Guard. She barely noted them. Only when the big red "Morrison's" sign popped into view did she shake loose from thoughts of Marie. Eggs. I need eggs.

Finding an empty space in the crowded lot, she parked then hurried inside.

"Ellen? Is that you?"

She turned at the voice. "Marta? How are you?" She embraced the older woman, who smiled and hugged her back.

"I haven't seen you for the longest time. I was so sorry to hear about Henry and sorry I wasn't at the funeral to pay my respects."

"Thank you," said Ellen, still holding the slender hand. "I heard you were in the hospital. Are you okay now?"

"Oh, much better. It was nothing serious. You know— one of those female things," Marta said, although Ellen had heard it was much more serious. She'd meant to visit her friend in the hospital. There were many things she should have done but didn't in the months after Henry died. Then she'd become so busy with her bread business and with Marie, she'd forgotten. What a terrible way to treat a dear friend.

Standing next to the dairy case, Ellen told Marta about her bread-making venture. "Can you imagine it, Marta— me, starting a business?"

"Absolutely I can. Henry would be so proud of you."

"Do you think so?" Ellen rubbed her wedding ring with her thumb, spinning it on her finger. "Sometimes I'm not so sure."

"Of course he would be."

Ellen sighed and glanced at her watch. "Oh my, I didn't realize it was so late. I have to go, but I hope to see you again soon. Maybe I can drop by and we'll have coffee. Like the old days."

The new oven had been delivered and Ellen was ready when Frank arrived with his box of tools on Saturday.

"Do you have time for coffee before you get started? These rolls are still warm from the oven."

"You bet—you think I'd turn down an offer like that?" Frank didn't hesitate before reaching for a roll stuffed with cinnamon and raisins and topped with a thin layer of icing. Ellen poured coffee.

"I'll take all this to the restaurant in a bit," she said, gesturing toward the cooling loaves and dinner rolls on the counter. I've arranged to use a friend's kitchen for the evening batch. You remember Marta Weitzel, don't you?"

"Didn't her husband die a few years back?"

Nodding, Ellen told him how they'd run into each other at Morrison's. When she'd called Marta and mentioned her dilemma, her friend had offered her oven. "I'm sure it's small." Ellen thought of the miniscule oven in Marie's and Paul's apartment. "But I guess it will have to do—or not. She's enlisted her next-door-neighbor's oven, too." Ellen smiled, remembering how eagerly Marta had organized everything. "I should be back by four-thirty or five. You'll stay for dinner."

Frank shook his head. "I have a better idea. You'll be bushed from being on your feet all day and the last thing you'll feel like doing is cooking a meal. Let's go out to dinner. With Marie still away, what do you say I call Paul and the two of us meet you at this restaurant of yours at five?"

Ellen was taken aback. She hardly knew what to say; she and Henry had rarely gone out to eat. "Why, I—"

"No arguing. Five o'clock."

Marta's apartment was in a new building on the outskirts of Platt City. Although it lacked the personality of her old home, her friend had done her best to bring warmth to the sterile rooms with flowers and pictures; a bowl of apples on the kitchen table brought back instant memories.

"I've set out all the other things you told me you needed."

Ellen, put the cardboard box loaded with flour, yeast and spices on the counter, enjoying the anticipation in Marta's sparkling eyes, the sudden lift of her friend's chin. She was also delighted to note Marta's oven was much bigger than she'd feared. She assumed the promised oven next door would hold an equal number of pans.

The afternoon passed faster than Ellen imagined possible. Although she enjoyed the solitude of her own kitchen, it was a pleasant change to have someone to talk with. The aroma of baking bread filled the kitchen as Marta brought her up to date on several town families. It turned out the woman next door was the mother of an old classmate of Ellen's. As the two older women chatted, Ellen thought of her mother and how much pleasure she would have taken in the day.

"I've enjoyed this so much," Marta said as they finished drying the bowls and pans for the last time, then repacking them in a large box. "I can't remember when I've had such a good time."

"It has been a nice day. What I'd have done without your help I surely don't know." Ellen looked over the baskets of bread and rolls and a flush of contented pride filled her. It had been a very good day.

"Well, it probably wouldn't have been the end of the earth if the restaurant had to do without your bread for one meal—after all, they never had it before," said Marta, picking up the box filled with pans and followed Ellen, arms also loaded, into the hall. "But, this was much better. And so much fun, too."

The two baskets of bread secured on the seat beside her and the boxes of pans and supplies in the back, Ellen leaned out the truck's window and waved goodbye. Marta was right. It wouldn't have been the end of things had she not been able to deliver her order, but she was glad she wouldn't be letting the restaurant down.

A sudden thought struck her. How had she not thought of it before—Marta's kitchen hadn't been inspected. A sigh slipped from between her lips—she'd have to tell Steve Richards, let him decide if the afternoon had been a waste of time.

She drove along the newly paved street, barely registering the young trees that bordered it, the cerulean sky overhead, the tree-covered mountains across the valley, and thought about her mother. Mama would approve of what I'm doing. Papa, too. But would Henry? Maybe he'd think she was well enough fixed with her parents' insurance money and those secret investments of his, that she shouldn't have to work. Maybe he'd be insulted she was baking bread for a restaurant. Without him to do for, though, how would I spend my time? I'd go crazy. Surely, he'd understand that.

She chewed on her lower lip, frowning with the realization that she had no idea what Henry would think. She began to wonder if she'd known Henry at all.

The restaurant was filling. Ellen spotted Frank and Paul at a rear table, waved and headed their way. Ian McCort and two men she didn't recognize sat huddled at a window table, deep in conversation. Ian didn't glance up and she didn't interrupt when she passed. Whatever they were talking about had his full attention.

She felt awkward sitting down to a table with two men, even though one was her son-in-law, whom she'd known since he was in diapers, the other a good friend she'd known even longer, almost since she'd been in diapers.

Paul's mouth was drawn down, his shoulders hunched forward. After a brief hello, he fiddled with the edge of his placemat and struggled even more than usual in his effort to make small talk. He soon gave up trying.

Frank, on the other hand, didn't seem daunted by his son's reluctance to join the conversation. "Your new oven is now fully operational," he told Ellen after the waiter had taken their orders. "I have a couple hours of work outside the house, but nothing that will interfere with your business. Tomorrow's Sunday. Paul can give me a hand, can't you son?"

Paul nodded, drumming his fingers on the table.

"I don't know how to thank you." Stifling her growing irritation with her son-in-law, Ellen forced a smile that included both men. "I'll have to promise you a lifetime supply of baked goods."

Frank grinned. "I wouldn't turn that down. How about you, Paul? Sounds like a pretty fair deal, doesn't it?"

"Sure," said Paul, but he didn't add anything.

Ellen glanced at Frank, wondering if he knew how adamant Paul had been in his disapproval of Marie going to Montreal, which was no doubt what lay behind his sullen behavior. She was about to ask Paul if he'd heard from Marie, when the waiter arrived with their meals. After he left, Paul didn't hesitate to cut into his steak.

Ellen and Frank dug into their meals, too, then the conversation between them picked up again. They discussed the high school wrestling team's prospects, which led to questions about Ken. Ellen told Frank how hot it was in Bahrain and about the gold bazaar Ken had described in his last letter.

Paul suddenly dropped his knife and fork onto his plate, startling Ellen and causing both her and Frank to stop talking and stare at him. "Have you heard anything more from Marie?"

Ellen shook her head. "Only the one phone call when they arrived. Hasn't she called you?"

"A few times."

"Has she told you what she's found out?"

Paul shook his head. "Only that she won't change her mind and come home early."

Ellen waited for him to say something more, but he picked up his knife and fork and returned to his meal. Poor Paul. It looked like they'd both have to wait for her headstrong daughter to come home before they would learn whatever secrets she'd unearthed.

Her earlier appetite gone, Ellen pushed her plate aside. When they were ready to leave, she noted that Ian and the two men he'd been talking with were gone, their table cleared. "Did you see those two men with Ian McCort?"

Frank nodded. "I didn't recognize them, though. Did you?"

"They were cops," said Paul. "City cops. Or Feds."

Ellen gave him a startled look. "In Platt City? What would they be doing here?"

Ellen dropped in to see Marta Weitzel twice in the following days and once Marta drove out to see her. "Just like the old days," Marta said, glancing around Ellen's kitchen. "Remember how we'd sit for hours talking about this and that?"

Ellen shared Marta's pleasure in their renewed friend-ship—as though it had never been interrupted by time, babies, life, and death. But she hated thinking of her old friend, a countrywoman from birth, cooped up in that soulless apartment—it wasn't right. It didn't take long before she knew what she must do.

"So, what do you think?"

"Ellen, I don't know what to say. I..." tears filled Marta's eyes and her voice shook. "To be in the country again...in a real home...I just can't believe you want me to come and live with you. It's too generous. You're too kind."

"Well, don't think I'm all kindness and generosity. I can use your help as well as your company. With Henry gone, and the children grown, the evenings are pretty long." That wasn't entirely true. Most evenings Ellen was so tired she dropped into bed before dark, but Marta's heartfelt response made her know she was doing the right thing.

The Sunday before Marie was due home, they rented a storage unit for Marta's excess furniture then, with Frank's and Paul's help, they moved the rest of her things out to Ellen's.

Ellen peeled her shirt from where it was sticking between her shoulder blades. The weather was still hot and dry, but thankfully, the wind had died and the forest fire raging out of control in the mountains east of Platt City had finally begun to taper off. "This gives me the chance to clear out some things, too. Maybe you and Marie want that tan chair in the living room, Paul. It was my father's then Henry's. You should have it now—and the lamp and table next to it. We can put Marta's rocker in that corner. What do you think?"

By evening, the furniture was in place, including a four-poster in Marie's old room next to a doily-topped walnut chest-of-drawers covered with black and white pictures in silver frames. What didn't fit—Marie's old bed, two small bedside tables and a straight-backed chair—had been taken to the storage unit.

"If you and Marie want any of those things, we can always get them out," Ellen told Paul as he and Frank prepared to head back to town. "Again, you two have been so much help. I wish there was some way I could repay you."

"Have us out to dinner one night, Ellen, and get Marta to make one of her famous blackberry pies." Frank turned to his son. "You probably don't know it, but you've been in the company of a world-class pie-baker. Marta Weitzel's pies always took first place at the county fair and brought in the most money at any bake sale."

"That's true. She can still make them, too." Ellen patted her stomach. "I'm living testimony." Paul gave a weak smile and Ellen was left with no doubt he was still brooding about her daughter. She put her hand on his arm and squeezed. "She'll be home soon, Paul. Everything will be back to normal in no time. You'll see." Even as she said the words, she wasn't sure who she was trying to convince, Paul or herself.

"Yeah. Well, see you Ellen." Paul turned the key in the ignition and the truck's engine grumbled to life.

Ellen waved goodbye, then turned and headed toward the house.

Inside, Marta was dusting off the furniture and adjusting pillows. She looked up as Ellen came into the room. "Oh, this looks so nice. Everything just fits, don't you think?"

Later, Ellen lay in her bed and listened to the sound of water running in the bathroom. It was good to hear someone else in the house. She hadn't realized how empty it had been.

Chapter Thirteen

KEN

Canned television laughter came from inside the house. Kamel stepped in front of Ken and knocked. After a moment, footsteps approached. The door opened and a man of medium height and dark complexion stood framed in the doorway. The look of inquiry on his face softened. "Ah, Mr. Kamel...and this is the young man you spoke to me of?"

Kamel made the introductions.

Khalid Soueif stepped back from the doorway. "Please enter. You are both welcome in this house."

Ken glanced around, taking in the high ceilings, thick white walls, and tile floors. The immediate drop in temperature they provided were a welcome relief from the sweltering heat on the street outside.

Kamel spoke a few words to their host then bowed to both. "I am sorry I cannot linger. I have another appointment."

After Kamel left, Soueif led Ken into a room with modern, Western-style furniture and thick, fringed carpets. A large television set on a metal stand stood in one corner. A little girl sat in front of it, staring at a rerun of *The Partridge Family*.

"Farida, you have a visitor." If she heard, the little girl gave no indication. "Farida," Soueif said again, then followed with several sentences of Arabic. The child continued to ignore him. With a sigh, Soueif turned back to Ken. "I'd hoped something unusual, like the appearance of a stranger, might bring her out of it."

Ken frowned. "Did the explosion damage her hearing?"

"No. She hears. But she doesn't speak. She only sits and watches the television. Even when it is turned off, she stares at it."

Ken held out the stuffed toy and candy. "I've brought her something. It's not much." What did anyone expect— she was supposed to slip into a new family without a backward glance, not notice her mother and father had been blown to bits?

"You are kind. Farida, your visitor has brought you gifts." Soueif took the toy and the candy across the room and placed them in the girl's lap. She didn't remove her eyes from the television screen, but her hand closed over both offerings.

A woman entered the room. Clad in the traditional black robes covering all but her eyes, she carried a large tray.

"My wife has prepared some refreshment."

Mrs. Soueif set the tray on a round table inlaid with mother-of-pearl. The tray held a hammered silver coffee pot and delicate china cups, a bowl with lumps of brown sugar, a dish of dates, a bowl of pistachio nuts and a plate of sugar wafers.

"Perhaps you'd prefer something cool?" Soueif turned and spoke in rapid Arabic to his wife.

She hesitated and Ken smiled at her. "No, thank you. This is fine. Perfect." She poured two cups of coffee and dropped a lump of sugar into each.

Soueif gestured to an overstuffed, upholstered chair. "Please sit."

Ken did so and Soueif handed him one of the delicate cups. A small spoon rested on the saucer. Ken felt clumsy taking the tiny cup and saucer in his unaccustomed hands.

Soueif sat in an identical chair. His wife served him then pulled up a low stool, placing the tray between the two men. She left the room without speaking.

Ken sipped the hot, sweet coffee. He'd thought the Navy and Marine Corps made the strongest brew possible, but it was nothing like this. Eyes closed, Soueif seemed content to sit and savor the hot drink. Holding the fragile cup between clumsy fingers, Ken did likewise. His eyes, however, traveled around the room.

A large, shuttered window below an equally large section of stained-glass occupied the center of one wall. Sunlight through the brightly-colored stained-glass fell in broken squares and rectangles across the already colorful carpet. Several open archways led off the room, allowing for a pleasant flow of air. From somewhere came the tinkling of water in a fountain.

Finally, Soueif roused himself, blinking several times. "How long have you been in Bahrain, Corporal Maris?"

Cautioned against giving specifics on the *Delivery*'s movements, Ken kept his answer vague. "In and out, a little over four months."

"And what do you think of my country?"

Ken had so many impressions—some good, some bad. "Well...there's the heat."

Soueif smiled. "Yes, of course. The heat is very hard for westerners to accustom themselves to."

"And the gold souk. We're not used to anything like that, either."

"And the people?"

"That's hard for me to answer. I don't really know anyone yet. You can't count the merchants or the taxi drivers. I think they are really like two people—the person who drives the taxi or sells the goods, and the other person—the person who exists for his family and friends… the person who stays hidden from foreigners."

"You are wise. We do not easily reveal our true selves to outsiders. Perhaps we are too suspicious."

"Do you and your wife have children?" If they did, Ken saw no signs of them. Maybe with someone her own age, Farida would come out of her shell.

"We have two. A boy and a girl—both are teenagers, in school now."

"What about Farida? Doesn't she go to school?"

"The doctor thinks school would be too difficult for her at this time. My wife is trying to work with her, reading to her from her school books. We're not sure what she takes in."

"She has no other family?" Ken knew nothing about caring for a traumatized child. He had to admire Khalid Soueif and his wife for what they were trying to do.

"No. But there would be plenty of people to take her in and care for her if we were unable to do so. Children in Bahrain do not go needy."

Returning to the base and the Delivery, in the back of a taxi summoned by Soueif, Ken wondered what more Marie had found out in Montreal. Like her, the idea of their father being penned up in prison for several months tied his stomach in knots. Angry as the old man used to make him, he couldn't bear to think of him being locked up and beaten, like Marie said they did to him. But imagining his father participating in anything like what had happened to Farida made his skin crawl. He didn't want to believe it. He couldn't, wouldn't believe it.

Twice more Ken visited the family, meeting the teenage son, but not the daughter. He learned Soueif's wife was an artist and Soueif a banker, though not the usual kind. He worked nights in the bank's international department, which explained why he occasionally nodded off in Ken's presence.

Both times Ken visited, he brought Farida a small gift. Each time she refused to acknowledge his presence.

Sharpe ridiculed his interest in the girl. "Why do you want to spend time on some kid you'll never see again? She got a good-looking cousin or something?"

Ken tried to remain impassive, but his fingers clenched, the muscles in his arms flexed. "If you don't understand, there's no way I can explain." He turned away. "I need to check with the gunny on something."

The days dragged on, the routine unchanged. The souks in Manama had lost their allure. At sea, it was more of the same—update manuals and off-load supplies. Twice he and his fellow Marines were put on alert, but nothing came of it. The temperature remained the same, in or out of port—unbearably hot and humid. Tempers grew short and boredom led to more than one altercation.

Then suddenly the ship came alive as word passed they were heading back to the Med. They'd been on another re-supply mission when the orders came. They didn't even return to port. Ken was disappointed he couldn't say good-bye to Farida's family in person. He had to rely on a written note. Still, he was happy to be leaving the Gulf behind.

"We'll be stopping in Yemen to refuel," the gunny said.

Chapter Fourteen
MARIE

Marie frowned at Emile. "Why did you insist on staying when she clearly didn't want us there?" Henry Reed had awakened and Marie used his fussing to end their visit with the mysterious Claudia. Now, still sleepy, he gazed at the long-fingered maple leaves dancing in the branches above their heads.

Emile shrugged. "She didn't mind."

"Of course she minded." Marie tried to hold her annoyance in check. As far as she was concerned, the visit had been a waste of time. "She wasn't in the least bit interested in telling me anything about my father, either."

"There's the bus. Let us hurry." Emile quickened his pace and Marie had no choice but to follow.

The bus pulled to the curb and a slender young woman with brown wavy hair was the first to step off. Pleasure lit the woman's large gray eyes when they fell on Emile. In the spate of French that erupted from her lips, the only word Marie recognized was maman.

When the woman paused for breath, Emile introduced her as Jeannine Turbot, Claudia's daughter. "And this is my American cousin, Marie Klein, and her son, Henry Reed."

Marie began to extend her hand, but the sound of the bus door closing interrupted the automatic gesture.

Emile banged on the door and the driver re-opened it. "Hurry, Marie."

"Wait…" Jeannine looked at Marie with a puzzled frown. "Cousin?"

"We have no time." Emile's hand on Marie's back urged her onto the bus. "I'll call you."

"Sorry." Marie threw a smile over her shoulder to soften the haste of their departure.

Marie made her way down the aisle. Behind her, Emile deposited their fare in the box. There were no seats together, so the subject of their unwelcome visit was effectively dropped—for the time being at least. She found a place next to a young man with a Walkman plugged into his ear.

After settling Henry Reed on her lap, she turned to the window. Jeannine remained standing where they'd left her, staring after the bus. Marie wondered what kind of relationship she had with her mother. She also wondered if Claudia was always as unhappy as she'd seemed during their visit.

Late in the afternoon, back at her aunt's house once more, Marie grabbed a tube of lip balm and gave it to Henri Reed, lying on her bed. She held his feet and tried to slip a diaper under his squirming hips.

"This would only take a couple of seconds if you'd stop wiggling."

The baby threw the tube aside, then twisted around and reached for it. Despite his frantic maneuvers, Marie held him down long enough to finish putting the diaper's Velcro tabs in place then pulled him onto her lap so that she could snap the legs of his coveralls together.

"Why do you have to make this so hard, you little rascal?" Her son's response was to reach up and stick his fingers between her lips, grinning.

His happy face went a long way to easing the tension generated by the visit to Claudia, also the ache in her heart whenever she thought about his father. Three times, she'd called Paul, and each time, the conversation was fraught with barely-disguised anger on his side and defensiveness on her own. He was being so stubborn and close-minded—he'd never acted like that before.

Up until now, they'd agreed about everything—at least all the important things. She thought they had, anyway. So had everyone. All their high school friends had claimed they were the ideal couple because they so seldom argued. But what if Paul had merely gone along with her to keep the peace? What if they really weren't as well-suited as she and her friends had believed?

It was enough to make Marie's head pound. She caught her lower lip and wiped away gathering tears with the palms of both hands. *I can't think about that now.*

The rumble of voices came from the kitchen, directly below her. Emile and Marie-Catherine. She was about to gather Henry Reed up and take him downstairs, when their voices suddenly rose. She felt unsure what to do, hoping their argument, and there was no doubt it was exactly that, wasn't about her. She hesitated, but only for a moment. Henry Reed on her hip, she left the bedroom and resolutely descended the stairs. The voices grew stronger as she drew closer to the kitchen.

Although Marie couldn't understand her aunt's words, she heard the anger they contained. Emile answered, defiance in his voice…something about *finalement*. Marie frowned. Something was final? What?

She pushed open the door and walked into the room. Her aunt quickly turned, her face filled with concern. "*Chérie,* I thought you were asleep. I hope Emile and I didn't waken you."

"You didn't. I dozed for a bit, but Henry Reed put an end to that. I came down to get him a bottle and help you with dinner. I hope I'm not interrupting." She glanced at both of their faces, trying to read them. The air almost quivered with the tension between them.

"Of course not, *chérie,*" her aunt said.

"I am just leaving," said Emile. He walked across the kitchen to his aunt's side and put his arm around her shoulder. "I'll call you later." Although Marie-Catherine's back stiffened at her nephew's touch, she nodded. Emile winked at Marie and left.

Her aunt, arms folded across her chest, stared out the window above the sink. After a long silence, during which Marie heard the snick of the outer door closing, her aunt turned from the window, a bright but obviously forced smile on her lips. "Well, how did you enjoy Montreal, *chérie?* Emile tells me you visited Old Montreal and Place Jacques Cartier."

"It was very nice. I bought some souvenirs for everyone, too." She hiked Henry Reed higher on her hip. "*Tante,* have I done something wrong, caused some sort of problem between you and Emile?"

"No, no. It is nothing like that, *chérie*. You must not think it. Emile and I have our ups and downs, you know. He's like a son to me. Like you and your maman, we sometimes have a wee tiff. It is nothing for you to worry about. Tomorrow we will be right as rain. You'll see."

Marie thought the argument was more than a simple tiff. She turned away so that her aunt couldn't read the doubt on her face, and at the same time swallowed a lump building in her throat. The day had started out so bright.

Marie's aunt had hired a car and driver for the day. "We will visit all the places important to your Papa."

Marie slid into the car's roomy back seat, next to Henry Reed. "Thank you so much for this. It means a lot to me."

Her aunt took the front passenger seat. "It is my pleasure, chérie. First we'll go across the bridge to Longueil. That's where Henri, Marc and I grew up." When they were settled, the driver pulled away from the curb and they were soon heading west, along the river.

Marie took in the passing traffic, the honking horns, muted slightly by the rolled up windows of the air-conditioned touring car, and the people hurrying along the sidewalks. "I've never lived in a city. It's hard to imagine my father living in one. He loved the outdoors."

"Papa thought Longueil was the countryside when we moved there," said her aunt. "It wasn't. There may not have been tenements and gangs like in the East End, where we'd lived before, but it was still a slum—a suburban slum."

"Emile said it is mostly warehouses now." Marie reached into the diaper bag and handed her son a bunch of plastic keys. He threw them to the floor and kicked his feet against his car seat. Marie retrieved the plastic keys and handed them to him. "Stop kicking." She put her hand on his feet to still them. He kicked against her hand.

They crossed the St. Lawrence River. "Look down there on the left." Her aunt waved toward the window. "Can you see? That's where Papa worked, loading and unloading ships." She turned to look at Marie. "Once upon a time, Montreal's economy depended on manufacturing and trade. When I was a child that harbor was always crowded with large ocean-going ships and barges. Papa gave me a piece of camphor wood from one of the ships. I still have it. Every time I smell it, I think of all the exotic places I'd like to visit one day." She sighed and faced forward. "Now, although shipping is still important—both by ship and by rail—our economy is built more around research, business, and tourism."

On the other side of the river the highway was clogged with cars, buses, and trucks. Marie stared out the car window at the pawnshops and bars lining the street along with barbershops, Chinese restaurants, and rundown shops with dreary clothes in their windows—all crammed together with dingy-looking apartment buildings. No wonder Dad fell in love with the mountains at home.

Her aunt pointed. "There…you see that arena? Your father and Marc used to play ice hockey there. Papa and I would often go to watch them."

"I didn't know my father could ice skate. Was he good?"

"He was very good. Marc, he knew no fear, never caring if someone were bigger. But your papa, he used his brain."

She tapped her temple with her index finger. "Like Emile, he was a short one, but very agile. While Marc was blasting through people, your papa, he went around. They were a good combination. Papa and I would cheer and cheer."

Marie shook her head. Even something as simple as ice skating and playing hockey he kept from us.

Her aunt signaled the driver to turn. "We lived down this street—though it wasn't a street then, but a dirt lane. Our house was just there—at the bottom of the hill, on the right."

The driver applied the brake as they coasted down the hill.

"A large lilac tree grew in front of our house," her aunt said, when they reached the bottom of the cul-de-sac. "When I was little, I would sit under it with my doll while Marc and Henri played baseball or football over there, with the other boys in the neighborhood." She pointed to a paved parking lot holding a dozen or so cars.

"They played their games every afternoon the weather allowed, the score see-sawing back and forth. Their games were frequently interrupted by scuffles or arguments." Her aunt's voice was filled with nostalgia. "But the next day they'd be back at it. In the winter, when they weren't playing hockey, they built snow forts and igloos and went sliding on garbage can lids down the hill—sometimes Henri would let me sit in front of him."

She was silent for a moment and Marie thought she must be remembering the thrill of that downward slide, the cold air rushing past her face. Marie could easily imagine it—sledding with friends had been a part of her winter childhood, too.

"Year-round, the boys played war. Papa was not the only one from our neighborhood to serve in World War II. Most of the boys had fathers, uncles and even older brothers who'd also experienced it first-hand."

Marie thought of the old men who rode at the head of the Platt City Fourth of July parade every year. They sat in the backseats of convertibles donated by Perkett Ford and waved at those on the sidewalks. She'd never paid much attention to them, instead waiting impatiently for the sheriff's posse and the high school marching band.

One of those old men could have fought beside her grandfather. She resolved to take Henry Reed to the parade the following year. He wouldn't be too young to start learning what his great-grandfather and men like him had done for their countries.

Her aunt's voice broke into her thoughts.

"Our house was a gathering spot." A wry smile played across her aunt's lips as she added, "often to *Maman's* dismay. Nearly every Friday evening would find Papa and two or three other men from the neighborhood sitting at our kitchen table, or out on the porch on fine nights, a bottle of wine between them. They mainly talked politics, but sometimes they reminisced about the war. Henri and Marc might pretend to be doing schoolwork, but really they were taking it all in. And I, of course, was always nearby. I was quite used to playing the mouse."

Marie smiled at the image of a little girl sitting in a corner, playing with a doll, perhaps, pretending not to listen to the grown-ups conversation—she had done the same when she was a child.

Gazing out the car window, she tried to imagine the house, the lilac tree and a little girl with curly black hair sitting beneath it. She tried to see a bunch of young boys playing ball. Or a group of men, roughened by hard work and a harsh society, sitting on the porch sharing a bottle of wine and talking about battles they'd fought in, battles that may have made some of them heroes. It was no use. All she saw was a big concrete building with small, mesh-covered windows, and a dozen cars in the paved parking lot.

Her aunt told the driver to head back to Montreal. "After Maman died and Henri left, Papa moved in with Emile and me."

Marie swallowed her disappointment. "Losing your mother must have been hard for you and your father." Henry Reed squirmed in his car seat, pulling at the belt holding him in place. She handed him a cracker.

"I think having Emile to care for kept Papa from being so lonely. *Maman* was hard to live with, but for Papa, she was harder to live without."

Marie sighed. "I tried to talk to my mother about moving in with Paul and me, but she won't think of leaving the house Dad built for her."

Her aunt clapped her hands to her cheeks. She turned to look at Marie, her eyes dancing. "Henri built a house? *Extraordinaire!*"

Seeing how her father had grown up, Marie was as surprised as her aunt. "It is, isn't it? I asked Mom where he'd learned to do carpentry and she said he'd just talked to people and figured it out. Another man helped him."

Her aunt tilted her head to one side, eyebrows raised. "Is it a big house? Tell me about it."

Marie mentally compared the house she grew up in to the one her aunt and Emile had described. "It's in the country. A ranch house."

Her aunt looked puzzled. "It is a ranch he built, with cows and horses?"

"Well, we often had one calf, in the summer anyway. I meant the style of the house though. It's spread out on one floor. No upstairs like your house. It has three bedrooms, a living room with a dining area at one end, though we rarely use it, and a really big kitchen. Mom is a wonderful baker and cook."

Marie-Catherine smiled, still shaking her head. "It sounds beautiful. I would like to see it one day. And I would like to meet your *maman*."

"That would be great. I'd love to have all of you come to Idaho for a visit." *Maybe not yet, though.*

They crossed the bridge again and turned west.

"This is René Lévesque Boulevard. It was called Dorchester Boulevard in your father's time. In the seventies, after the *Parti Quebecois* finally came to power, they changed the names of many streets and parks to show Quebec's French-Canadian heritage."

Marie chuckled. "I can only imagine how confusing that must have been—at least for a while."

Her aunt laughed. "Indeed it was—a boon for map-makers, though." She nodded to a large, boarded up building. "There is where your father worked for many years. Unfortunately, the newspaper went out of business ten years ago."

No sign of life glimmered. Only a faded sign reading *Le Journal Quotidien* painted along the top of the building told of its earlier glory. Marie tried hard to imagine her father, young, alive, and part of the once thriving newspaper. But the place looked like nothing other than what it was—closed and empty—with no connection between it and her father.

She looked away, lips pressed tight. To be so close, to see the things he must have seen, be where he must have been and still not really see it. If only she could put herself in his place, see all this through his eyes, experience what he experienced. Feeling utterly defeated, she slumped against the back of the seat and let out a long sigh.

Her aunt motioned the driver to move on then reached back and patted Marie's knee, as though sensing Marie's unspoken disappointment. "We're going to the East End, now. There's something there you must also see."

Marie nodded, not trusting her voice to speak.

Twenty minutes later, she gazed at the fourteen-story high Rue Parthenais Detention Center and the seventeen-foot chain-link fence topped with barbed wire that surrounded it. The muscles in her arms quivered.

"Your father was in there for eight months." Her aunt's voice was flat, showing no emotion.

Marie's nails bit into her palms. "So long?"

"He and his editor thought it would only be for two or three weeks. Instead, they kept him, without charge, from December, 1969, until August, 1970. This place had a terrible reputation then. Henri was purposely kept with drug addicts and the insane."

Marie gasped and shivered, trying to shut out the images her aunt's words invoked. "Why? Why would they do that?"

"Henri said it was to break him down."

Tension spread from Marie's shoulders to her neck and she felt the first twinges of a headache. "Were you able to visit him? Did he at least get to see his family during all those months?"

"I came here once, but your father made me promise not to come back. I don't think he wanted any of us to see him there."

Tears once again welled in Marie's eyes. Her throat thickened. She took a deep breath, trying to ease the constriction.

"Enough of this place," said her aunt. "Now I wish to take you to where I think Henri was most happy."

"Where?" Marie asked, glad to be moving on.

"The University of Montreal."

It wasn't anything like Marie expected—nothing like the University of Idaho. No big trees with students beneath them, reading or talking. No rolling lawns or ivy-covered walls, either. Just a bunch of tall buildings on a bluff. They looked like office buildings. At least her father was happy there. She was glad. Because from everything else she'd seen that day, once he'd left childhood, there wasn't much else for him to have enjoyed.

That night, after dinner, when dishes had been washed and dried, when René and the old man had gone to bed and she'd put Henry Reed down for the night, Marie and her aunt once again sat alone in the kitchen, sharing a pot of tea.

Marie took a deep breath, her heart pounding. "Tante, I need to know what made my father the man he was—the man I knew. Can you tell me?"

PART TWO

Henry / Henri

*"They have sown the wind,
and they shall reap the whirlwind."*

From
The Book of Hosea

Chapter One

ELLEN

Ellen was drawn to the box, again, and again, picking up a notebook, reading a page or two before returning it and picking up another. Each time she wondered how Henry would have reacted to her reading his most private thoughts. He'd never said they were off-limits, though, and if he hadn't wanted her to read them, why hadn't he destroyed them? Or he could have written in French. Some part of him must have wanted her to know. That was the conclusion she armed herself with as she prepared to read all the journals.

She sat cross-legged on her bed and sorted through the books, arranging them as well as she could in chronological order. Most were small spiral-bound notebooks that could fit into a shirt pocket, but some, especially those he'd written in when he first came to the United States, were larger. The way he'd written in them varied as well. Sometimes he skipped weeks at a time or dashed off a few lines of incomplete sentences. Other entries were long and thorough. Some dated, some not, but all in the spidery penmanship that looked as though it belonged to a different age.

Since the restaurant was closed Mondays, Marta had gone into town to visit her former neighbor. With no bread to bake or deliver, Ellen normally used the day to shop for supplies and plan, and for bookkeeping—Mr. Baker had cautioned her to do her own books, at least in the beginning. "That way you'll know where every penny comes from and where every penny goes," he'd said.

She wouldn't be doing any of those things today.

She put on a fresh pot of coffee, then brought the box from her bedroom and set it on the floor next to the kitchen table. As the coffee perked, she sliced some ham and chose a tomato from several ripening on the windowsill. The coffee was done when she finished making her sandwich. She got a clean mug from the cupboard, filled it, then carried coffee and sandwich to the table. She went back and wiped off the counter where she'd spilled coffee, rinsed the dishcloth, and wiped away the breadcrumbs.

She could delay no longer.

Picking up the first notebook, she gazed for a moment at its brown cover, corners dog-eared with time, opened it and began to read.

Slowly, she put together the bits of Henry's arrival in the United States—on a cargo ship at a dock near Rochester, New York. She found a map in Ken's room and traced the route the ship must have taken up the St. Lawrence River, through the locks and into Lake Ontario. He'd hitchhiked from there to Chicago, arriving just before winter set in.

People say I should have gone farther south, where it isn't so cold. Warm would feel good now. I found a job washing dishes in a restaurant. The pay is poor, but they don't ask questions. At night, after closing, I sometimes go for walks, even though it is bitter cold—made colder by the wind. I look across

Lake Michigan and for a second or two can believe the lights I see winking out of the blackness are Canadian, but of course they're not. I think often of Claudia. I was never worthy of her love—am sure my leaving must finally have killed it. How will my family survive my defection? I miss them every hour of the day.

That simple statement brought tears to Ellen's eyes—how he must have suffered. She sniffed and wiped her tears with the back of her hand, her brows drawn together as she read the words that puzzled her once more. Not worthy of Claudia's love? It must have been the other way around; if Henry had felt truly loved, he would have stayed with her.

I left Chicago as soon as the weather warmed. I keep to the back roads and occasionally pass through a small farm town. When I'm fortunate enough to get a ride, the talk is often about Vietnam and friends who fled to Canada, or others who've come back from the war, broken in spirit or body or both. Rarely is there any news about Canada. It seems that for most Americans, the country to the north of them doesn't exist.

South Dakota is huge. It seems I've been walking across it for days. The few rides I get are of short duration. As usual, this morning I started walking before sunup. Fields spread out from both sides of the road—cornfields, the stalks not even knee-high. I came to a large farm. The early morning sun gilded the house, the barn, and the fruit trees surrounding them. It looked so beautiful, like something in a painting, I had to stop and study it.

It already bustled with activity—a tractor started up, a screen door slammed, Elvis's "Return to Sender" poured from an open upstairs window. A black and white dog, its long hair flopping over its eyes, raced across the wide sloping lawn, barking and keeping pace with me as I walked on. A piercing whistle split the air, the dog barked one more time then turned and trotted back toward the house.

I didn't hear or see anyone after that—not even a passing car or truck. Around noon I spotted a van far ahead, parked at the edge of the road. It seemed to float in the shimmering heat. There was no movement around it, and I wondered if it had been abandoned. Suddenly, a man about thirty feet into the cornfield, stood and pulled his jeans over his naked buttocks. Then a woman sat up, struggling to untangle something from her hair. I called out and the blank faces they turned toward me were comical to see. The woman stood, brushed down her long skirt and blouse, then both made their way out of the field.

Trent and River are their names. Their van doesn't have much speed in it, but they take turns driving, so we make good time. We stopped at Mt. Rushmore. I took a picture of them against a railing—Theodore Roosevelt's profile in the background. The camera is a cheap one and I doubt the picture turns out. They wanted one of me, too, but I said no.

Last night we camped in a place called Ten Sleeps Canyon in Wyoming. I never thought I'd be in Wyoming. Some others were camping there, too, in vans and old trucks, with makeshift tents and blankets instead of sleeping bags. We shared a campfire with two other couples and a young woman with long brown braids. I said no thanks to the marijuana being passed around. And the woman. Not because I'm philosophically opposed to either, but because I was enjoying the star-filled sky and the clear air and didn't want to do anything that would alter my mood. I felt like I was in a state of suspended animation, floating between the past and the future. At least for the present, I felt no guilt.

Ellen's mouth went slack. She read the words a second time, then a third. *Not philosophically opposed to sharing a woman? Who was this person?* She wanted to slam the journal closed, throw it into the box with the others and shove them all to the back of the closet. Instead, she sucked in her breath and read on.

My first sight of the Grand Tetons, with their immensity and grandeur, robbed me of speech. They are so unlike anything I've seen before. Quebec's Laurentian Mountains are as nothing by comparison. I was struck dumb by these giants that rose in front of me, spearing nearly straight up from the meadow and lake at their feet. My awed gaze swept from where the white, slab-sided peaks disappeared into the southern horizon, to the north, where one large peak filled my view. I'd seen pictures, but nothing prepared me for the reality of what lay before me.

I decided to stay by the lake for a while and told River and Trent to go on without me. They were headed south, toward Jackson Hole, on their way to California. I have hollowed out a space by a fallen log and made a sort of tent with a blanket that River left with me. I've built a small fire and now sit writing in my journal. The stars are so bright, it's hard to believe they're real. I am nothing compared to these mountains, these stars, this place. What happened before, what happens next…it changes nothing, means nothing.

I've been here for a week, hiking around the lake, exploring. There's a little town with a general store at the north end. Also, a small hotel and restaurant. Tourists stay there. Each day, a bus takes a load of them to Yellowstone Park, a few miles to the north. Today I bought a larger backpack from the general store, also a warmer sleeping bag and a fishing rod along with some food. I plan to skirt the parks and all their tourists, and head into the heart of the mountains. The man at the store cautioned me about late snow storms, but I'll chance it.

It is easy to understand how these mountains got the name Rockies. They are all granite. Huge boulders and slabs of rock— I must find a way around or over. I thought I was prepared, having walked so many miles this spring, but the muscles in my legs and shoulders are close to giving out. I don't travel nearly as far as I expect to each day. Every evening, I am asleep before the sun sets. Nights are cold, but at least the sleeping bag keeps me warm.

I'm eating the beans first—straight from the can, tilting my head back to allow every bit of juice to drain into my mouth— partially to lighten the load. Also, partially because, aside from their being filling, my luck with the fishing rod is proving elusive. Saving the granola for later.

When I woke this morning, I saw what I think was a cougar. Golden coat, powerful-looking chest. Magnificent creature.

Blinked my eyes and he was gone. It's like that with so many animals I've come across here in the mountains. One moment they're there, behind a tree or shuffling through the underbrush, and the next moment they're gone. The birds are the same.

I'm running out of beans, but my luck with the fishing rod is improving. By trial and error, I'm learning the best way to cook what I catch—on heated rocks. I tried threading the fish on a stick, but as the fish cooked, it broke apart and fell into the fire. I had to be quick to get it out before it burned.

I'm on the western slopes now. No fishing spots for days. Eating granola. Have been trying to trap a rabbit. No luck so far. But what a country. The views are awe-inspiring. Last night, around midnight, a storm came up. The sudden crash of thunder woke me. The sky was lit to near daylight by the lightning. The noise of thunder and the howling wind made my ears ring. I huddled in my sleeping bag beneath a lone tree. The wind was so fierce, the tree's network of roots made the ground heave. I was quite sure the end was near—but what a glorious way to go.

I awoke in the morning to complete calm. It was as though the storm had never been. The only sound, a chipmunk in the tree above my head chattering what sounded like some kind of alarm. Don't know about what—some animal, I suppose. I've been in these mountains nearly a month and sometimes wonder if I shall ever see another human again.

Even with the occasional hint of loneliness, Ellen sensed the burden of Henry's past slip away the farther he trekked into the mountains. Fewer entries referred to his guilt-ridden past. Instead, they detailed the birds and animals, the splendor of the mountains, sunsets and sunrises. She could almost feel his hope beginning to blossom.

I've reached eastern Washington and what is called The Palouse. The rolling countryside is covered in fields of wheat— an undulating golden carpet. I don't think I've ever been so hot. It's nothing like summers in Montreal where the heat is sticky from all the moisture coming off lakes and rivers. The heat here is dry enough to singe the hair on my arms. I've decided I've come too far, so plan to turn back toward mountains.

Yesterday, passed through a town called Lewiston, where the Snake River and the Clearwater River merge in a golden trough of wheat fields. Too bad a paper mill east of town ruins it by spewing yellow smoke that fills air with noxious odor of sulfur. I will keep pushing south and east until I am back in the mountains.

Ellen smiled softly, thinking of Henry's love of Idaho's mountains. Then, without any warning, she came to an entry that had her hands shaking.

I can't forget seeing Pierre Laporte's body in the trunk of that car, strangled with his own gold chain, the St. Christopher medal still dangling from it, knowing things I wrote for the newspaper or proclaimed in speeches may have escalated the violence that led to his murder. What must I do to atone?

Someone was dead and Henry had been part of it? Ellen frantically skipped ahead, hoping to find an explanation, but there was no further reference to the man named Laporte.

Reluctantly, she closed the notebook and returned it to the box. Marie would be home soon with who-knew-what to tell her. She'd said she needed to find out who her father was. Ellen was beginning to feel a similar need—who was this man she'd spent over half her life with?

Chapter Two

MARIE

Eyes glowing, Marie followed her aunt to the living room where each settled into a comfortable chair. She leaned forward, almost rubbing her hands together, waiting for her aunt to begin the story she had come to Montreal to hear.

"Your father was a wonderful brother, chérie. None finer. Whenever I needed him, he was always there for me. Papa used to say I was his shadow, because as soon as I could walk, I trailed after him like a baby chick following its mother. As I grew older, the bond strengthened. He taught me how to tie my shoes. He bandaged my hurts and wiped away my tears. His patience was endless; I cannot tell you how many times he extricated me from problems I had created for myself." She paused and sipped her wine. "Are you sure you don't want a glass, chérie? It's quite good."

"No thanks." Marie wanted nothing to cloud her brain now she was finally about to learn the secrets her father had kept locked in his past. Her eyes willed her aunt, a born story-teller, to continue.

"I am sad to say it, one couldn't confide to Maman. Henri—I could tell him anything and he would explain or sympathize or offer to help, whichever was called for at the time."

"He was a wonderful father, too." Marie's voice bubbled her eagerness to share her own version of her father, to contradict the version she'd seen since arriving in Montreal. "Just like with you, he was always there for me."

"Yes, I can imagine. You are a great deal like him, you know, and not just in looks."

Marie blinked. "How do you mean?"

"Like him, you need to know the whole story. You ask questions and you aren't satisfied until you know all the answers."

Marie's fingers rose to her lips. Was her aunt criticizing her and her father?

Her aunt cocked her head to one side. "It's what made your father such an excellent journalist."

Marie's shoulders relaxed. "Ah."

Not giving Marie time to enjoy the comparison to her father, her aunt's mouth pressed tight. "Marc was nothing like Henri. He had no time for me. He was tolerant when it cost him neither time nor patience, but otherwise, no."

"I'm sorry to hear that. But he and my father were friends growing up, right? What were they like back then?"

"Well, as you know, chérie, your papa was eight years older than me, and Marc ten years. Many things happened when they were boys and I was either not there to see or too young to remember."

Marie twisted a curl around her finger; she hadn't thought of that.

"One thing I do recall, because it happened without fail every Saturday night: the family bath ritual. It is my first clear memory."

Marie's eyes widened. "You bathed together?"

"Not together…well, not entirely."

Marie remained silent, but her eyebrows raised in question.

Her aunt took a sip of wine then leaned her head against the back of her chair. "A large woodstove separated the kitchen from the parlor, where Marc and Henri slept on bunks hinged to the wall—like bunks on a ship. The only other room in the house, our parents' room, was barely large enough to contain a bed, a small chest-of-drawers and my narrow cot. When I got older, Papa and a friend he worked with on the docks put in a loft over *Maman*'s and Papa's bedroom and I slept up there. Right under the roof, where it was hot in the summer and freezing in the winter. At least I had a little privacy, which was more than Marc or Henri enjoyed."

"Such a small house for five people. How did you manage? Well, I guess lots of people live in even smaller places."

Her aunt shrugged and nodded. "Indeed they do. But I digress. I was telling you about the bath ritual. Every Saturday night, *Maman* dragged out a battered tin tub and placed it in the middle of the kitchen, then filled it with water heated on the stove. Being the youngest and a girl, I was the first one in. I must have been a little over two the time I first remember.

Henri sat on the edge of his cot and kicked off his shoes, revealing holes in the heels of both socks. He peeled them off

then stood. Casting a glance at Marie-Catherine, in her nightgown, her hair still wet and curling around her ears, as she dragged her doll under the table. He removed his clothes, dropping them in a heap before stepping into the tub. He hopped up and down in the over-heated water as goose-bumps broke out on his thin arms and back.

"Sit," Maman ordered.

"It's too hot."

"Sit."

Henri eased into the water and Maman immediately poured more water over him, wetting his hair and shoulders.

"Ow!"

Marc, who was next in line, sat on his cot, kicking off his shoes. "Don't be a baby."

Henri shot him a glowering look. "Shut up."

Maman ignored them and rubbed soap into Henri's scalp. She began to scrub. Henri winced, but refrained from further complaints. Complaints did no good.

He braced himself as she worked soap and washcloth downward over his scrawny body, paying methodical attention to ears, fingernails and anywhere dirt might lurk, until she came to his private parts. "Here," she said, handing him the soapy cloth. "Clean yourself."

When Henri finally completed his ablutions to the apparent satisfaction of his mother, he escaped the tub to make room for Marc. He grabbed the towel Maman held out to him and quickly wrapped its skimpy length around his waist, sending another quick look in Marie-Catherine's direction. She scuttled farther under the table, still cradling her doll, humming a tuneless song. Henri dropped the towel and stuck his legs into underpants then pulled an undershirt over his still-damp body.

His father sat next to the stove, reading a newspaper. Fully clothed but still shivering, Henri went to stand beside him, waiting for Marc to be finished.

"They are saying we'll have a sewer here by next fall," Papa said. Henri's mother didn't reply. "Did you hear me Anne-Marie? If they put in a sewer that means we can have a toilet and a bathtub."

She didn't bother to look at him. "And where would we put them?"

"We'd find a place."

"Humph," was all she said. It was as though his mother already knew the city's politicians would get no further than digging a ditch next to the lane leading down the hill.

When Marc was done bathing and dressed, the two boys dragged the tub outside and emptied it, then pulled it back inside and their mother refilled it for their father.

Marie rubbed her upper arms and shook her head. No wonder Dad was so emphatic about Ken and me having our own space.

"Although I don't remember it specifically, the next morning being Sunday would have been like every other Sunday of my youth, and which was probably replicated across Quebec. We would form a line at the door, hair slicked down, or in my case braided, dressed for church. Papa, too. Maman would then inspect us, looking into and behind our ears, checking our fingernails—as though we could have gotten dirty overnight. Amusing, no?"

She paused for Marie to nod before going on.

"At church, we sat in the third row—always the third row on the end. Your grandmother was a big woman and insisted on sitting next to the aisle. But not in the front row, mind you, which would have been far easier. That would have been too forward. No, we must sit in the third row, with Marc and Henri in the middle, between *Maman* and Papa, and me, until I became too big, on Papa's lap. If Marc or Henri squirmed or didn't listen, they would get a cuff on the head or a twisted ear from *Maman*." She stopped and drained the last of her wine. Her voice turned somber. "The last time we were at church together was to bury Marc." She abruptly rose to her feet. "Nature calls, *chérie*. I must leave you a moment."

Marie remained in the living room, thinking of the similarities in hers and her aunt's childhoods: an adoring older brother, not much money, rather primitive living conditions—though they'd always had a bathroom, at least for as long as she remembered. Both had lost a parent.

There, the similarities ended of course. Marie-Catherine had been forced to raise a child on her own, something Marie was thankful would never happen to her. And her aunt was a professional woman with a college education, not a thing Marie was likely to attain any time soon.

Marie-Catherine returned with a full glass of wine and quickly resumed her story.

"Henri was a difficult student I think—at least I would not have wanted to be his teacher. He and Marc were so different. Marc had his own opinion about everything, just as Henri. But, in Marc's mind, at least, that was enough. He never cared what anyone else thought, whether they agreed with him or not."

She sipped from her wine glass and set it on the small table next to her chair.

"Not so with Henri. He could never let anything go unchallenged. When he believed something, he wanted to convince everyone of the rightness of his opinion—including his teachers. As a young boy, it led to many raps with a ruler across the knuckles."

Marie fingers curled. "Poor Dad."

Marie-Catherine nodded. "In secondary school—high school—it became worse. Canings were not uncommon and more than once Henri was threatened with expulsion. Long before, Maman's doctor had taken a special interest in Henri and his schooling. Several times he had to plead Henri's case to the headmaster."

Marie pictured the quiet, non-aggressive father of her memory and tried to align him with the rebellious teenager her aunt described.

"Being younger, I took it all in," said Marie-Catherine. "Several of my teachers had Henri as a student. Even though eight years separated us, they no doubt remembered and dreaded my arrival. But I learned from Henri and Marc and found a road between the two." She smiled and nodded to herself then looked at Marie. "What of you, *chérie?* What kind of a student were you?"

The question caught Marie off guard. "Well…I got pretty good grades. Ken had straight A's." She looked down at her hands, folded in her lap, and felt ashamed of her lack of effort—she should have gotten all A's as well. "I was too social, I guess. My husband was a good student, though. He planned to be an engineer and me a teacher until I got pregnant with Henry Reed. That kind of put the kabash to our plans."

"Kabash? What is that?

"Putting an end to something—in this case, Paul's and my university plans. We can't afford it now."

Her aunt gave her a questioning look but didn't comment before continuing with her story. "I was telling you of Henri's schooling. Despite his ongoing war with the priests, he graduated at the top of his class. Papa and *Maman* and I were in the audience. We were stunned when Papa was called forward to pin on the ribbon Henri had earned in Latin. If there was irony in the fact that Papa had only a fourth-grade education, it was lost on him; his pride in Henri was boundless. He often said education was our road to success, claiming those in power had used our lack of education to keep us in our places for decades. For 'those in power' you can read 'English-speakers.' As I mentioned before, every meal was served in our house with a discourse on French-Canadian subjugation. Is it a wonder Papa's children were caught up in the struggle?"

Marie couldn't answer the question; she was too surprised by her aunt's earlier revelation. "Dad spoke Latin?"

"Oh, yes. The Jesuits stressed the classics. They wanted him to be a priest, though how they thought they would handle his rebellious nature, I don't know."

"A priest? Dad? Oh, I'll bet that didn't go over well." Marie couldn't help laughing.

Marie-Catherine chuckled. "You are right. Henri would have no part of it. But to celebrate his graduation, Papa took us out to dinner—the Boar's Head Restaurant on Sherbrooke Street. It was the first restaurant I'd ever eaten in. It's gone now, but I remember as though it were only yesterday when we climbed out of the taxi onto the sidewalk and I gazed in awe at its imposing front door—at least I thought it was imposing. In retrospect, it was a small, quiet place that must have been built as an afterthought between an office building and an old house that long before had been converted to apartments. The other diners were mostly office workers."

Marie nodded, easily seeing the place in her imagination.

"Once inside, Henri looked around the room as though searching for someone, probably Marc. No one had been surprised when Marc had given the feeble excuse of being busy that night—education meant nothing to him. Still, your papa must have hoped he'd changed his mind." She folded her lips and for a moment stared at the silent and empty television screen. "Maman looked at the menu and claimed she could fix the same meals at home for pennies. She did nothing to modulate her voice. I inwardly cringed and exchanged a look of embarrassment with Henri."

Marie joined her aunt's soft laugh. "I can name a few people in Platt City who would have had the same reaction."

"Papa told *Maman* money wasn't important that night. 'We've never had so much cause to celebrate,' he said. 'Henry's graduation marks the end of our servitude. After this, we can only go up.'" Marie's aunt shook her head. "*Maman* was not convinced. She claimed she didn't know why Papa believed knowledge of a dead language was the key to Henri's future and ours. 'If you ask me, it's all a waste of time. Nothing will change, no matter how much you declare it so.'"

Marie-Catherine took another sip of wine and gave Marie another sad smile. "That was your grandmother, *chérie*. She could never allow herself to be happy."

Marie stood and crossed to the window. She looked out on the small front lawn and the sidewalk, lit by a streetlight, to the vacant street beyond. Did she pass on that inability? Is that why Dad couldn't let go of the sadness?

Chapter Three

ELLEN

Haying season was underway when I arrived in Platt City, Idaho. It is a small town near a lake and a river, in a valley surrounded by mountains. I knew right off I wanted to stay. The second day here, I spotted a sign in a store window and had no trouble joining a crew that goes from ranch to ranch 'bucking' baled hay onto a truck, then unloading it again and stacking it in big covered sheds. The crew chief is a broad-shouldered, barrel-chested fellow, whose belly is beginning to hang over his silver belt-buckle. He introduced himself as R.T. I had to look up a good six inches to meet his eyes, the color of blue ice.

Ellen, her coffee grown cold and her sandwich only half eaten, was sure the man Henry referred to was R.T. Haines, the grandfather of one of her classmates. She remembered R.T. once picking Tina up after school. Her friend had hopped up onto the running board and clambered into the high cab, her short legs stretching to reach. Once seated, she shouted goodbye to Ellen before R.T. shifted into gear and the big truck moved away from the curb.

The haying trucks were even bigger now and were loaded by machines instead of crews of young men. She'd heard R.T. had Parkinson's disease and wondered if, before he became ill, he'd made the transition to the new way of hauling hay—the huge trucks they used nowadays must cost a fortune. She didn't care much for them, hated meeting one barreling down a narrow country road, bits of loose hay and wind in its wake. She also missed seeing all those young men loading the bales, their shirtless torsos bronzed in the sun, working together as though part of a choreographed dance.

She'd ask Marta what had become of Tina, and if R.T. was still alive. Marta would know; it seemed she had a line on everyone in the county.

Most days R.T. drives the truck through the fields while the crew loads. This morning, he got down to help load and let someone else drive. As the newcomer, I have the worst job— standing on the truck's bed, catching the bales the others heave up to me.

Using a couple of borrowed hay hooks, the one-hundred-pound bale R.T. lifted appeared weightless. It knocked me off my feet. The rest of the crew, who'd known what was coming, hooted as I staggered and sat down hard. If I were the only one they laughed at, I would have been offended, but their humor is democratic and each must take his turn at being the butt of their jokes. I stood, brushed the hay from the seat of my pants, grinned at my tormentors and braced myself for the next bale R.T. was preparing to throw at me.

Although the job is hard and I am exhausted at the end of each day, I find I love it here—the people, the town, the surrounding mountains. I can't get over how the mountains change colors: from blue-black in the early morning hours to hazy blue during the day, to deep lavender and purple at night. And I enjoy the camaraderie of the crew. Except for R.T. and me, they are all teenagers, still in high school.

Their seemingly carefree existence fascinates me. It is as though they had never heard of Vietnam, never watched the war on the nightly television newscasts. Don't they have brothers or friends who have been drafted? Won't they be drafted when they turn eighteen? Why don't they protest? It seems all they talk about is girls and football or girls and wrestling. I envy them their self-confidence and easy assurance, but I don't envy what they will have to face if this war is not ended soon.

I bought a small tent with my first paycheck and set it up in a campground along the river outside of town. I walk in each morning to wait outside the coffee shop where R.T. picks up crew at 5:30. Occasionally I find one or two other tents pitched along the river when I get back at night. One young couple stayed for a week. Twice we shared our evening meal.

Ellen knew the place and imagined Henry spending evenings fishing or swimming, walking along the riverbank. She was glad he'd had someone to share an occasional meal. It seemed such a lonely way to live. She wished she'd known him then. Of course he wouldn't have looked twice at her. She been only twelve when he'd first come to Platt City.

We drove out to the Hartley ranch this morning. He's a friend of R.T.—they "rodeoed" together, riding bulls, when they were both "too young and too goddam stupid to know any better" according to R.T. The ranch is at the north end of the valley, about ten or fifteen miles outside town. We turned off the highway, under an H&H Ranch sign hanging above the gate. We had to drive nearly half-a-mile before reaching the ranch buildings.

I find it hard to describe the perfection of the place. The ranch house spreads along the top of a small knoll and overlooks the valley in both directions. A mountain appears to rise directly behind it. The barn and all the other outbuildings (and there are many) are painted grey and trimmed with white to match the house. The three-slatted board fences are white, too. Stretching from the barn to the road is a large pasture—I can't estimate the number of acres, but more than fifty, I think— where Black Angus cattle graze contentedly on emerald green grass. If ever I were to imagine a ranch belonging to a cattle baron, the H&H would be it.

R.T. drove past the house and stopped in front of the barn. The small cloud of dust following us drifted upward and in front of the truck. R.T. swung down from the cab to shake the hand of a tall thin man with a head of thick black hair falling nearly to his shoulders. At his side was a boy close in age to the teenaged crew in the back of the truck with me.

From the similarity of their facial features, I was sure the man and boy were father and son. R.T. clapped his old friend on the back before shaking hands with the boy.

The boy—Scott, R.T. called him—was thin and pale, as though he'd been sick or spent most of his time indoors. His expression was both sullen and wary. None of the crew said anything to the boy, though they must all have known each other from school. Instead, they confined their talk to the start of *football practice the following week and the tough workouts their coach would put them through.*

Scott, standing a few feet away from his father, kicked at a tuft of grass. Although he appeared not to notice what the boys on the truck were saying, I sensed he was taking in every word.

When R.T. and Hartley finished their reminiscing, R.T. climbed back in the truck, backed up a few feet then drove around the side of the barn to a wide gate. Scott was there before us and held it open as the truck went through. I nodded my head and lifted a hand in thanks as he watched us drive off. No one else acknowledged him.

We bounced down a dirt lane and across a rough stubble field before entering the field where bales of hay were strewn.

It is strange to see the hay baler at work. It lumbers along like some science-fiction monster, scooping up the hay—cut several days before and left to dry in long rows—then shooting it out behind, compressed into tight rectangular loaves. It stays about a day ahead of us in the field, but we frequently see it before it finishes and goes on to the next field or ranch.

We've been at Hartley's for three days. Each day, we're served lunch by Glenna, a large woman with dark hair beginning to go gray. The first time I saw her, for a painful moment she reminded me of Maman. As usual, we ate at two white picnic tables set up in the shade of a towering walnut tree. Glenna brought out a heaping platter of roast beef and ham sandwiches, which disappeared before she had the chance to return with pitchers of iced tea. She was well prepared though, because she quickly returned with another heaping platter along with a large bowl of potato salad.

The second platter and the salad slowed us down a little. While finishing my third sandwich—I am always amazed how hungry I get by noon—Mr. Hartley came out of the house and joined us, reaching for a sandwich as he sat.

He and R.T. discussed the progress we'd made that morning and the prospects of rain—which seems a constant concern during haying season. As they talked, I tried to imagine growing up in this place, surrounded by these mountains. I'd expected to see the boy, but there'd been no sign of him. I wondered if he was riding fences or whatever ranchers' sons did here.

What a difference from the congested streets of Montreal, and the tarpaper-covered shack in Longueil I once called home. When we were young, Marc and I planned to run away and live with the Montagnais, learning to hunt, fish and trap as some Native People still did—even as the government is taking more and more of their land. Ironic if the Hartley boy dreams of running away to the city.

The rest of the crew finished lunch and moved toward the truck, pushing and jostling each other, jeering and poking fun as they always do. I was the last to get up from the table. A rustling noise came from above my head and a walnut, still encased in its green covering, landed on the bench where I'd been sitting then bounced to the ground. I looked up and spotted the Hartley boy standing on a branch high above me. We stared at one another for a moment before I hurried to catch up with the others. I was still shaking my head when I climbed onto the back of the truck. He was the strangest boy I'd ever come across.

This morning, the last we're scheduled to work at the H&H

Ranch, R.T. asked me to sit up front in the truck cab on the drive out. It surprised me. R.T. is pleasant enough, but most of the time he keeps aloof from the rest of the crew. Aside from hiring me and giving me directions, we rarely speak. Tooth marks from the comb he'd drawn through his hair that morning were still visible—he always combs his iron-gray hair into a neat dip above his right eye. And he was clean-shaven—the scent of bay rum filled the enclosed space of the air-conditioned cab.

As we passed the small airfield north of town, R.T. asked what I planned to do over the winter. That's another thing I like about the people here. They speak straight out. I answered in kind and told R.T. that I didn't have any plans, though I've been trying to come up with something that will keep me in the area after the haying finishes, which will be soon. When R.T. asked how far I'd gotten in school, I hesitated for a moment before telling him I'd completed university.

R.T. said he'd guessed as much and that I was probably wondering why he asked. I nodded.

He said it was Hartley's boy, and that he isn't like most boys his age. He jerked his head toward the crew in the back of the truck, but he didn't need to. I already knew exactly what he meant. He said Hartley is worried about his son. He sent him to a private school in Spokane the year before, but now the boy is refusing to go back.

I sensed R.T.'s reluctance to talk about it, but apparently the boy's mother ran off with another man—some cowboy that caught her eye when the boy was still an infant. Of course, I immediately thought of Emile. Not that Bunny abandoned him because of another man. But she did abandon him.

After the mother left, Hartley brought the boy back to the ranch, which has been in his family for generations. He only left it to go rodeoing as a way of letting off steam, R.T. said.

I wondered what it all had to do with me. When R.T. repeated that the boy didn't fit in at school—private or public—it finally dawned on me where the conversation was going; Hartley wants a tutor for his son.

But why me? Aren't there others more qualified? I was amazed to learn it was the boy who demanded I be the one. I didn't hesitate to accept.

Ellen was equally amazed. Though she'd always known there was a history between them, Henry had never mentioned that he'd once tutored Mr. Hartley's son. When she was a girl, everyone had known about Scott Hartley and talked about him, often in whispers—he was such a strange one and a complete loner. Though he was older than her, she'd felt sorry for him. He didn't seem the sort to accept sympathy from anyone, though—some would have wondered why he'd aroused any. After all, wasn't his father one of the richest men in the county? So what if he didn't have a mother when he had Glenna? Still, Ellen's heart went out to him. Having Glenna wouldn't have made up for the loss of the mother who'd abandoned him.

Once I came to know Glenna, I couldn't imagine how I'd seen any resemblance to Maman. Although close in age and both big, the similarities ended there. Unlike my taciturn mother, Glenna is a hearty woman who laughs easily, frequently at her own jokes. She keeps up a running stream of conversation. I am often confused by her descriptions of neighbors or ranch hands, knowing only a few of the people she refers to, but that doesn't stop Glenna once she launches a story. Confused or not, I enjoy hearing her stories as much as she enjoys telling them.

There is an ease with which she allows me to see the people she tells about. Like Scott's mother. She said the woman didn't want to live on a ranch—not even one as nice as this.

"They say she liked to party too much 'n Platt City isn't much of a party place. It was Ben's fault, too. He loved her about as much as he loved to rodeo. Gave her whatever she wanted. Spoiled her rotten, his mother said."

Scott was a difficult baby; he was allergic to cow's milk and cried a lot. I was again reminded of Bunny when Glenna told me his mother left without warning.

"They always say you got to walk a mile in the other person's moccasins 'n all that, but seems to me she was a pretty sorry piece of business."

I think Glenna's feelings for Mr. Hartley run deeper than merely being his housekeeper. I can see it in the way her hand runs over the back of the kitchen chair when he gets up and moves away, or the way her eyes linger on the door after he's left the room. She's a bit older than him I think, but not much. And she's apparently been taking care of him and his son since Scott was two or three. I wonder if her feelings are reciprocated.

Ellen closed the book, wondering the same thing. Glenna Owens was still the housekeeper at Hartley's ranch. She was something of an institution, in fact. Built like a mountain, with a booming voice and laugh, she kept the ranch hands in line and they never seemed to resent it. Growing up,

Ellen had often seen Glenna at her parents' store, coming in to buy supplies for the ranch. But the most memorable image had to be Glenna sitting in the stands at every Fourth of July rodeo, cheering for H&H hands at the top of her lungs. Everyone, including Ellen, thought the world of Glenna. But a romantic liaison between her and Mr. Hartley—Ellen blushed to imagine it.

Before winter sets in, I asked Scott to teach me to ride and was surprised when the boy agreed. I was also surprised at how good he is with the horses—both gentle and patient.

He didn't extend any of that patience to me.

I have never been so sore in my life. Twice the horse threw me off its back—once before I was even properly mounted. It gave a little hop and off I went. Scott showed nothing but disdain. I'm sure he can't imagine someone my age never having been on a horse. But I think I brought him around, finally, by persevering. I've made him promise to take me out for two hours every day. As well as teaching me to ride, it is good for him to take time from our studies together and to be out in the autumn air.

His relationships with the others on the ranch are strange. Not surprising, he's most at ease with Glenna. Who isn't? The ranch hands, a good-natured bunch, pretty much leave the boy alone, and he all but ignores them. What I find most intriguing is how he behaves around his father. I don't think Mr. Hartley knows what to make of his own son. And I don't think Scott has any better idea what to make of his father.

It was a pleasant surprise to find the ranch has a library with books on a variety of subjects. When I looked inside a book on art history, I saw a woman's name on the flyleaf and wondered if it had belonged to Hartley's mother.

I was in my bedroom, reading one of Hemingway's Nick Adams short stories, when Scott appeared at my door. He held back when I invited him in, and instead looked around the room as if suspicious of my intentions. Finally, he edged inside and slid down the wall to sit cross-legged on the floor.

It took forever to coax from him the reason for his visit to my room: he wanted to talk about his mother. He is convinced she is a frail flower who couldn't take the roughness of either his father or life on a ranch. He believes she lives in New York or Boston and that she'll send for him one day. I can't believe he got any of that from Glenna and wonder if his father told him something of the sort, trying to soften what had actually happened—that she'd run off with a bull rider.

Ellen had never known what happened to Mr. Hartley's wife. Her parents wouldn't have spoken about it around her when she was young, and by the time she was old enough to understand, it would have been old news. Perhaps with Scott the same thing had happened. And in the absence of knowing—of someone telling him what had become of his mother—he'd made up a story that suited him.

After two winters working with Scott, and two summers haying, I continue to feel more a part of this country each day. Scott and I have managed to build a bridge of understanding. He's very bright and I am sure he is now ready for university. His father talks about the University of Idaho, but Scott seems reluctant to discuss it. He insists he hasn't made up his mind. I am pleased that he has grown more comfortable around his father, enough to hold his own in an argument, at least, and has even taken to joking with some of the ranch hands. He's never discussed his mother with me since that night, nor did I ever tell anyone what he'd confided to me.

Scott didn't go to the University of Idaho. He didn't go to college at all. In the summer of 1974 he enlisted in the Marine Corps and was killed a year later in the rescue of the *SS Mayaguez* off the coast of Cambodia.

The memory of a newspaper photo of Scott Hartley in his uniform, standing straight and proud beside his father, brought tears to Ellen's eyes. Poor Mr. Hartley. First his wife leaves him then his only child is killed. What has all the money and that huge ranch brought him but grief?

Chapter Four

MARIE

Marie's aunt, seated comfortably with her recharged wine glass at hand, pushed a straying curl behind her ear. "As I told you earlier, *chérie,* after putting childhood games aside, I believe your papa's years at the University of Montreal were his most carefree. And yet, he was always busy, either with schoolwork or his political interests."

Marie cleared her throat. "What about his love life? Didn't he have girlfriends?"

"Oh, there were always girlfriends—for both Henri and our brother, Marc, although the way Marc treated women, well...maybe some women like to be treated as though they have no worth."

Marie folded a leg beneath her. "What about Emile's mother—was she like that?"

"Bunny? No. Surprising even to me, I liked Bunny. Despite the silly name, she was not one of those women who seemed to thrive on Marc's disrespect. She was very strong."

"But she gave up her baby. How did she know he would be well-cared for?" Thinking of Henry Reed, asleep in the borrowed crib upstairs, Marie frowned, shaking her head. "I could never do that. No matter what, I'd find a way. You did. You took care of Emile on your own. Why couldn't she?"

"I felt the same as you, *chérie.* For years I had nothing but contempt for what Bunny did. As I grew older, though, I realized that giving him up may have been her gift to him."

Marie pursed her lips, unconvinced.

"But, we were talking about your father and about his university years. As I told you, Father Thomas wanted Henri to be a priest, convinced he had the academic background for Laval University. Laval is in Quebec City and was the keystone of Quebec's social, political, judicial and ecclesiastical systems in those days. Though it was no surprise to anyone who knew him, poor Father Thomas was dismayed when your father would have no part of going to Laval." Her aunt chuckled. "Henri claimed he wanted to rub shoulders with all types of people, not just breathe the rarified air of the *haute bourgeoisie.*"

A Canadian Harvard or Yale and her father had turned such an education down on principle? Marie wasn't sure whether to applaud her father or shake her head at his foolishness—how could he have walked away from something like that?

"Henri told Papa that the changes about to happen in Quebec weren't going to come from that quarter. Students at Laval might rebel against their parents, he said, but they wouldn't rebel against their class—not when they held all the power. He insisted on going to school here in Montreal, where he was persuaded the changes would come."

Her aunt twirled a graying curl around her index finger, something Marie noticed she did when thinking. "Henri was correct. Although the call for Quebec independence created a political and social maelstrom across the whole of Canada,

Montreal became the epicenter of battle." She flashed Marie a bittersweet smile. "It is hard to believe now, but for nearly ten years, riots, bombings, labor strikes and other violence were part of our daily life." She closed her eyes, perhaps re-envisioning that violent past.

Marie pictured Montreal's loud, horn-honking yet smooth-flowing traffic, the tourist boats on the river, the sidewalks crowded with people going about their business. How was it possible to reconcile what she'd witnessed over the past two weeks with the mayhem her aunt described? She stared unseeing at a framed poster of red poppies on the wall across the room, trying to puzzle out an answer.

Her aunt straightened her shoulders. "Henri told me that Papa was absolutely right about education being our key to freedom and he threw himself into his studies. He also threw himself into his work on the school newspaper, *The Forum*, with such enthusiasm he almost got expelled."

"Expelled! My goodness, what happened?"

"I wasn't there, of course," said her aunt. "I can only tell you the story as I heard it from Henri."

Henri sat with eight other students around a large table in The Forum office. Papers and red pencils were scattered across the table along with several empty coffee cups. Henri's jacket hung over the back of his chair. Steam from the radiator, intermittent in its hissing, covered the window above it with moisture and made the room as hot and stuffy as a second-rate gym.

"We're not going to run your article, Henri," said René DuPont, a senior and The Forum's editor.

Henri scowled. "Why not?"

"*Sontag says it contains too many derogatory statements about the Church. He said the university could neither condone nor print it.*"

"*What!*" *Henri threw down the pencil he'd been twisting between his fingers. "I turned in harsher indictments when I was at Sacred Heart—to the priests, no less." He narrowed his gaze and looked around the table, then back to René. "Every one of us here knows there's not one word in that article that isn't true.*"

"*Henri's right.*"

Henri glanced at Claudia Chartier. Her support surprised him. He didn't know her well—she rarely spoke out at the Monday evening meetings and whenever she did, she seemed tentative in offering her opinions.

"*Nobody's saying he isn't right,*" *said René. "What we're saying is we can't print it.*"

Henri snorted. "That's bullshit."

His friend, Denis Haimard, shoved his fingers through the tight curls of his blond hair. "Why should Sontag decide what we do or don't print?" Several others nodded their heads in agreement. "Why should we listen to him? We should print it anyway."

"*Denis is right. Whose paper is it, anyway—the school's or ours?" The vehemence of Claudia's response again surprised Henri.*

He shoved his chair back and stood. "Denis and Claudia are dead on, René. This is supposed to be a student newspaper. I say we run it."

Cheeks flushed, René stood, pushing his own chair back, and faced Henri. "I'm just telling you what Sontag said. I'm the editor. I make the final decisions."

"So make it. What's it going to be?"

Rene looked around the table, appearing to seek an ally. He found none.

Henri pressed his advantage. "Make a decision, René. What's it going to be?"

René swallowed, his face still flushed. "We'll run it."

Henri and René were called into the Chancellor's office on Friday, after the newspapers with Henri's article were distributed. In a brief five-minute interview, Sontag let them know they were through at The Forum.

Walking down the steps of the administration building, René tried to brush it off. "I've got so many other things to do I really shouldn't have accepted the position in the first place. It will be a relief not to worry about deadlines."

"Don't give me that shit, René," Henri said when they reached the bottom step. "Being the editor of The Forum is a plum position. Of course you wanted it."

"No, it will be a relief. Really."

René's weak protests failed to convince Henri, who looked around the editorial table later that day, gauging the reaction of the others. "René took a stand for our editorial freedom. I'm only off for the rest of the year—I can come back to the paper in the fall. Not René—he graduates in the spring. This is his last chance to win the Bracken Trophy." Henri paused to let that sink in. Universities all over Canada competed for the trophy, given for the best editorial page in a student newspaper. "I think we should do something about it."

"What are you thinking, Henri?" Claudia's brown eyes focused on him. Her dark brown hair hung straight to her narrow shoulders and framed her face. She had the largest eyes

Henri had ever seen. Dark lines drawn on with pencil accentuated their size. She made him think of a doe.

He gave himself a mental shake. "I think we should show a united front."

"You mean all of us go out on strike? Like a union?"

Henri nodded. "Solidarity."

Denis, fiddling with an empty cup while the others spoke, raised his head and grinned. "I like the idea. Let's do it."

Marie eyed her aunt, sensing by the half-smile on her face that she was enjoying the memory of her brother's jousts with authority.

"At first the student newspaper strike failed to move the administration," her aunt said. "Later it led to long drawn-out negotiations. Students from all over campus rallied to support the 'Group of Nine,' as Henri and the others on the newspaper staff ended up being called. That marked your papa's first year at the University of Montreal, *chérie*." She gave a little dip of her chin as punctuation.

Marie took a perverse pride in her father's defiance. "He must have been very persuasive."

"*Oui*, your father was a very persuasive man—both on paper and in his speeches. He went with a group of students to Quebec City when he was in his third year of university and spoke in front of a huge crowd. It was on television and in the newspapers. I was so proud of him. Papa was, too. Even the English-language newspapers said Henri was a natural leader. Just a minute. I'll show you."

Marie's aunt crossed the living room to where a small desk and filing cabinet were nestled into a corner. She came back with two files, one slim, the other bulky. She opened the first and handed one of several clippings inside to Marie. "This is from The Montreal Star. There is your father, standing on the base of a flagpole in front of the Parliament building. Quebec's National Assembly meets there. Look at that sea of faces, all turned toward him. Only the week before, during a visit by Queen Elizabeth, people lined the streets of Quebec City to watch her motorcade, including a group of French-Canadian protestors. They were so badly beaten by the police that it's since been referred to as Bloody Sunday. Many of those protestors are in this crowd Henri is addressing."

Marie's brows furrowed as she read the accompanying article. Although her pride in her father grew stronger with each paragraph, the event the article described, Bloody Sunday, appalled her.

"That was your papa, *chérie*. You have every right to take great pleasure in his accomplishments."

Marie handed back the clipping, which her aunt returned to the file.

"Henri was tireless in his efforts to unite his fellow students in the cause of separatism and sovereignty. Some, especially those from the northern rural areas, were more difficult to convince."

Marie leaned forward, puzzled. "Why?"

"Tradition has always played a large role in Quebec politics. For a hundred years or more, French-Canadians stayed on the land raising crops and babies. The entire time they supported, and were supported by, conservative governments and the Catholic Church."

"What about separation of church and state? Don't you have that here?"

"It varies from province to province, but is not part of our constitution like in America."

"Oh," Marie said, surprised that something so basic wasn't a right of everyone, especially in a modern country like Canada. Obviously, she had a lot to learn.

"When all those babies grew up and there was not enough land to support them, many moved to the cities. The English-speakers, however, owned most of the businesses, so those grown-up babies from the farms were forced to join what many called a pool of cheap labor. As a consequence, most changed their political allegiance. The families who remained on the land did not."

"That's kind of like in the United States. I've never taken a big interest in politics, but I know that people who live in the country are more apt to be Republicans, conservatives—Idaho is mostly a Republican state—and people who live in cities are more apt to be liberal or Democrats."

"Exactly," her aunt said and Marie felt like she'd just been given a star on her report card. "Eventually most of the students agreed with Henri. By the time he'd graduated, he'd built such a name for himself as a speaker and writer, André Maurault was eager to rehire him; I think I explained to you that as a teenager your papa worked for the *Le Journal Quotidien,* running errands and such. After he went back to work for them, in no time he rose to become their number one reporter, with a regular by-line." She picked up the bulky file that had remained in her lap and handed it to Marie. "This contains many of his articles, most of them translated into English. Also, the letters he wrote from prison. You need to read them. Perhaps they will help you to understand."

Marie clasped the file with both hands. "It's so hard to believe. Dad a famous journalist and so interested in politics he even went to jail for his beliefs...to change so much...it just doesn't seem possible."

"I don't know what to tell you, *chérie*.   It was his whole life when he was a young man. He lived and breathed politics. He was an ardent believer in Quebec independence and worked hard for it. Nothing was allowed to interfere. In his own way, he was perhaps even more determined than Marc. I didn't see it then, because Marc's way was so different."

Marie tensed. Not wanting to, but knowing she must, she asked the question that had hovered in the corner like an unwanted guest all evening. "Tell me about him, *tante*. Tell me about my father's brother, Marc."

Chapter Five

ELLEN

Ellen threw her half-eaten sandwich in the trash and poured a fresh cup of coffee. She stepped out on the porch, stretching the cramped muscles in her back as she went. A gray-blue haze hovered over the mountains. Another forest fire. Every year, fires burned thousands of acres in the Northwest. Fighting them was dangerous work, often deadly. When fire struck the mountains around Platt City, a local team of volunteers worked the fire lines. Henry always joined them—just as he'd done that past summer. Ellen hated fire season.

She returned to the kitchen, sat, and picked up Henry's last journal.

Smoke fills the overheated air. Eyes stream with tears. Above all is the noise of heavy equipment, the fire spitting and cracking. Animals crash through underbrush, attempting to escape. There is an acrid stench of burning flesh—animals not quick enough to get away. Yesterday I came across the carcass of a large buck. Its antlers were still smoldering. I wanted to sit down beside it and weep.

Just when we get one hotspot under control, another springs up. The fire is jumping from crown to crown. It leaves nothing but blackened carnage in its wake. Working the south side of the mountain—picks and shovels proving of little use. Around noon told to fall back to Pinto Creek, near the fork. Later, left line and went down to lower camp to eat and get some rest.

Heard the heavy drone of engines long before I saw them— two big DC-7s and a C-130. Loaded with retardants. Flew so low—ground beneath my feet shook as they passed overhead— headed to the worst of the fire. Please, God, it works. Can't go on much longer without some luck on our side. If only winds would die.

The fire finally tamed, I dragged myself into the back of the Suburban, joining the rest of the crew slumped onto two hard bench-like seats running along opposite sides of the vehicle. All eyes were closed, heads falling forward or back. No one spoke. I climbed over the tangle of legs and charred boots and dropped into the last seat, next to Ian McCort. Like the rest, his face was blackened and weary.

Once we got down on the highway, the tires a hypnotic hum on the pavement, Ian started talking in that low drawl of his. I only half-listened. Was too exhausted to feel alarm when he first mentioned seeing a documentary on television. But when he said the documentary was about a couple of political kidnappings and a murder up in Canada back in 1970-71, my heart jumped and my palms began to sweat. I forced my breathing to even out and asked where in Canada.

His answer came as no surprise. Montreal. He said a journalist was involved, a man whose name was quite a bit like mine. Henri Morais. He wanted to know if I'd ever heard of him. I told him no. He didn't probe further. I closed my eyes and feigned sleep.

Ellen remembered the hot afternoon Henry arrived home from that fire. She'd been listening for the sound of his pickup coming down the lane—as soon as she heard it, she hurried outside to greet him.

Shutting off the engine, he'd leaned his head back. Soot and grime filled every line and pore on his face. His eyebrows and hair were singed. Shoulders slumped and looking wearier than she'd ever seen him, he'd dragged himself out of the truck. Leaning on her shoulder, he crossed to the porch and dropped onto the bottom step. For several long moments, he sat unmoving and unspeaking, period-ically taking deep breaths. Finally, he leaned down, unlaced his charred boots, and kicked them off. After peeling his dirt -encrusted clothes off, he sprayed himself down with the garden hose then came inside to shower.

Just when Ellen began to think he'd fallen asleep stand-ing under the spray, Henry emerged from the bath-room, steam billowing around him. He passed her as though he was sleep-walking. Naked, he dropped onto their bed and slept for eighteen hours straight.

I'd barely gotten home from the fire when the woman, Pearl Whitebear, approached me. I was leaving the hardware store in Platt City. My first instinct was to deny everything. I was sure she was a government official—a policeman or someone from INS. After she convinced me she was not connected with the government, but rather a friend of my family in Montreal, I agreed to talk with her. It had been almost thirty years. I was hungry for news of home.

We sat on a washed-up log on the bank of the river, near the spot where I'd camped when I first come to Platt City.

Right away, she told me Maman died—a few years after I left Canada. Heart failure. I hadn't thought I could feel more guilt. I was wrong. I threw pebbles into the shallow water, watching their circles widen and disappear, and thought of Maman. For some reason, I kept picturing her hands, fingers thick, knuckles swollen. They were the symbol of a lifetime of hard work.

Pearl told me Marie-Catherine is a successful writer now. Good to know she is happily married, her husband, a professor at McGill University. Glad to hear news of Emile, too. I've often thought of Marc's son, wondering what kind of man he'd turned into, hoping he'd traveled a far different path than his father.

My eyebrows shot up when Pearl told me Papa lives with Marie-Catherine and her husband. I was glad to know he wasn't on his own in that miserable house in Longueil, but I wondered what M.C.'s husband thought of having thundering lectures served with every meal. Pearl assured me that Papa has mellowed. Then she said Papa blames the government for Maman's death. I gave a shout of laughter. That would be Papa.

Pearl tried to give me Marie-Catherine's phone number, saying they wanted to hear from me. I told her it was too late, thirty years too late...

Ellen's hands shook when she recalled an evening about three weeks before Henry died. She was cleaning up after dinner. Henry told her he was going elk hunting. She asked how long he would be gone.

"About a week, I guess. Maybe ten days."

"Will you be going alone or with someone?" She'd stood at the sink and scrubbed a skillet, her head down, her back to him.

"Alone, like I always do. Why do you ask?"

"I just wondered." She continued scrubbing the skillet, even after all signs of fried chicken were gone.

Later that night she sat on the stool in front of the dressing table and mirror she'd inherited from her mother, brushing her hair as she had done every night of their marriage. "I was talking to Mr. Samuels today."

"Who?" Henry sat on the edge of the bed, pulling off his boots.

"Mr. Samuels. From the post office."

"Oh yes. I don't see him around very often. His son still playing football for that big east coast team?"

"The Redskins." Blood pounded at Ellen's temples. Her hands shook as she continued to run the brush through her hair. It was turning gray now. Mostly she wore it pulled back in a clip at the nape of her neck, but loose, like now, it tumbled past her shoulders. "You may not have seen him, Henry, but he saw you."

"Oh? When was that?"

Through the mirror, she saw the puzzled look on his face. She turned her eyes away. "A few days ago. He said he passed you on the highway. You were heading out of town as he was coming in. There was a woman in the truck. He thought it was me. I didn't tell him different." Her cheeks flushed. She finally lifted her eyes and looked at him through the mirror, challenging.

Henry's eyes dropped and a flash of guilt slid across his face.

Ellen's heart raced. So it was true.

"Ellen." He came to her and squatted in front of her. He took the brush from her limp hand, set it on the polished surface of the dressing table then held both of her hands in his. "I love you. Don't ever feel that love is threatened by anything or anyone. Her name is Pearl Whitebear. She's a consultant for Marrick-Pacific, and she does some work for Ian McCort. I was giving her a ride."

"Oh." She wanted to be convinced. "But..."

"What?"

"It's just you've been so moody lately. I can't seem to reach you."

He stood and placed his hands on her shoulders, his eyes looking deep into hers. "I'm sorry." He seemed to want to say more, then straightened and moved away. "I've had a lot on my mind lately." His back to her, he crossed to the bed. "There's a big argument between conservation groups and the government over logging in the national forests. Ian has been telling me about it. There are some unpleasant characters, some real radicals, involved."

"Is that why the woman is here?"

Seated on the bed once more, Henri pulled off his socks. "Not really. Well, maybe partly. She teaches forest management at the University of Idaho."

"My goodness, isn't that an unusual field for a woman?"

"I don't know, but you may be right. Anyway, I thought I'd scout around for Ian while I'm up in the mountains."

"You'll be careful, though?" She was suddenly frightened, remembering stories she'd heard of spiked trees and burned logging trucks. "Maybe you should have someone with you."

Henry smiled reassurance. "Don't worry. I know those woods better than anyone. I'll be fine."

Ellen rested her forehead in her hands. Tears stung her eyes. She almost wished he had been having an affair. Instead, he'd been frantically trying to keep his past buried…buried alive.

Twice more Pearl Whitebear approached me, and twice more I told her it was too late. First Ian McCort and his probing about Henri Morais and the FLQ, and now Pearl Whitebear. No matter what I do, no matter how hard I try, my past keeps coming back. But I've caused too much damage there. As soon as Ian mentioned the kidnappings and killings, I saw Laporte's strangled body again, the chain cutting into the flesh of his neck. God. How will I ever forget that, knowing part of it was my fault? And if I give in, if I go back or call Marie-Catherine, I'll cause damage here. How could Ellen go on loving me—how could she even stand to look at me—if she knew I was responsible for the maiming of my sister and the deaths of two people—Marie-Catherine's friend, Dora, and that policeman; both had families.

And I AM responsible, no matter what anyone says; I could have stopped Marc, but I chose not to. I CHOSE not to. All because I was so sure my way was the right way. And what would Ellen think if she knew about the people I've abandoned?

She'd never understand. Never forgive me. But I've tried to change. My God, I've tried to. What more can I do?

Feeling as if her skin had been peeled back, leaving her raw and unprotected, Ellen returned the last notebook to the box and closed the lid. What could she have done to heal the wounds the past inflicted on Henry? What could she have offered besides her love and support—and he'd always had that. She'd given it freely.

But Henry hadn't trusted her love, not enough to share his burden. She'd need to live with that fact. She returned the box to the back of the closet with determined finality.

Chapter Six

MARIE

The clock on the mantle ticked away the minutes as both women sat without speaking. Marie had fixed a pot of tea, worried that more wine would put her aunt to sleep. To appease her, perhaps, her aunt had agreed to a cup. Finally, she began.

"By the time I was seventeen and had finished secondary school, your father was well established with *Le Journal Quotidien*. But still he made time for me. Even his girlfriend indulged me." She chuckled, but quickly sobered. "It should have been enough that I had Henri's support, but somehow it wasn't. I wanted Marc's good opinion too. The more he withheld it, the more I wanted it. You understand, *chérie?*"

Although she nodded, Marie didn't really understand why her aunt should have needed or wanted her bomb-making brother's approval for anything. Especially not when she already had Marie's father's support. That should have been plenty.

Her aunt didn't seem aware of Marie's unspoken censure and instead went on with her story. "Like many people my age, I was convinced that the FLQ was in the right. I was proud of how they stood up to the English-speaking establishment. They said the bombs they planted in buildings and mailboxes targeted property, not people, and I believed it. So when Marc asked me to go with him to North Carolina to buy explosives for the FLQ, I was eager to go, thinking I'd finally proved myself worthy of his notice."

Her aunt's lips thinned.

"As I told you the other day, when we returned from North Carolina, Marc insisted I tell Henri where I'd been. I called him and we arranged to meet in the park. It was a beautiful fall day. Ducks paddled about in the lake; small children were there with their mothers or nannies; the leaves had begun to turn red and orange. Henri waited for me on the path—by then my university classes had already begun and I was a few minutes late. I told him I'd needed to talk to one of my professors, but that was not true. I delayed because I didn't want to face him. Telling him was the most difficult thing I'd ever done."

Marie understood her aunt's dread—she'd felt the same when facing her parents and confessing she was pregnant—several weeks before her high school graduation. It struck her that she and her aunt would have been the same age, eighteen.

"I couldn't tell Henri exactly where we'd gone—we got there in the middle of the night. All I knew was that it was a cabin somewhere on the western shore of Albemarle Sound. Marc told me to stay in the cabin, out of sight. The men he was meeting were the scum of the earth, he said. They bought and sold everything from people, to drugs to guns."

Marie's hand went to her mouth as a frisson of fear rippled through her.

"At Marc's instructions, I stayed well-hidden, watching from the cabin window as Marc and two men shifted the boxes from a small fishing boat to the back of a rental truck Marc and I had picked it up the day before in Norfolk, Virginia. It was an eerie sight—just before dawn, the moon lighting up the beach, a chorus of frogs and cicadas. Peaceful, almost. But so important to the movement. Even though I was only watching, I was elated—I was part of the future of a new Quebec."

At her aunt's words, a sour taste filled Marie's mouth. She fought with the urge to run up the stairs, gather up her sleeping son and flee.

Her aunt studied her face. "I've shocked and disappointed you."

Marie swallowed. "You have, *tante*." She shrugged her shoulders, feeling helpless. "I just don't get how you could have gone along with Marc—he built bombs. How could you have wanted to be part of that?"

"Your father felt the same. I'm sorry to say, I just didn't see it at the time. Sorry, too, that there is even more you must hear."

A car passed in front of the house, its headlights a momentary flash on the living-room window.

"Henri was furious with me when I finished telling him. 'Bombs are built for one thing,' he said. 'To kill people.' I tried to protest, parroting about the FLQ targeting property not people, but he dismissed my claims, which made me angry and entrenched me further in my conviction that the FLQ was in the right."

Marie straightened in her chair. At least her father wasn't taken in by his brother. "So why did Marc insist you tell Dad, when he knew it would upset him? Just to be mean?"

"He was blackmailing your father and using me to do it."

Marie felt more lost than ever. "I don't understand."

"No, you wouldn't. I will explain." Once again her aunt leaned her head against the back of her chair. "The FLQ wrote what they called '*communiqués*,' which they wanted published in the major papers. Most newspapers refused, English and French alike. Marc told Henri that he would keep me from becoming more involved with the FLQ if he, Henri, would use his influence to get a new *communiqué* printed in *Le Journal Quotidien*." She turned to Marie, her head cocked to one side. "Of course your father knew that even if he could accomplish that feat, Marc wouldn't keep his word—not unless it was in his interest to do so."

Marie frowned. She could understand sibling rivalry when her father and his brother were boys, competing in sports or for their parents' attention, but not as adults.

A crease appeared between her aunt's eyebrows. "That is when Henri and his editor hatched their big idea for Henri to pretend to be fired so that he could join the FLQ—with the goal of getting himself arrested. On Henri's part, it was an indication of his desperation. He thought he could somehow show me by example that civil disobedience and peaceful protests were better than the violence Marc espoused. His editor's only interest was getting a good story—about how so-called political prisoners were treated. Well, to give him credit, he wouldn't have known about Henri's true purpose. Neither of them thought Henri would be in jail more than a week or two.

"As I told you before, *chérie,* Henri agreed one-hundred percent with the FLQ's goals of a free and independent Quebec. It was their methods he abhorred." She gave Marie a sad little smile. "Marc was suspicious of Henri's defection from what he called 'the other side,' but the FLQ put your father to work making speeches against the government and leading demonstrations. The last speech I heard him give was where we were a few days ago—the University of Montreal. In spite of it being a miserably cold and snowy night, hundreds of young people gathered, cheering Henri."

Marie had seen pictures in textbooks of students protesting the Vietnam War and imagined the demonstration her aunt described must have been similar. Still, to think of her father leading something like that, giving speeches...

"You should have seen your papa. He stood on a half-wall next to a set of steps leading into the administration building. The crowd was eating from his hands, shouting Morais, Morais, Morais." Her aunt's face lit at the memory, but like a switch had been turned, the light in her eyes went out and her voice became grim. "Then the police, the RCMP, arrived. And then it became terrible."

Hundreds of uniformed men had poured from behind the two wings of the building, shields and clubs poised. They marched double-time into a line, trapping the students in the square in front of the building; there was no way out except up the steps, into the building itself. The RCMP's appearance was anticipated by some students—veterans, no doubt, of previous demonstrations—because rocks and bottles were soon flying through the air. Most of the missiles were deflected as the line of police steadily pressed forward, their shields upraised and their nightclubs slashing downward, frequently onto unprotected heads.

"It was a bloody conflagration of two equally determined but unequally armed forces. The police said little, but young people were yelling and screaming. I saw one young woman clubbed, then kicked in the stomach when she fell to the ground. I tried to go to her, but Henri pulled me to shelter behind the wall he'd earlier been standing on. 'It's no use,' he yelled to me. 'You'll only get yourself beaten.'"

Marie shuddered at her aunt's words.

"Later, when the police had the crowd dispersed—the more adamant were hauled off to jail—Henri walked out from behind the stairs and turned himself in, exactly as he and his editor must have planned it." Her aunt twisted a curl with a finger that trembled.

"I could not believe it. I tried to hold him back, but he shook me off. They took him to Jeffers's precinct. Jeffers was a pig of a policeman who had a special hatred for Henri. He and his partner were brutal in their treatment—later, when Henri got out, he wrote about it. You'll see some of the articles in that file."

Marie fought a wave of nausea at the image of her father being dragged off to prison, at the mercy of a monster. "But...the police are meant to protect people."

Her aunt shook her head. "Not here, not in those days, I'm afraid. And as I told you, Henri and his editor greatly misjudged the amount of time he would be imprisoned. When he was transferred to Rue Parthenais, they put him in with the psychologically damaged and the drug addicts, trying to break his spirit. Even so, he was able to write letters to the editors of various newspapers, including his own. His lawyer got them out and posted them. People read the letters and the articles Henri wrote later, when he was finally released, and they compared him to Gandhi."

Her aunt smiled, pride glowing in her eyes before a self-deprecating smile appeared on her lips.

"What happened then, you will ask. Did I not finally see that Henri was in the right: we could accomplish more with civil disobedience than with all the FLQ's bombs?" The irony in her voice turned to self-disgust. "Unfortunately the answer is no. I was still convinced of Marc's way—Marc's and the glorious FLQ. By then it was spring and I believed the train for Quebec independence was leaving the station without me. I complained to Marc that while he and Henri were doing so much, each in his own way, I was doing nothing."

Her aunt picked up her teacup then set it down, the tea untouched. "That was when Marc told me about the Arrow Shoe Factory, where the workers were out on strike. He wanted me to apply for a job during my spring break." She fingered a wrinkle in the slip-covered arm of her chair. "He told me he needed a mole—someone to find out what was going on inside."

"But why you? You were a student. Why not someone else?"

Marie-Catherine shrugged. "Perhaps he was merely indulging my naïve longing to be part of things. More likely, it was another opportunity to use me in his undeclared war with Henri. Whatever his reason, I fell right into his trap."

Disgust filled her aunt's voice. Marie wondered if it was for herself or for Marc. Personally, she thought they were equally to blame—her aunt for having allowed herself to be used, and Marc for using her.

"Marc was right when he said I'd be hired. The work was hard and far from glamorous—sorting hides and loading boxes. After the first day, I was so exhausted I didn't think I could possibly continue. But I did. And I made a friend. Dora. She was from London. Her family had emigrated when she was a teen-ager. She was beautiful—with wavy red hair and creamy white skin and freckles. Her laugh would have you joining in, even when you didn't know why she was laughing."

She dabbed at a tear that slid out at the corner of her eye and when she started speaking again, there was a tremor in her voice. "Dora had been at Arrow Shoes forever, but she hadn't joined the strikers. She had a husband and four young children and said they couldn't afford for her not to work—no matter how badly she was paid."

This time the pause was even longer. Marie reached for her aunt's hand, squeezing it.

"A friend of Henri's, she was a friend of mine, too, got word to him what I was doing, that I'd quit school even, because I had by then, and Henri made a deal with the warden."

She paused a moment and Marie got the impression she was about to say something on a different subject, but changed her mind and went on. "The warden and Jeffers knew all about Marc. They'd tried to get Henri to make a deal before. Each time he'd refused, but when he found out I was spying for Marc, telling him everything that was going on inside the factory, he told the warden he'd find out what Marc planned. So they let him out."

Marie swallowed, not sure she wanted to hear more.

"Although he came to the factory several times, the guard outside wouldn't let him in and I refused to see him. Marc was no help to him either. He told Henri he didn't know where I was, even though I was sleeping on his couch every night. It was a week before I finally spoke to Henri. He called Marc's apartment one evening and I answered the phone. We were both shocked to hear the other's voice. He wanted to know why I hadn't contacted him, why I'd quit school and what I was doing working in that factory. He was bewildered and I couldn't blame him. While he was away, his little sister, the very one he'd gone to prison for in the first place, had shut him out of her life."

Marie's eyes filled, thinking how forsaken her father must have felt—as though everything he'd gone through had been for nothing.

"I told him Marc and the others needed to know what was going on inside with the workers who remained, that I was observing only. Your father would hear none of my feeble excuses. He knew Marc and the FLQ had plans for the factory, but he didn't know exactly what or when. And because I was involved, refusing to stop working there, he couldn't, wouldn't tell Jeffers or the warden as he had promised."

A crooked half-smile appeared on her aunt's face. "Your poor papa, *chérie*—he was caught in the middle. He loved both of us, you see—Marc and me, no matter that neither of us deserved his love and his loyalty. And Jeffers wouldn't stop pressuring him."

Marie's heart ached for the pain her father must have felt. She was surprised at the strength of the anger and resentment she felt toward her aunt. It didn't help that she knew her aunt blamed herself, perhaps more than anyone else could.

"I had a day off coming. I was very much looking forward to it when my supervisor told me I had to come to work the next morning anyway. He was a nasty, hateful little man, not above touching a girl's breast or putting his hand between her legs when no one was near; it was easy for Dora and me to hate him.

"The next morning it was raining. Despite the weather, Dora stood on the sidewalk waiting for me to get off the bus. She was wearing a bright yellow raincoat; the hood hid her red hair, but I knew it was Dora. We always hooked elbows to get through the picket line. And the line was there—along with the police, who, as they did every morning and evening, just stood and watched while we were jeered and pinched and spit upon. I was such an innocent and I hated that part so much. I wanted to tell them, the strikers, *'don't you understand I'm doing this for you?'* But I didn't, of course—Dora didn't even know my true purpose. She thought I was at Arrow Shoes for the same reason as her own—because I needed money.

"When we got inside, I breathed a sigh of relief. We slipped off our wet coats and were walking across the factory floor, just passing the area where they wrapped the shoes in tissue and put them into boxes, when Dora pointed to an object wedged into the conveyor belt. The instant I saw it, I knew what it was and I knew who had placed it there. Just as Dora reached for it, I yelled 'No!' But I was too late."

Marie gasped and a tightness filled her chest.

Her aunt barely paused for breath before going on. "I woke up in the hospital three weeks later, with my eye bandaged, my head immobilized in a metal cage, and no memory of what had happened. No memory of my friend, Dora—the mother of four young children and the wife of a loving husband. She was gone. Dead. From massive head and chest wounds, as I later learned." She swallowed; a sad smile wavered on her lips and she reached up with a shaking hand to wipe away the tears. "I will have another cup of tea, *chérie*."

With trembling fingers, Marie managed to pour them each a fresh cup of tea. Could her aunt see how appalled and sickened she felt? Surely it was written all over her face. The ticking of the clock filled the silence until once again Marie-Catherine began to speak.

"For several months, I'd have flashes of memory, but it was so frustrating—like trying to put together a giant puzzle without the picture on the puzzle box to guide you. Everyone told me to relax. The doctor said my memory loss was my mind's way of protecting me. My parents and Henri didn't want me to remember. Probably Marc didn't, either.

"*Maman* never left my side, either in the hospital or later, when I finally was able to come home—we became closer during that time than we'd ever before been. Still, I could remember nothing of the accident, and it haunted me. As I said, little pieces floated through my mind, but no matter how hard I tried, I couldn't put them together. When I was strong enough to be out on my own, I took the bus to McGill University. I went to the library and asked for all the newspaper articles that dealt with the accident.

"In a stuffy room surrounded by shelves stacked with books and files, staring with my one good eye at a picture of my friend Dora, a glorious smile on her freckled face, my memory flooded back and I remembered everything. I knew what happened to Dora. I knew what they'd been keeping from me. And I knew, too, that Henri had been right all along: Marc would stop at nothing, including murder, to get what he wanted. A terrible thing to say about one's own brother, *n'est-ce pas?*"

Disgust, bewilderment, anger, outrage. Marie trembled as one emotion followed the other.

Her aunt drew a breath. "I refused to talk to any of the others at the North Montreal precinct while I waited for Inspector Jeffers to show up, just as I refused to let myself back down. I wanted to. I was terrified of the man, but I knew what I had to do. Suddenly he was there—swaggering through the door to the precinct, his face beefy red, his forehead shiny with sweat, even though it was autumn and the summer heat had passed. 'You wanted to see me?' he said and it was too late to change my mind." She gave a slight shiver. "I told him about the building near the airport, where Marc and I had delivered his cache of explosives, where I assumed most of it remained." The determination in her aunt's voice matched her words. "If I hadn't told, Marc would have gone on using it. More people would have died."

To know that about your own brother. Marie thought of Ken and the muscles in her chest tightened.

"Jeffers told me to let Henri know he was off the hook. He said I'd made up for Henri not keeping his side of the bargain." Her aunt drew a deep breath. "It was clear he knew Henri had been protecting me. And because of that, because of me, Dora died. Because of me, Dora's children grew up without her. Because of me, Dora's husband grew old without her."

In the long silence that followed those words, Marie wondered how her aunt had been able to live with all the guilt. It seemed too much. But there was yet more.

Marie-Catherine spoke in a matter-of-fact voice when she continued. "They set a trap for them, for Marc and the others in his cell. Marc, who got away, later managed to steel explosives from a construction site in Montreal. He planned to use it to blow up a busy bridge connecting Quebec to Ottawa—a grand, symbolic gesture, his *pièce de résistance.*"

"Blow up a bridge? With cars and traffic on it?"

"The police trapped him there. He was charged for the deaths of two people: Dora, of course, and a bomb expert who was killed trying to dismantle a bomb Marc and his cell had placed in the Palace of Justice. Marc had built it specifically to go off if anyone tried to disarm it."

Her aunt reached across the space between them and took Marie's hand for a moment. "I know you must find it nearly impossible to believe, to even imagine, the horror of those years, chérie, including the terrible things your uncle, my brother, did. Even I, who lived through it, sometimes think it must have been a terrible nightmare, wished it was a terrible dream. But it was not. It was very real."

She released Marie's hand and sat back in her chair.

"The charges against Marc, his imprisonment, devastated my parents. While I hated to see them suffer, I was glad, glad there would be no more chance of Marc hurting someone." She paused, but only for a moment. "Montreal was calm for a while—only an occasional incident to remind us of the unresolved conflict. Then another FLQ cell—there were many of them—kidnapped James Cross, a British diplomat. A few days later a different cell captured a second man, Pierre Laporte."

Her aunt's voice turned grim once again. "Both cells demanded the release of all political prisoners, including Marc, in return for the two men's lives. Plus, they wanted a great deal of money and a plane to fly them to Cuba. They placed deadlines and extended them as the Government negotiated. Things were stalled for several days as everyone held their collective breath. Then, finally, the Government issued a statement refusing all the FLQ's demands."

Her aunt straightened in her chair. "They killed Laporte. They strangled him with a gold chain he wore around his neck, and left him in the trunk of a car. Because of a tip—someone had called the newspaper wanting publicity for their cowardly deed—Henri was there when the trunk was pried open. He wrote the story, of course. He had no choice. But it sickened him so, he would never again speak of it."

Marie thought she would be sick herself. What kind of people would do such a dreadful thing? Only days ago, she'd been proud of her new-found heritage; now…. She shook her head. Now she felt only revulsion.

"Everyone knew then that the FLQ had gone too far. Before, many had thought those in the FLQ were just idealistic and well-meaning young people—this despite the bombs and terror. But after the brutal, despicable murder of Pierre Laporte, any support they had vanished overnight.

"Trudeau enacted the War Measures Act and Quebec was put under martial law. Armed soldiers and tanks streamed down the streets of Montreal. Doors were broken down without search warrants. The police rounded up hundreds—most of whom had nothing whatever to do with the FLQ—and held them in jail for weeks on the flimsiest of charges. It felt as if we were living in a foreign country—the very landscape of the city seemed to have changed overnight; apprehension and fear hung as wood smoke over Montreal."

"Tanks and armed soldiers on the very streets you and I walked on just yesterday?" Marie said. "It doesn't seem possible."

"It may seem unfathomable now, *chérie,* but I assure you, it happened." When Marie said nothing further, her aunt went on. "I made Henri take me to see Marc in prison. My brother showed no remorse. He was indifferent to Dora's death. To my injuries he would only say, 'you weren't supposed to be there.' All my youthful and naïve ideals were shattered like a glass windowpane struck by a brick. Although I wanted to place all the blame on Marc, I knew I shared much of it."

Marie could tell by the pleading tone in her aunt's voice that her aunt wanted her understanding, her forgiveness. Marie wasn't sure she could do that. Between them, Marie-Catherine and Marc, they'd nearly destroyed her father.

Tears again filled her aunt's eyes, but she quickly wiped them away. "It was the last time I saw Marc alive. The last time any of us saw him alive."

PART THREE

Home

I have been a stranger in a strange land.
From
The Book of Exodus

Chapter One
MARIE

Marie had already packed Henry Reed's bag and her suitcase—they were to fly home to Idaho the following morning. Her son reluctantly down for his afternoon nap and her grandfather dozing in front of the television, she sat once again with her aunt. Even though she understood that Marie-Catherine regretted the past and was trying hard to make amends, their conversation seemed stilted—nothing like the ease they'd shared before Marie-Catherine had revealed the extent of what she and Marc had done to make Marie's father's life in Canada intolerable.

"I'm making *coq au vin* for your farewell dinner. I hope you will like it. Emile will be joining us. He said he would be here around six."

"You shouldn't go to so much trouble, *tante*."

"It is no trouble, *chérie*."

Emile surprised them by arriving two hours early. He didn't bother to sit. "Have you told her about Claudia?" He asked Marie-Catherine the question in English and without preamble.

Her aunt gave Marie a worried glance. "Leave it alone, Emile."

"I'm not going to leave it alone, and if you don't tell her, I will."

Marie jumped to her feet. "Stop! Neither of you needs to tell me. I already know. Claudia was Dad's girlfriend." She looked at her aunt and attempted a smile. "The one who indulged you and who told Dad about you working at Arrow Shoe factory."

Emile spoke first. "Not his girlfriend. His wife."

Marie's eyes widened, darting from Emile to her aunt. "His wife?" She shook her head, finding it impossible to think of any woman besides her mother as her father's wife.

Emile, apparently satisfied he'd said enough, crossed to his grandfather's chair and roused him. "Let's go for a walk in the park," he said the old man, helping him to his feet. A moment later, they were gone, the television left flickering in the corner, the sound muted.

His wife. The words continued to swirl around Marie's head, echoing gong-like in her ears. It couldn't be...could it? She looked once more to her aunt.

Her aunt's voice trembled, hesitant at first. "They dated for years, beginning when they were at university. They lived together in Quebec City, after Henri left the newspaper and went to work for the *Parti Quebecois*."

Marie took a deep breath, trying to remain calm. She felt her aunt's eyes on her, gauging her reaction. When Maria made no comment, her aunt went on, her voice stronger.

"Claudia was crazy about your father. She would have done anything for him. And did, I believe, or at least tried to. They married that summer. I was happy for them, but also concerned. Henri was always caught up in some political passion. He didn't have enough time for Claudia when he worked on the newspaper and even less when he went to work for the *Parti Quebecois*. And when he wasn't embroiled in some political maneuver, he was immersed in feeling guilty. I loved your father, too, chérie, but he was a difficult man to live with, much less live up to."

Marie shook her head, her curls bouncing. "I don't understand this guilt thing you keep saying he was consumed with. Didn't he try to keep his brother out of trouble? Didn't he help you with Emile after Marc committed suicide? Didn't he do his best for the newspaper and for his country?"

Her aunt smiled in sympathy. "I don't understand it myself, chérie. I think some people are born with an overdeveloped sense of responsibility. Henri was like that. Everyone and everything, he would be responsible for, then consumed with guilt when something went wrong. You couldn't talk to him about it."

Marie scowled. "He wasn't like that, though." She bit hard on her lower lip. Why couldn't her aunt understand?

"He was convinced my injuries were his fault—not Marc's, not my own, only his—because he hadn't found a way to put a stop to Marc's plans. He also became convinced his articles and speeches had led to Pierre Laporte's murder. He even blamed himself for Marc committing suicide. For months, he was plagued with self-doubt and recrimination. Then the *Parti Quebecois'* opposition brought up Marc's and Henri's involvement in the FLQ and Henri's period in prison, completely misrepresenting the reason he'd gotten himself arrested. It appeared to cost the Parti seats in the election." Her lips thinned. She sighed. "It all became too much for him and he left."

"What do you mean 'he left'?" An even heavier feeling descended on Marie.

"Just that. One day he was here, the next day he was gone."

"But, he can't have gone just like that. You just said—he had a home, a wife." A sudden flush of adrenalin made Marie's skin tingle; her hands opened and closed convulsively. "There would have had to be a divorce."

"No *chérie*. No divorce. Even though divorce had finally become legal in Quebec, they were hard to acquire." Her aunt's concern was evident in the sorrowful look on her face and in her eyes.

"I don't understand. How could he just walk out like that? He was a good man, a decent man. He was. He wouldn't have done what you're saying." Her voice rasped on choked emotion. Tears dammed behind her eyelids, shut against the pain of a truth she didn't want to acknowledge. It's not true. *Oh, Daddy, can't you somehow show me that it's not true?* But there was no revelation, no bright shimmering light denying her aunt's charges. Instead, there was another question—she didn't want to ask it, but she needed the answer.

"And Jeannine? There's no way Dad would have left his child."

"He didn't know. Claudia was waiting for his birthday to surprise him with the news of her pregnancy. He left two days before." Her aunt's unrelenting voice kept on, piercing the thick armor of denial Marie sought to hide behind. "Claudia was devastated. She went to the police, hired detectives. She quit her job and for months did nothing but search for Henri. We were fearful she might lose the baby.

Finally, she gave up and moved back to Montreal, into her parent's home, where you met her. There, she devoted her life to her daughter."

"Did she never remarry?"

"No, *chérie*. How could she? She was still married to your father."

Marie gazed out the plane window to the pile of cotton-candy clouds below. They looked solid enough to support her weight and she felt an overwhelming desire to be in them, lolling, sprawling—forgetting everything she'd discovered. They'd been right, her mother and Paul. She should have left well-enough alone, never have gone to Montreal. How could she tell her mother her marriage had been a sham and that her husband was a bigamist—a bigamist and the father of another woman's child?

When they finally touched down in Idaho, Marie's stomach was so tied in knots she didn't want to get off. She had to, though. By the time the plane rolled to the terminal she'd gathered Henry Reed's things from the floor and from the seat next to her, tucked them into his diaper bag and was ready to leave with the rest of the passengers.

She'd called Paul the night before, but like all the telephone conversation they'd had while she was in Canada, it too had been laced with his anger. What was happening to them? It was as if Paul had become a stranger to her—like she knew him no better than she'd known her father. At least he was eager to see their son. She just hoped that beneath his anger he was a little eager to see her as well.

He stood a short distance from the others awaiting relatives or friends. The way the hair above his forehead defied taming, even with comb and water, brought a small jolt, almost like an electrical shock. Warmth infused her. He gave her a tentative smile and that's all it took for her to rush into his arms. He enfolded her. She closed her eyes a moment and reveled in the comfort of his familiar smell and feel. She pulled her head back and saw tears pooled in his eyes. "Oh Paul. I'm so sorry we've been quarreling. Forgive me?"

Before Paul could answer, Henry Reed stiffened, signaling his displeasure at being squeezed between them, forcing them to break apart. Paul reached for him. After a moment's hesitation, Henry Reed leaned forward and allowed his father to gather him up.

"Let's go get your stuff."

Once home, Marie quickly fell into the routine of her old life—taking care of Henry Reed, fixing meals, doing laundry, shopping. When she could no longer delay, she drove out to see her mother.

Paul had warned her, so she wasn't surprised to find Marta Weitzel in residence—helping pack the lunchtime order for the restaurant. Even forewarned, it still seemed weird to find the older woman not only in Marie's childhood home, but occupying Marie's old bedroom. Not that it was a bad idea—it was just, well, weird. It made home feel not like home.

But home might never seem like home again. Marie was afraid nothing would feel the same. Ever. It wasn't just what she'd found out about her father's past, it was her mother, too. Her mother wasn't the same person. With this bread-making business, all the changes to the house. Even her mother's appearance had changed. Gone were the old-fashioned housedresses she'd always worn and Marie had secretly made fun of. Even before she'd left for Montreal, her mother had started dressing in jeans and tank-tops, claiming jeans didn't get in her way in the kitchen, and the tops were cooler. Now Mrs. Weitzel. Where was it going to end?

She answered her mother's questions about what she'd found in Montreal with a degree of vagueness that brought a sharp look to her mother's eye, but no further questions. She still hadn't told Paul everything. She'd relayed much of it—what the city was like, her father's job, his obsession with politics, Marc's terrible deeds, even her father's time in prison and how she'd felt when she saw the place where he'd been held.

She hadn't told him about Claudia and Jeannine. She didn't know what to say—how could she explain it to Paul when she hadn't a clue herself? The word bigamist kept echoing in her brain. Her whole being wanted to reject it. Her father wasn't—hadn't been—a wicked or cruel man. He was a loving husband, a loving father.

But when she thought about the sadness she often saw in his eyes, when she thought about his retreats to the woods, his need for solitude, she knew in her heart all the things Marie-Catherine had revealed were true.

She had to tell Ken, but wondered if it would be better to wait until he was home. How could she put it in a letter and what could he do, anyway? And yet, she would explode if she didn't tell someone soon. The time came one night after dinner. She'd been home for a week.

"Something's on your mind," Paul said, as she poured him a second cup of coffee. "It's been on your mind since you got back—you haven't been sleeping well."

He was right. She'd tried keep still, not awaken him, but she couldn't conceal the smudges under her eyes or the yawns she attempted to hide behind a quickly raised hand.

When she finally sat back in her chair, feeling both empty and tense, he wasn't as shocked as she'd expected. "I knew there was something more. That's one of the reasons I was against you going there. At least now you know and can put it behind you."

"Well, not exactly put it behind me." She raised her hands, palms upward. "My God, Paul, I have a sister—I can't exactly ignore that. I need to decide what to do about it, like how and when to tell Mom." She relaxed somewhat. "I've already decided to wait to tell Ken."

Paul pushed his chair back. "You can't be serious. How in hell can you think about dumping this on Ellen? What good would that do? Jeez, Marie. Try to think from someone else's point of view for a change."

Marie stared. She hadn't even considered not telling her mother. "I couldn't keep that from her and she wouldn't want me to. It's too important." She smiled, trying to soften her words. "Besides, now some of the shock's worn off, I'm dying of curiosity. I want to get to know Jeannine and I'll bet she wants to know me. Ken, too—assuming Emile has told her about us. I couldn't stand having such a secret and not telling Mom. Wouldn't you want to know if I had a life you weren't part of and kept it secret from you? For years and years?"

"Sometimes, Marie, I'm not so sure you don't."

Her forehead furrowed into a frown. "What do you mean? You know everything about me. We've been together since we were babies. We grew up together."

"Maybe so. But I sure don't know how you think anymore." He shook his head. "I haven't got a clue what's important to you. I'm beginning to wonder if I'm important to you."

"How can you say that?" Marie's cheeks burned and her heart began to beat hard. "What have I done to make you doubt that you're important to me, to doubt that our life together is important?"

Paul stood, bracing his hands on the kitchen table. "Going to Montreal when I asked you not to, for one thing." His eyes and voice were granite hard. "And now you come up with this crazy idea that just because you know something you have to inflict that knowledge on someone else. I mean, don't you care about your mother's feelings? Don't you think she's been through enough this last year without rubbing her nose in your father's past? She loved him, for God's sake."

Marie stood as well. "I loved him, too. I don't think telling my mother the truth will change her feelings. But she always knew there was something he was hiding. She had to have known. I think she deserves to hear the truth, finally. And not just about Claudia, but about his whole life." Voice shaking with emotion, she stared at him. "His life in Montreal was not something to be ashamed of—he was an important man, a caring man, with deep-seated values." Her conviction of this was absolute.

Paul's eyes narrowed. "And the fact that he didn't want her to know, didn't tell her himself, that means nothing to you, does it? You'll just barge in there with your mighty 'truth', whether she wants to hear it or not, and you'll be satisfied, is that it? You'll have done your duty, right?"

Her chin lifted. "Yes."

Paul's eyes narrowed. "Have you noticed that this is really all about you? You needed to go to Montreal, so you went. You need to unburden what you know, so you'll tell your mother." He gazed at her as though trying to read something in her face, in her eyes. "Well," he finally said when she made no reply, "actions have consequences."

"What is that supposed to mean?" She knew she sound -ed belligerent, but it was too late to back down.

"I don't know. I guess we'll both have to wait and see. I'm going for a walk. Maybe I'll stop by and see Dad. Don't wait up."

Marie was too stunned to respond. She stared after him as he crossed to the door, opened it and walked out. From the window she watched his familiar, long-legged figure make rapid strides up the block to the corner, turn and disappear from view.

Chapter Two

ELLEN

Ellen pushed aside a low-hanging branch and ducked into her favorite viewing spot. If she stayed quiet, she might see the doe and her two fawns again. The fawns would be bigger, but still they would heed their mother, moving with quiet caution through the woods. It never ceased to surprise her how, with no warning or sound, they'd appear as if from nowhere. She might blink her eyes or turn her head a few inches one way or another and there they would be, one foot delicately placed in front of the other, tails, ears and noses twitching. The slightest sound from Ellen, hidden behind a moss-covered log and draped with overhanging branches, would send them crashing through the underbrush and out of sight.

Her wait was rewarded when the doe and her offspring appeared, single file along the path. Sunlight, breaking through tree branches, dappled their coats. The doe's head and nose were raised, testing the soft air, redolent with the smell of evergreen and earth. A smile played across Ellen's lips as she watched the trio cross in front of her then disappear. A chipmunk moved cautiously along a nearby branch; blackbirds flew from perch to perch, as though to claim a better spot to view the parade; above the canopy of trees the sky was a clear, periwinkle blue.

Fall might be approaching, but it was still warm and would be even warmer by afternoon. Surrounded by tall pine trees, white-barked alder, a tangle of vine maple and witch hazel, her hiding spot was a few degrees cooler.

She sighed, resisting the urge to stretch out on the carpet of soft needles. Despite the knowledge that her daughter hadn't revealed everything she'd learned in Montreal, Ellen was content. Her business was going well, she enjoyed Marta's company. And busy as she was, she still seemed to have more friends than she'd had since high school. Ian McCort continued to drop by every week or two—he was a good man. There was Frank, willing to lend a hand whenever she needed it, and the people at the restaurant. They always had a joke or a good word to say to her.

She missed Henry, even though his diaries had shown her how much she didn't truly know him. Maybe she simply missed the man she thought he'd been, the man who, for over twenty years, had been her life, her rudder, her guide, her lover, her best friend. Part of her would always love and miss that. But…she was content. It was a good feeling.

From a distance came the slam of a vehicle door, followed by the softer slam of the kitchen door. It was too soon for Marta to be back. It must be Marie. Ignoring the urge to stay where she was, the sense of duty ingrained over a lifetime drove her to her feet and back to the house.

The moment she saw her daughter's face, she knew something was wrong. "Marie? What is it? Has Paul been hurt? Have you heard something from Ken?"

Marie shifted the baby on her hip, avoiding Ellen's eyes. "Is Mrs. Weitzel here?"

"She's gone into town to deliver the lunch order, then she plans to stop at Morrison's for a few things on the way back. Why? What's wrong, Marie?"

Marie put Henry Reed on the floor and gave him her keys to play with. "Is there coffee made?"

Ellen's heart raced. Her daughter was never at a loss for words—she always blurted out whatever she had to say. That Marie was stalling now frightened her. Silently, she went to the cupboard and got down two cups. She filled them with coffee and placed them on the table. "Sit. And tell me."

Marie sat. She picked up the coffee cup and brought it to her lips then set it down without tasting it. "Oh, Mom, I don't know what to do. Paul and I had a horrible fight last night. Now he's refusing to talk to me. He's blaming it all on me."

Ellen drew a patient breath. A fight she could deal with. Though not common, this wouldn't be the first time she'd counseled her daughter following a spat with Paul. "He's blaming what on you, Marie?"

"Going to Montreal when neither of you wanted me to go. He says I'm selfish and bull-headed and think only of myself. But that's not true. It isn't." Her daughter stared at her, as though daring her to disagree.

"Of course it's not true. He knows that. He missed you. Sometimes finding yourself vulnerable like that can make you angry with the other person."

"It's not that. He says everything I do is about me. But I didn't go to Montreal only for myself. I went for you and Ken and for Henry Reed, and for Dad, too. You know that,

Mom. And I told you how important I think it is for Henry Reed to grow up knowing he has family besides us."

"I remember what you told me. Paul will get over it, Marie. Just give him some time."

"He won't. Oh, God, I wish I'd never gone. I wish I'd never heard of Montreal." And with that she burst into tears. Henry Reed dropped the keys and crawled over to his mother's chair, whimpering.

Ellen reached down and picked him up. "There, there," she said, unsure if her comfort was for the baby or her daughter. "Let's get you a cookie. Would you like a cookie, sweetie?" When she'd gotten a cracker out of the plastic tub in the cupboard, she brought a box of tissues to the table and set it next to Marie, then broke the cracker and gave a piece to the baby.

Her sobs subsiding, Marie pulled a tissue from the box and blew her nose.

Ellen sighed. "Tell me. Tell me what you discovered in Montreal that Paul doesn't want me to know."

While Marie told her about Claudia, her words hesitant at first, then gathering speed, Ellen stroked Henry Reed's cheek and hair.

When her daughter finished talking, Ellen remained silent.

Marie stared, her face a picture of bewilderment. "You knew."

Ellen nodded. "I always knew."

"Then how...? I don't understand."

"I knew Henry was married and I knew he couldn't get a divorce—because of her religion and because of the laws in Quebec."

It had been so long ago—all the years they'd lived together. She'd all but forgotten about it. Until Marie started to dig it all up. In her own mind, she and Henry had been married, as surely as if a minister had said the words.

"We pretended to elope. Mom and Dad were already upset about his being fifteen years older than me. They would have had a fit if they'd suspected he'd been married before—was still married, technically."

At first, she'd been sick with worry that her parents would find out; they'd think she was a sinner—living with a man outside the bonds of marriage. Perhaps she had been, but she'd never felt like one—until now.

"We went away for the week-end and when we came back, we told everyone we'd gotten married. No one asked for a marriage license. Why would they?"

"I met her. I met Claudia."

"You met her?"

"Yes. And there's something else. Something you couldn't have known, because Dad didn't."

The wary look on Marie's face told Ellen that the news her daughter was about to impart was significant— something her normally fearless daughter was reluctant to say. "What?" She braced herself for the answer.

"They had a daughter."

Blood drummed in Ellen's ears. "Dear God."

"Her name is Jeannine."

"Oh, dear God." Ellen closed her eyes, pressing back on the tears threatening to flood them. "I never thought we were hurting anyone." She'd told herself Claudia had her chance and somehow proved she wasn't worthy, so it was okay for her and Henry to be together. *But if it hadn't been for me...* "He might have gone back." She rubbed her forehead with her free hand, trying to ease away the tension. "My God, my God. What have we done?"

And why can't Henry be here when I need him? But he wasn't there, would never be there again, and she would have to muddle through this on her own.

She straightened her shoulders and looked at Marie, her mouth drawing tight with determination. "I won't feel sorry. Maybe that makes me terrible in your eyes, but I'm not going to regret my life with your father." A sudden defiance filled her voice. She thrust out her chin. "Do you think I should? Do you think I should feel guilty for living with a man who loved me and gave me two beautiful children?"

"I don't know what to think." Marie's voice trembled. "I've been so worried how to tell you about Dad being married before and not divorced. It didn't occur to me that you might already know."

Ellen settled back in her chair, Henry Reed, now asleep, a warm and comforting weight on her lap. "I knew."

Fall 2000

Chapter Three

KEN

The weather in the Mediterranean was a perfect, balmy, seventy-two degrees—an amazing thirty degrees cooler than the Gulf. An island, Crete someone said, loomed on the northern horizon. Egypt's coast now lay hidden a few hundred miles to their south. In a matter of hours, they would be in Malta, rejoining the float they'd been part of when they left Norfolk, Virginia, nearly six months before.

Ken still marveled at being in such exotic places, so far from the mountains of Idaho. So far from home. He leaned against the ship's rail and closed his eyes, tilting his face to the sun a moment before pulling from his pocket the brief letter he'd received from Marie. He read it through for what must have been the tenth time.

Dear Ken,

There's so much to tell you. I don't know where to begin. I got back from Montreal a week ago. I'm so confused about things there. It was nice. Marie-Catherine, our aunt, made me feel like I was visiting royalty. But besides all the stuff I already told you, there's something else I found out. It's pretty mind-boggling, but I have to wait until you're home to tell you. I hope that's soon. As promised, I haven't told Mom you're coming. She's changed, Ken. It's too much to explain in a letter, but you'll see. Her business is doing well, though. They're even selling her bread by the loaf, and another restaurant has contacted her to see if she'll bake for them. I think she's going to take them on.

See you soon.

Love,

Marie

As he read the lines, trying once again to puzzle out what she was hinting at, the public- address system squawked into life. A CNN announcer spoke, his voice tense:

"An American destroyer, the USS Cole, has suffered severe damage in a surprise attack this morning. The Cole was in the port of Aden, Yemen, for a routine fuel stop. At 11:18 a.m. a small craft approached the port side of the destroyer, and an explosion occurred causing a huge gash in the side of the ship—forty-feet by forty-feet according to eye-witnesses. The numbers of dead and wounded are not yet known. Efforts are underway now to assess damage and manage flooding; divers are going down to inspect the hull."

There were a few more details followed by some inter-views with Pentagon brass and analysts' comparisons to the Marine barracks bombing in Beirut in 1983—it, too, had occurred in October.

After the P.A. system went dead, off-duty sailors and Marines gathered in clusters, unsure what to do. No general alarm had been sounded, but everyone seemed to feel they should be doing something, Sharpe included. "What the fuck?" he said. "Do you think we're at war? Shit."

Another Marine shook his head, his expression as awed

as Sharpe's. "It coulda been us. There was somethin' about that place gave me the fuckin' creeps."

They'd reached the port of Aden in the early morning hours, before the worst heat of the day. Unlike flat Bahrain, beyond a narrow coastal plain, hills and rugged-looking mountains filled the horizon.

No one was allowed ashore while they waited to refuel. Ken hadn't want to go into town anyway. It wasn't only Yemen's landscape that was different. It looked peaceful enough and the water traffic seemed to run smoothly, but there was something in the air, something not quite right. For one thing, the harbor-crew was short-staffed, and those on the docks were strangely silent. Coupled with the closed faces of the men who passed by on small boats and those that eventually helped with the refueling, Ken was on edge. He was glad when they finished refueling and left the port, headed for the Red Sea and the Suez.

"They'll probably send us back to the Gulf," someone speculated in a voice filled with tension and excitement.

"We've already been out here six months. Can they do that?" asked another man. His nervous gaze darted around the group.

Ken understood. He was as prepared as the Marine Corps could make him if they had to go to war, but he was plagued with doubts. Was he physically brave? He didn't know. Sure, he could ride a bucking horse. Lasso a bull. He was a state finalist wrestler. But those things were nothing compared to war. If someone were shooting at him personally—actually aiming at Kenneth Maris, Corporal, United States Marine Corps, ready to pull the trigger—what would he do?

Later, they heard the *USS Donald Cook* and the *USS Hawes* had been close enough to get to the Cole within a few hours, in time to give repair and logistical support.

"Did you hear how many bought it?" Sharpe said, when it was announced it had been a suicide attack. "Seventeen. Plus thirty-nine wounded. What gives with these people? What have we ever done to them?" His voice contained both bewilderment and rage.

In his bunk that night, Ken considered Sharpe's questions. Were Middle Easterners that much different from the rest of the world? Was there something inside them, something they got with their mother's milk that made them believe killing innocent people was okay? Then he recalled the gentleness of Farida's father and the kindness of Hamid Soueif, and knew that wasn't true.

One thing he was sure of: the kind of hatred that leads someone to drive a boat filled with explosives into a ship, killing himself and seventeen others, the kind of hatred he saw in those three young men's faces that day in Manama, the kind of hatred that would throw a bomb into a café filled with innocent people enjoying an evening of talk and music—that kind of hatred was something that would have to be dealt with. The question was, how? And by whom?

What would his father have said? Given his own history, would he have sided with the terrorists? At the thought, a bad taste came to Ken's mouth. Surely his father wouldn't condone anything like that. But he could almost hear the old man say something like, *"to deal with it, first you need to understand it, put yourself in their shoes."* That was probably true, but how could anyone understand the kind of violence these people inflicted on each other? It was crazy. And even if a person could understand it, how in the hell could anyone in their right mind approve?

Despite rampant rumors to the contrary, rumors that kept them all on edge, they left the Mediterranean a week after the *Cole* attack and headed west, back across the Atlantic. Ken was glad to put thoughts of the Middle East aside, at least for a while. He looked forward to the thirty-day leave he'd earned.

"We never even got to see them Eyetalian dames," said Sharpe. "They never fuckin' let us go ashore."

The two were leaning against the ship's rail. Ken shrugged. "Guess that'll have to wait until next time."

"Next time? What next time, man? You ain't thinking of re-upping?"

Sharpe's look was so incredulous, Ken almost laughed. He shrugged again instead. "I don't know. I'm not sure."

"They won't get me to sign away another four years, man. They can take their re-enlistment bonus and shove it. I'm outta this green machine."

"It's a lot of money." More money than Ken was ever likely to get at one time; he wasn't sure he could turn it down.

"Not enough for this guy. Jersey City, here I come, baby."

"I've got thirty days leave coming," Ken said. "While I'm home I'll decide."

The late afternoon sun reflected from the windows of his childhood home, visible from the highway. Fir and pine trees behind and on each side gave the house's dark brown rambling form the setting it needed to look complete. Ken knew when they got closer he would see the signs of wear that were as familiar to him as his face in the mirror each morning: the same cracked pane of glass, the summer garden beginning to fill with weeds and dead plants, the shed still unpainted. The shed had stood for as long as he could remember, listing slightly to the right, as though a strong wind would cave it in upon itself.

Marie hung back, letting him go inside first. He should have known where he'd find his mother—in the kitchen kneading bread dough, just as he had found her a year ago when he'd come home to bury his father, and a hundred times before that, when he'd come home from school or in from some chore.

When she saw him, she threw her flour-covered hands to her face.

Ken laughed. "Surprised?" He swept her up in a bear hug and swung her around. She and the kitchen smelled as they always did—of yeast, coffee, and spices.

"Why didn't you let me know?" she said when he finally set her down. "Let me look at you. You're so brown! Oh my goodness. I'm such a mess. Look, I've got flour all over you. Why didn't you let me know?"

"I wanted to surprise you." He grinned.

"Are you surprised, Mom?" Marie set Henry Reed on the floor and he took a few unsteady steps to Ellen then grabbed her leg.

"You should have told me." Tears filled his mother's eyes. "Oh look. Now you've made me cry."

"Cookie," Henry Reed said, pulling on a loose fold in Ellen's jeans.

"Oh, sweetie, give me a minute. Gramma needs to catch her breath."

"Cookie," Henry Reed said again.

Ken chuckled. "There's a man who knows his priorities."

After Marie and Henry Reed had headed back to town and Ken had stowed his gear in his room, he and his mother sat on the porch and he tried to tell her all he'd seen.

"I can't imagine it," she said, when he finished recounting a description of Manama and the island it was situated on. "I just can't imagine so much heat and sand." She fingered the delicately woven gold chain he'd given her. "The souks, the Street of the Gold Merchants—it sounds like something from a movie or some fairy tale."

"It was no movie, Mom."

Chapter Four

MARIE

Long after the lights were out, Marie stared into the blackness above her. Though he remained silent, she knew Paul was awake, too. She couldn't get back into rhythm with him. Since her return and their big quarrel, their conversations had seemed normal—they were about normal things, anyway—but the subject of Montreal, what she'd found out there, was always between them.

The day she'd told her mother about Claudia, Paul had known the minute he saw her face.

"You told her, didn't you?"

"Yes."

He hadn't said another word, just turned away and went to take a shower.

Several times she'd begun to explain, but each time she'd hesitated, unable to find the right words. It was as though a wall had sprung up between them and she didn't know how to get around or over it. It made her unsure of herself. She didn't like the feeling.

She'd been relieved when Ken had been more interested in seeing their mother than discussing what Marie had found in Montreal. She still wasn't sure how she would tell him. Would he feel like she did—as though she'd lost both her parents, as though she didn't know them and never had.

"You still awake?" Paul said, startling her out of her contemplations.

"Yes."

"How was Ken?"

"Good. Very tan."

"Did you tell him?"

"No."

"Are you going to?"

"Yes."

After a while the evenness of his breathing told her he'd gone to sleep. Hours passed before she did.

Chapter Five

ELLEN

Marta pulled the pans out of the oven and set them on the wire rack to cool. "He must have been exhausted."

Ellen slid the next batch into the oven then glanced at the clock—it was nearly ten. "I've never known him to sleep this late."

"Maybe he's still on Bahrain time."

"Maybe." Ellen washed the empty bread pans and set them on a towel to dry. She liked the plainness of their conversations when she and Marta were working in the kitchen. She was still surprised at how much she enjoyed their easy companionship.

Marta poured them each a cup of coffee. "Ellen, I've been thinking about something," she said when they were seated at the scrubbed pine table.

Ellen propped her feet on an empty chair and set her coffee cup down. Her friend sounded serious. "What?"

"I'm wondering how the people at your restaurant would like my pies."

"Why, Marta, they'd love them. Who wouldn't? But are you sure? That's a lot of work."

"It's not work when you enjoy it."

Ellen grinned. "Oh, my, we're getting to be quite the team, aren't we?"

"We'll have to add on to the kitchen soon."

"Hire someone to help us."

"Move over Nabisco. 'Ellen's Breads and Pies' are on the move."

"What's going on?" said Ken, walking into the kitchen on bare feet, wearing a pair of jeans but no shirt. "Sounds like a bunch of giggling schoolgirls in here."

Ellen took her feet from the chair. "We're just plotting our business strategy. Pour yourself some coffee and have a seat." He did so, trailing a hand across her shoulder as he passed. She smiled after him. "I'm glad you're finally up. You can drive me into town with the lunch order."

"Sure. I'm at your disposal for thirty days."

Marta rose from the table. "I'll leave you two. I need to make my bed and put some things away. I'm so glad you're home, Ken."

Ellen watched her son savor his first sip of coffee. Pride bubbled inside her, giving her a feeling of lightness. He'd changed in the past year, grown up. He'd always been responsible, always done everything he could to make things easier for her, but now there was a new confidence in him, a new maturity. *I wish Henry could see what a fine man he's become.*

"This sure tastes better than the stuff they serve in the Marine Corps. I think they mix it with diesel fuel."

Ellen laughed. "That bad?"

"Yep. So, what were you and Mrs. Weitzel plotting when I came in?"

"She wants to add desserts to our bread business."

"Will the restaurant be interested?"

"I think so." They were impressed with what she was already giving them. Homemade pies would be an easy sell. When people were on vacation they wouldn't mind splurging on extra calories. "We were talking about enlarging the kitchen and hiring someone to help us. We were joking, but I'm thinking that may be something we'll need to consider. Not right now, but down the line."

"That's fantastic, Mom."

"Yes. It will be different, though." It had been a big change when Marta had come—one she enjoyed, to be sure—but wouldn't there be times she'd miss being on her own, having the house entirely to herself?

"Things are already changed with Mrs. Weitzel here. And isn't that why you started the business? To succeed and grow?" Ken went to the stove and refilled his coffee cup.

He raised the pot toward her, but she shook her head. "I'm not sure what I was thinking—maybe just that I liked doing it. Making bread, I mean. And I needed to have a reason to get up every morning, something to do with my time." She looked at her watch. "Speaking of which, it's time to load up."

"I'll get a shirt and shoes."

He seemed content to let her drive as he gazed out the window.

"What are you thinking?" she asked.

"Fall is definitely here."

"You're right. It's dropping into the low-thirties at night. We may have snow before you leave." She thought about what he'd told her the night before—about the heat in Bahrain. "Do you think it's true that your blood thins out in warm weather?"

"I guess we'll see." He grinned. "How are you for firewood?"

"I don't want you spending your vacation chopping wood."

"I don't mind."

"Well, I wouldn't say no. It's all in a pile out back. I haven't had the time to take care of it." Actually, she couldn't bring herself to look at the place where Henry had his stroke. She forced that thought away, glanced at her son and smiled. "The problems of a small business owner. There's never enough time."

"You're loving it."

She didn't even try to suppress the grin. "Yes, I guess I am."

They came to the outskirts of town. She tried to see everything with Ken's eyes. Would he notice the changes— the newly opened book and art supply store and the men's apparel shop in the middle of town, the trees that had been planted near the park, the bronze pig on the corner of Third and Aspen? She couldn't get over that herself, but the mayor called it art and maybe he was right. She turned into the restaurant parking lot and drove around to the back where garbage cans were lined up, their lids dogged down to keep raccoons and bears out of them. The kitchen door was wide open.

"In there?" Ken asked.

"Uh-huh," she said, parking the truck and turning off the engine.

Ken jumped out before she could open her door. "I'll get them."

Watching him disappear inside the restaurant a moment later, Ellen wondered how much he knew. Marie had written to him, of course, but she didn't think he knew everything yet. That would end soon—he was going over to see Marie and Paul that evening. Marie would tell him.

Ellen had considered telling him herself, but had put it off. An act of cowardice some might call it. She gave a slight shake of her head. No, it was better for Marie to be the one—those two had always been close conspirators, especially where Ellen was concerned. Trying to protect her. Later, after Marie broke the news, she and Ken could have a long talk. *And then, just maybe, we can be done with it.*

Chapter Six

KEN

Ken picked up the axe and tested the edge with his thumb, surprised to find it still sharp. Like his mother warned, the woodpile was a scattered heap, untouched since his father's death. His mother thought his father died from the exertion of splitting wood. Ken figured it was more likely related to the stress of keeping so many secrets.

It didn't take long to work up a sweat as he split each round into halves, quarters, and finally eighths. Reaching for another round, he wondered what Marie had planned to reveal the night before, when Paul left for Morrison's to get them all ice cream for dessert. The baby was down for the night, so it was just him and Marie when she asked a question that surprised him. "Is Jordan anywhere near Bahrain?"

"Not really. It's in the Middle East, but Saudi Arabia is between them. Why?"

"Dad's brother, Marc, went there to learn how to build bombs."

Ken's mouth turned down. "From someone in the PLO, I'll bet. There are thousands of displaced Palestinians in Jordan. Many of them hate Israel and they're famous for building bombs." He wondered at how the lines of history seemed to cross and re-cross like the silken threads of a spider web, waiting to capture the unwary—his uncle, his father. Him, too.

"Marie-Catherine talked about them—the PLO, I mean. There were some others, too—the Red Army, the SDS, Black Power. I guess they were all inter-connected in a way, trading secrets and strategies. She told me Marc learned to booby-trap the bombs he built from someone in the IRA."

"Jesus." Ken shook his head. "I thought the sixties and seventies were just about Vietnam."

"Marie-Catherine said violence was going on all over the world back then. She's writing a book about it. She promised me a copy when it comes out in English. You can read it, too."

Ken was impressed his sister wanted to read a book that sounded more like a history text than the novels she usually read. "You've grown up a lot this last year." His words brought a pleased smile to her lips.

They'd talked a little more about Montreal and their father. Marie was telling him about going to see a woman named Claudia when Paul's footsteps sounded outside the door. She quickly changed the subject.

Ken picked up another round of wood. Something was going on between those two; they weren't easy together. He was sure it had to do with something Marie had found out in Montreal. But while they ate the ice cream, they talked of old high-school friends—who'd gotten married, who'd had a baby, who'd moved away—and Marie hadn't referred to their father or Montreal again.

Marie was right about one thing. Their mother had changed. She looked and talked differently. She even moved differently. He wasn't sure what he thought about her bread-making business. He was glad she enjoyed it, but, my God, she wasn't kidding about being busy all the time. If she wasn't making bread, she was delivering it or shopping for it. He'd have thought she would feel tied down. And now she was thinking about expanding? He was really pleased she had some money to rely on—the insurance money from her parents his father had invested and added to—but why didn't she use it to get out and see the world? That's what he'd do and he'd told her so a year ago. He had to admit, even though he'd tried, he couldn't picture her anywhere but in the house where he'd always known her.

It was strange with Mrs. Weitzel there. He couldn't get used to seeing her in her bathrobe, coming out of Marie's room, sitting at the breakfast table. Just being there all the time. His mother seemed to enjoy her company, so he guessed he'd better get used to it. At least she was a good-hearted old biddy.

Finished with another round of wood, he straightened up and wiped his brow. He'd barely begun and already was dripping—showed what sitting at a desk updating manuals did to a person. Grabbing another round, he let his mind drift back to a long-ago summer when his father had given him the job of bringing in wood.

Ken looked up at the Ponderosa Pine towering nearly one-hundred feet above his head. The tree remained upright for a few seconds then slowly began to sweep a huge arc across the sky, building up speed as it began its downward plunge, then crashed against the forest floor, jarring the ground beneath his feet. The tree's branches waved in the air and their odor filled his nostrils; despite the muggy heat, for a moment the pungent smell made him think of Christmas. Bits of needles and dried grass stuck to his skin and gnats flew in circles near his face.

Earlier he'd twisted his white skivvy shirt and tied it around his forehead to keep the sweat from running into his eyes. Even so, the sweat ran down between his shoulder blades and evaporated into salty dryness that pulled at his skin. Walking toward the creek that ran through their property, he rolled his shoulders, liking the feeling of the muscles he was building. He'd be more than ready to start training once wrestling season started in the fall. He knelt and splashed cold water onto his face, then cupped his hands and drank. On his way back to the tree, a couple of wasps hovered then flew off.

It would take him all day to cut the tree into lengths he could manage, but first he needed to trim off the branches and twigs. As he'd moved with the axe up the length of the tree he fell into a rhythm. Again, and again, the axe blade bit into the green wood. Each time, a quiver of resistance traveled up the long handle, all the way to his shoulders.

While he swung the axe, he thought about his father, over in Montana taking some rich guy fishing. He'd quit his job to do it, of course. Typical. The guide job might pay well, for the time it took, but would he get his old job back—the one that paid the bills month in and month out? Not that the old man ever kept a job month in and month out. Ken didn't know how his mother stood it. She wouldn't hear any criticism of his father, either; if Ken said anything, she shut him down. Why? The old man was the one supposed to be the adult. Instead, it was Ken who had to worry about his mother having enough money to pay the bills. It never seemed to concern his father—he just up and quit whenever the spirit moved him to take off to the mountains. He didn't care if someone needed him at home. He didn't care if people were lonely without him. He didn't care if people depended on him. Well, fuck him. Fuck him and his fucking mountains. Tears blurred Ken's vision as he plunged the axe into another limb.

After dinner that night, leaving thirteen-year-old Marie washing dishes and his mother in the garden pulling weeds and picking off some over-ripe tomatoes, Ken walked the three miles to Hartley's place. He needed to arrange to borrow a horse from the neighboring rancher. He'd use it to pull the logs he'd finished sawing to a clearing he could reach with the truck.

Although Hartley's foreman told him the big gray gelding—Smoke was its name—was used to pulling from the saddle and shouldn't give him any trouble, Ken was a little nervous when the horse danced around as he climbed aboard the next morning. But as they made their way back home, a pickup truck loaded with fence posts rattled past and Smoke didn't spook or shy away. After that, Ken relaxed his grip on the reins.

All morning he worked Smoke, securing one end of the rope around a log and snubbing the other end around the saddle horn, then dragging the log through the trees to the clearing he'd chosen. There he planned to cut the wood into shorter rounds before hauling it down in the back of the pickup, once the old man got back with it. Then he'd split and stack the wood behind the house, where it would need to age until the following winter.

At noon, Ken sat with his back against a tree trunk, eating a roast beef sandwich his mother had packed. Smoke was ground-tethered nearby, pulling up tender shoots of grass wherever he could find it, his bridle jingling as his jaw muscles worked. Clouds had been building to the west all morning. A clap of thunder rolled in the distance. Smoke's head swung up, his ears cocked forward. Ken stuffed the remains of his sandwich into a paper sack, the sack into a saddlebag. "We'd better get with it, boy, if we're going to finish before that storm gets here."

Two hours later, Ken looped the rope around the saddle horn for the last time and clicked his tongue for Smoke to go forward. The rope pulled taut and the log slowly began to move. Pulling the reins to the left, Ken urged Smoke between two pines. With dainty precision the horse lifted one foot after another over a branch that had fallen to the ground the year before.

The branch was beginning to rot. All that spring and early summer, along the ground next it, wasps had been building a nest of mud and sand, collected from the banks of the nearby creek, and a papery material of masticated vegetable matter. When the log crashed through their nest, the wasps came pouring out, disoriented and angry. In a flailing, swarming cloud they attacked log, rope, horse, and rider. At virtually the same moment, thunder crashed overhead and lightning filled the air with a metallic smell. The horse screamed, twisting and kicking out at a world suddenly gone mad and vicious. Ken clung to the saddle horn with one hand and tried to bat off the attacking wasps with the other.

Smoke fishtailed and bucked. Ken held on with his knees. If he got thrown against a tree trunk, it could kill him. "Whoa, boy. Steady." His words did nothing to calm the crazed horse. Instead, Smoke twisted his head back toward Ken's leg, teeth bared, eyes red-rimmed and frantic. Ken kicked both feet from the stirrups and pushed off. The last thing he remembered was a sharp crack of pain in his head and shoulder.

He awakened in the hospital with a dislocated shoulder, a concussion and multiple wasp stings. It was two days before they let him out. When he got home, his mother insisted that he take the pain medication the doctor had prescribed and go straight to bed. With a fierce headache and pain jabbing his shoulder whenever he moved his arm, Ken didn't argue.

When he opened his eyes a few hours later, Marie was sitting on a pile of dirty clothes in the corner of his bedroom, reading a book. She must have heard the change in his breathing because she looked up. "You're awake."

"Sort of."

"Mom was scared to death."

"Was she?"

She nodded. "Yeah. Me, too. Smoke ran home to Hartley's. The log was still dragging behind him. Mr. Hartley's foreman drove you and Mom to the hospital. I had to stay here—there wasn't enough room in the truck." She looked crestfallen and still indignant at being left behind.

"I'll be okay."

"I know. Want me to get you some water or something?"

"No thanks. Right now, I gotta take a leak."

"Do you need help to the bathroom?"

"I can make it. Thanks, anyway."

"Okay."

When his father came home a couple of weeks later, they hauled the wood down to the house, then split and stacked it.

A drop of rain on his forehead brought Ken back to the present. Once again, he hadn't noticed the clouds rolling in. It was like that in the mountains—the weather could change in a minute. Not like in Bahrain where each day was the same: hot or hotter.

By dinner time the rain came down in buckets. "I wonder how long this will keep up."

"The weather report says it will dip down to freezing by tomorrow," his mother said. "We could even get a skiff of snow."

They had more than a skiff; six inches fell during the night. Ken heard his mother and Mrs. Weitzel in the kitchen and knew they were setting bread dough to rise. So what did they do when the snow was too deep to get out of the lane? He doubted his mother could maneuver the blade onto the front of the truck so that she could clear it.

"Good morning," she said, when he wandered into the kitchen a few minutes later. "Did you see our snow?"

"Yeah. A little more than a skiff. Is the blade still in the shed?"

"You don't have to worry about that—Mr. Hartley sends someone over with a small Cat whenever it snows. He's already called to say they'll be here in half-an-hour—as soon as they finish with their lane."

"Great, but I was kind of looking forward to doing something useful."

"How about delivering our bread order this morning?"

"Sure. Maybe I'll go see Marie while I'm in town. Is something going on between those two? Things seemed a little strained the other night."

"They've had a quarrel. They'll get over it."

But Ken felt it went deeper that a spat.

She answered the door as soon as he rang the bell. "Mom called to say you were coming. I was watching for you."

Ken looked around. "Where's the kid?"

"You just missed him. I put him down about ten minutes ago."

"And he's already asleep? I thought babies were supposed to cry a lot when they had to take naps."

"Not so far, knock on wood. He's really a good baby. The only time he fusses is when he's cutting a tooth."

The pride in her voice amused him. He grinned. "Probably takes after his uncle."

"Right," she said, grinning with pretended sarcasm. "Hey, do you want a Coke or something? Or I can make coffee."

"A Coke sounds good—I get enough coffee at Mom's." He sat down on the worn couch while she crossed to the kitchen and took two cans out of the refrigerator.

She handed him the Coke and nodded toward the kitchen. "Would you believe the size of that thing?"

"Don't even talk to me about size. Until you've tried to sleep in the troop compartment of a Navy ship, or store everything you own in a space smaller than a gym locker, you have no idea what small is."

"No, I guess not. I shouldn't complain." Her voice trailed off.

Ken frowned. "Okay, what gives with you and Paul?"

"Is it so obvious?"

"It is to me. I'm your big brother, remember? I know you too well for you to hide anything."

"You're right. It's all to do with Montreal, starting with how he didn't want me to go in the first place. Now he's mad because I told Mom what I found out."

He gave her a questioning look, mentally urging her to stop beating around the bush. She took a deep breath then began. Ken sat in stunned silence as she recounted what she'd learned. Finally, it seemed she'd finished.

"Mom knew all about Claudia, about Dad not being a U.S. citizen and his not having a Social Security number. He was here illegally—that's the reason she was so reluctant to go to the Social Security office. She knew there wouldn't be anything from them since she isn't Dad's legal widow; she just didn't know how to get me to back off without telling me the truth. I feel like such a fool. I kept pushing and pushing to find out what was going on, and she knew all the time."

Ken was still back on the issue of his father being married to someone else, on the whole 'previous life' business. The fact that their mother knew didn't bother him that much. At least he didn't think it did.

"But I haven't told you all of it." Marie stared at him with even more intensity than before. "I haven't told you the biggest surprise of all." She paused then blurted it out. "We have a sister."

"What?" The word exploded from his mouth.

"You heard me. We have a sister. Her name is Jeannine Turlot. She's a teacher and she's married to an airline pilot. They have four-year-old twin girls."

"Jesus Christ, Marie. Why didn't you tell me before?" He sprang up from the couch and began to pace the room. "A sister…holy shit. Did Dad know?"

Marie shook her head. "He left Canada before Claudia could tell him she was pregnant."

"What's she like, this sister, this Jeannine? Did you meet her? Did you talk to her?"

"I met her, but only for a minute and neither one of us knew who the other was. She still might not know, though I expect Emile will have set her straight by now." Marie went on to explain that, according to their aunt, for years Claudia maintained someone from the FLQ was angry with their father for exposing them, killed him, and hid his body. "She made Dad into a political martyr. I guess it would have been hard for her to admit he merely left her to make another life for himself. I wonder what she's telling her daughter now."

"Jesus. So, what was she like, this Claudia person?"

"Well, I don't really know. I only met her once and she was pretty resentful of me being there." She took a sip of her Coke. "Who could blame her? But she struck me as lonely. She lives in this big old house—it's beautiful, I guess her parents were pretty rich—but now it's just her, because Jeannine is married and has her own family."

"What does Mom make of it? You did tell her about Jeannine?"

"Of course. Who knows, someday Jeannine might show up on our doorstep—kind of like I did on theirs."

"What did she say?"

"She was upset—seemed to feel guilty, like maybe Dad would have gone back to Canada if it hadn't been for her, for us. She got over it pretty quickly, though."

"He was in Platt City for years before he and Mom got together—there's no reason she should feel guilty." He quit his pacing and returned to the couch. "So how do you feel about her?"

Who? Claudia or Jeannine?"

"Our sister," he said, still trying to come to grips himself.

Marie gave a half-smile. "Really, really curious. I wanted to meet her again, after our aunt finally told me, but then I didn't. When Emile introduced me to her as his cousin, she was clearly puzzled, so I knew she had no idea." Marie shook her head. "To think, if it hadn't been for Emile taking me to meet Claudia..."

"You think he just did it to make trouble?"

"No. And in retrospect, I think he was right to take me there—for her sake and mine. I don't think Marie-Catherine

296

would have told me otherwise. She said maybe on my next visit we can all get together."

"Will there be another trip?"

"I don't know. Part of me wants to go back, but part of me is still angry at learning about all the pain they caused Dad. You should go, though."

Ken shook his head. He was curious, sure, but he wasn't like Marie. "You're the one needs to dig for all the answers. Maybe you take after our big-time journalist father more than anyone knew."

"Do you think so?" Puppy-like eagerness was in her voice, in her eyes.

"Yeah." He couldn't resist patting her on the head. "Maybe someday I'll go and size things up myself." *Not yet, though.* "So, what happened to Emile's mother?"

"She came to Dad's boarding house when Emile was just a few days old and told Dad she was leaving Montreal and she couldn't take a baby with her. She just shoved him into Dad's hands, turned around and ran out. They never heard from her after that."

"No wonder the guy's screwed up."

"Could be. But despite being a lousy sister to our father, at least to my mind, I think Marie-Catherine would have been a good mother." She paused a moment and looked at him. "You haven't told me what you think of our mother. About her knowing and all."

"Well." He thought a minute before he went on. "I guess maybe it doesn't bother me so much, that she knew. It doesn't surprise me that much either. I mean, how many years were they married? Together, I guess I should say.

Anyway, it's natural he would have told her—at least some of it."

She gave him a fishy look. "Don't you feel like she should have told us? Don't you feel betrayed?"

Ken pulled his head back, his brows furrowed together. "Betrayed? Why would I feel that?"

"Because we're illegitimate. We're bastards."

His brows shot up. "That's just a word, Marie. You don't really feel that way, do you?" He was sure she didn't. "What if you and Paul weren't married? Henry Reed would still have a mother and father, wouldn't he? Would you or Paul love him any less?"

"No. Of course not. That's not what I meant. Oh, I don't know what I mean. It's just that nothing feels the same anymore. I don't feel like I lost a father, I feel like I never had one—not the one I thought I had. And here Mom knew about it all the time, went along with it, so I don't feel like I knew her, either. Or know her now. She's just changed so much."

She looked like she was about to cry. Ken wasn't sure what to do. He patted her shoulder, but she didn't seem to notice. "And now Paul is mad at me for going to Montreal, no matter how many times I've tried to explain I went for all of us, especially Henry Reed. He didn't think I should have told Mom what I learned—even though she already knew about Claudia. He says she's been through enough and I should have just kept my mouth shut. Now he'll hate me for telling you." And then she stopped trying to hold back—the tears started flooding down her cheeks. She turned and buried her face in Ken's shoulder.

After a few more awkward pats, Ken decided to let her cry it out.

"I need a Kleenex," she finally said, her voice muffled.

There was a box of tissues on top of the television. He gently disengaged himself, got up and handed it to her.

"Thanks." She took several, scrubbed at her reddened eyes then loudly blew her nose.

"Feel better now?"

"I guess. Sorry I got you all wet."

"No problem." He rescued his Coke can from the floor and took another long drink. "So what are you going to do about you and Paul?"

"I don't know. I just don't know."

Chapter Seven
MARIE

Marie spent the afternoon cleaning the apartment. It should have been easy, given how small the place was, but the dark brown tile floor, which showed every footstep, every scuffmark and every spill, was a monster to clean. There wasn't near enough storage space for their things, either. Even so, she scrubbed and polished, washed and folded, and when she was through, she stood in front of the kitchen counter and surveyed her work. Except for a tilted lampshade, which she carefully straightened, everything looked nice.

She'd put Henry Reed in his crib for an early afternoon nap so he would be ready for bed soon after Paul got home. She wanted the evening to be perfect, and for just the two of them. A roast and potatoes were in the oven, the salad was made, and fresh lima beans were simmering. Henry Reed was content in his playpen. At the last minute, she jumped into the shower. When she finished drying, she pulled on a pair of clean jeans and a green sweater that set off the gold flecks in her eyes. Down to her pre-baby weight, she didn't need the mirror to know she looked good.

Running gloss over her lips, she heard the front door open and close. That's when everything fell apart.

"Marie! What the hell?!? Jesus!"

She rushed out of the bathroom. "What?" Then she saw. Henry Reed had somehow climbed out of his playpen, gotten his pajama bottoms and diaper off and had smeared feces along the front of the couch and on the top of the coffee table. "Oh, my God! No! Henry, baby. No." She grabbed him up and, arms held out straight to avoid the poop, she ran into the bathroom and stuck him into the tub. He let out a wail. She pulled his pajama shirt off and turned on the water. He cried louder.

Paul came into the bathroom. "Why weren't you watching him?"

"I was taking a shower. He was in his playpen, playing with his toys. I thought he was okay."

She soaped Henry Reed then rinsed him, crooning. "There, there, baby. You're okay."

"He could have hurt himself. You should have checked on him."

"I did, Paul. He's never climbed out of his playpen before. I didn't know he could."

Henry Reed's cries grew louder.

"You're scaring him."

"No. You are. He's not used to hearing you raise your voice." Marie grabbed a towel off the rack and started drying the baby. She was getting angrier by the minute at Paul. Was he just going to stand in the doorway and criticize? "Get me a fresh diaper, will you? If it's not too much trouble."

He disappeared and came back with a diaper and clean pajamas.

"Thanks." She already regretted her earlier sarcasm. Paul didn't say anything. When Henry Reed, still whimpering, was dry and dressed, she put him back in his playpen. Tight-lipped, she set about cleaning the couch and coffee table. From the noises coming from the bathroom, Paul was taking a shower.

Over the smell of feces came the acrid smell of something burning. The beans. She rushed to the stove and jerked them off the burner then held the pan under cold water. Steam rose up and burned her wrist. Tears sprang to her eyes as she ran cold water over her arm. "Shit. Shit, shit, SHIT!"

Venting expletives didn't help. She checked the roast and found it had cooked down to almost half its original size. The potatoes were wrinkled and overdone. She drew a breath and turned the oven off with shaking fingers.

Henry Reed hiccupped and sniffed. His whimpers had stopped when he found his thumb. With a baleful look on his face, through the netting of his playpen he watched her resume cleaning the couch.

"Is it coming off?" Paul stood in the bedroom doorway toweling his hair.

"I guess so." She scrubbed harder.

"What's that smell?"

"Besides the baby poop?" She sent him a quick glance over her shoulder. "I burnt the beans. I put the roast in too early, so it's ruined, too."

Dinner was a mostly silent affair, though Marie tried. "How was your day?" she asked between bites. At least the salad was okay, because not even horseradish helped the dried out roast beef. Paul merely shrugged.

The next morning, following another sleepless night, Marie stared out the living room window as a pickup truck with two brown and white hunting dogs in the back passed along the street below. Paul hadn't even noticed how pretty she'd looked the night before. Were all marriages like this after a year or two: people stopped talking to each other, nothing was special anymore? But she feared it ran even deeper than that. It wasn't that Paul was taking her for granted—it was like he was looking at her for the first time and realizing he didn't like what he saw.

She curled her arms over her head, feeling as frightened and confused as a fledgling bird being pushed out of the nest. What could she do to make things right between them again? And what about Paul...was he even trying? It didn't seem like it. Maybe he'd already given up on them.

Friday night, when Paul got off work, they drove out to her mother's, for dinner. He spent most of the evening talking to Ken about Bahrain. He was full of questions about how the country was governed, what kind of work people did there, how they lived and more. Her mother even commented on it. "Paul looks good tonight. It's nice to see him enjoying himself." Though she didn't add 'for a change', Marie thought she might as well have done.

Driving back home Paul quickly fell back into the remote silence that was making her crazy.

When they got home, she wrestled Henry Reed into his pajamas. After going through the normal routine of reading him a story and tucking his 'lamby' blanket around him, she switched the bedside lamp on low, then left the bedroom, clicking the door closed behind her.

Straightening her shoulders, she crossed to the couch, sat and took a deep breath. "Paul. I have to know what's going on."

He looked up from the airplane magazine he was looking at, though he hadn't turned a page since she'd brought Henry Reed in to say goodnight. "What do you mean?"

"Am I being punished for something? You've barely spoken a word to me in two weeks, other than things like 'pass the salt' or 'where's my blue shirt.'. It's like I'm getting the silent treatment and I don't know why."

"I didn't want to tell you until after Ken left."

Her chest tightened. "What do you mean? Tell me what?"

"I think we should separate for a while."

"What? Why?" Her face felt flushed, then suddenly she was icy all over.

"Nothing. It isn't you." He stood and faced her. "Look at me. I'm not even twenty-one and I feel like an old man already. I'm tired of it, Marie. I'm tired of feeling like this. I think about what's in our future and I want to howl. Don't you think about it? What is it going to be? Another baby in a year or so? Driving out for Sunday dinner with your mom once a week? Dinner with my dad every Wednesday? Maybe I'll get to be a department manager at the lumber yard. I could always quit and drive a logging truck. Or go to work in the lumber mill. But I don't want to, Marie. I don't want to do any of that. And it's killing me."

"But, Paul, what else can you do? You've got responsibilities. Henry Reed. Me." Tears burned and her eyes filled with pleading. How could he be thinking of leaving them? She covered her mouth with her hand to keep the howl that was building up inside her from coming out. What would she do?

"I've talked to Dad. I'm going to move back home for a while. Until I get my head straight."

Her ears rang. Everything in the room seemed to whirl around her. A huge lump formed in her throat. She swallowed. "Don't you love me anymore?" It took extreme effort to get the words out.

"It's not that. I do love you. You and Henry Reed both. You mean more to me than anything." Tears were in his eyes, too. "But I can't go on like this, Marie. I just can't."

Chapter Eight

ELLEN

While Marta drained the sink, and wiped down the counter, Ellen dried the last dinner dish and put it in the cupboard. "I haven't heard from Marie for a few days. I'm surprised she hasn't been out; Ken will be leaving before we know it."

Marta rinsed the dishcloth and draped it over the sink. "She's probably busy with the baby."

"Maybe." Ellen didn't think so. Something wasn't right. If Marie didn't call or come by the next day, she'd stop in and see her, find out what was going on. She turned as Ken came into the kitchen. "You look sharp," she said, taking in the wet hair, the clean shirt and jeans. "Going out?"

"With Larry Peters—you remember him don't you? Class between Marie and me."

"He was on your wrestling team as I recall. Red hair and glasses, right?"

"That's him. We arranged to meet at Rose's and shoot some pool. Mind if I take the truck?"

"Of course not. Have a good time."

"Thanks, Mom. Don't wait up."

"I won't."

She didn't intentionally wait up for him, but she couldn't stop thinking of what Marie had discovered in

Montreal: the daughter Henry never knew about. She wondered how much responsibility she bore for the child growing up fatherless. She dismissed the idea; Henry had been in Idaho six years before the fateful day he'd come into her parent's store for supplies. In all the time they were together, he'd never given any indication he wanted to go back to Canada, back to his legal wife.

She rolled over and punched up her pillow as her thoughts turned to Claudia, wondering if she'd been a good mother and what kind of life she'd given her daughter. Now the little girl Henry never knew, had never known about, was grown up and had children of her own—twins no less. Henry had been a grandfather long before Henry Reed was born.

Henry Reed. So precious. What was going on with his parents? They'd been downright frosty with one another at dinner the other night. Thinking about Marie and Paul had her still tossing and turning when she heard the slam of the truck door then Ken's footsteps on the porch. She was surprised when, instead of tiptoeing past, as he usually did when he came in late, he stopped outside her door and rapped softly.

"Mom. You awake?"

She snapped on the bedside lamp and saw it was nearly midnight. "Come in." He was disheveled, but excitement gleamed from his eyes. "What is it? What's happened?"

Chapter Nine

KEN

Ken was glad he'd run into Larry Peters in town that morning, when both were filling up at the Jackson gas station. He looked forward to spending the evening with his former teammate, admitting to himself that he'd begun to grow bored with little to do but chop wood and make his mother's bread deliveries. It seemed most all his high school friends had moved away—for college or jobs or, like him, to join the military. It would be fun to catch up with where they all were and how they were doing. He figured Larry, who'd been in Boise attending a Human Resources class for the last two weeks, would know. Besides his job with Platt City's largest employer, Merrick-Pacific, Larry had been the one person in their crowd who, at any given moment, could share the latest rumor, knew who was grounded, or who was dating.

It was a beautiful night with the stars out and a full moon. It had snowed, stuck, thawed and snowed again, drifting up the ditches and along the fences. He had to brake suddenly when a doe bounded across the road, lit up in the truck's headlights like a dancer on a stage, jumped a fence and took off across a field of wheat stubble. Wild and free. What would that be like?

He neared the airport and the end of the runway. The long, low bulk of the Marrick-Pacific building, made soft by the pile of snow on its roof, was on his left. In front of it were the silhouettes of the two CH-46s used for logging. Completely relaxed, his heart ticked up suddenly when he saw what looked like a shadowy figure dart behind a small hangar adjacent to the Merrick-Pacific building. What the hell? Before he could consider further, a burst of white light, then flames engulfed one of the helicopters. A moment later another flash of white light and the second helicopter erupted in flames. Ken, nearly blinded by the sudden brightness, stepped down hard on the brakes and skidded across the road before sliding to a stop.

"Jesus Christ." Heart pumping, he jumped out of the truck and ran toward the snow-filled ditch separating the highway from the burning helicopters, but the intense heat brought him to a halt.

A single fire truck tore across the runway from the direction of the terminal, careening to a sideways stop twenty yards from the roiling flames. Black, oily smoke filled the moonlit air. Sirens wailed from the direction of town and soon a second and then a third fire truck arrived on the scene. Their arrival was too late; by the time they rolled up, there was little left of the helicopters but the blades and a melted, twisted pile of metal.

Ken stood with Sheriff Bill Tate in front of the Merrick -Pacific building and stared at the helicopters' smoldering remains, shaking his head. He'd been there, seen them go up, but still couldn't believe it.

"Did you see anything suspicious before the fires?" Tate asked.

Ken had known the sheriff all his life, but never before in an official capacity. Hands stuffed into his jacket pockets to control their trembling, he hunched his shoulders. "I can't be sure. I think I saw someone running toward that hangar over there." He nodded to the Quonset hut-shaped building fifty yards away. "It was pretty dark. Then everything lit up and for a minute I was blinded. I couldn't see anything."

Tate was a heavyset man. Maybe mid-forties. Younger than Ken's father, but he knew they'd been friends. "The fires were deliberate, weren't they?"

"The Feds—FBI probably—will have to make that determination," Tate answered, cigarette phlegm rattling in his throat.

"Marrick-Pacific must have been the target."

Tate sighed and put aside his official persona. "M-P has contracted with Ian McCort to do some old growth timber thinning on government land. Some of those earth-first types, namely ELF, are opposed. They haven't been shy about making their feelings known, mostly with graffiti and other kinds of monkey business—that's what they call damaging bull-dozers, trucks and other equipment."

Ken gestured toward the smoldering remains of the helicopters. "That wasn't monkey business, or petty vandalism either. It was a deliberate act of sabotage."

"They're escalating their attacks, all right. Who knows what's coming next."

Ken thought about the bomb thrown into the café in Bahrain, killing innocent people, including the café's owners, and the attack on the *USS Cole*. Seventeen people had died with that one. "Damn. I feel like I'm back in the Middle East, not Platt City, Idaho. At least no one got killed."

They stood in silence for a few moments, each thinking what could have happened.

"How much longer will you be home on leave?" the sheriff asked, appearing ready to change the subject.

"Another ten days."

"Your enlistment should be up soon."

Ken nodded. "Five months." He was surprised the sheriff knew so much about him.

"You going to re-enlist?"

"I'm not sure. That's one of the things I came home to decide."

"Your mom would probably like to see you get out and settle down here."

"I expect."

"Maybe you think you've outgrown Platt City," Tate said, not unkindly.

Ken shrugged in semi-agreement. "What's that old saying about you can't go home again?"

"Has it changed so much?"

"Yeah. A lot."

"Good change or bad?"

"Mostly good." Ken was again surprised at Tate's interest. But maybe that was just part of being a small-town sheriff—knowing what was going on with everyone.

Tate nodded, appearing satisfied. "The Feds will probably want to question you before you leave."

"Sure. Though I don't think I can tell them much."

By the time he was finished with the sheriff it was too late to meet Larry. Still pretty much in a daze, Ken turned the pickup around and headed home. He was way too keyed up for sleep.

"The craziest thing happened," he told his mother after she'd turned on her bedside lamp and told him to come in. "When I was driving past the airport, on the way to town....you know that area where Marrick-Pacific keeps their helicopters staged?" When she nodded he went on. "Anyway, I was driving past there when one of the helicopters burst into flames. Then the second one."

His mother sat upright on her pillows. "My goodness—was anyone injured?"

Ken shook his head. "No one got hurt. I'm pretty sure I saw someone running away, but he disappeared behind one of the hangars."

"Maybe he was running to get help."

Ken shook his head again. "Not running for help, Mom. More likely, the one who started the fires. They looked for his footprints in the snow, but there were too many people trying to put out the fires and any footprints he left may have been trampled. There was no one else, at least no one I saw. But the helicopters are destroyed. Bill Tate's calling in the Feds. He thinks it was sabotage."

His mother frowned. "He thinks someone did that deliberately? In Platt City?" Her questions echoed Ken's own thoughts. She leaned back against the pillows. "He must be wrong. It had to have been an accident of some kind."

Ken shook his head one more time. "It was no accident."

The next morning Bill Tate called and asked Ken to stop by his office. Ken was sure it was about the fires, but doubted he could add anything more to what he'd told the sheriff the night before. When he drove past the airport, yellow crime-scene tape was draped across the fence and all around the burned-out helicopters. Several people, with FBI or ATF written on the backs of their jackets, were sorting through debris.

Tate's two deputies were out at the airport directing traffic, but Ken was surprised when he found Ian McCort in Tate's office.

McCort shook Ken's hand. "I hear you were up close and personal at the fireworks last night."

Ken nodded. "It was something, all right."

"Bill said you didn't see anyone you could identify."

"It was too dark." Ken turned to Tate. "Looks like the FBI and ATF are on the scene."

"Joint Terrorism Task Force—got here before dawn." He walked around his paper-covered desk and prepared to sit. "Take a seat, both of you." He waved them to chairs positioned across from him. Ken leaned to one side to see around a stack of files on the corner of the desk. Tate moved them. "Had they decided the explosions you saw were accidental, the case would be handed back to me, but because all agree it was deliberate, the FBI is the lead agency; they've taken over the investigation lock, stock and barrel." Both disgust and relief sounded in Tate's voice.

McCort cleared his throat. "That isn't why me 'n Bill wanted ta see you, Ken."

Ken's eyebrows went up, his head cocked to one side. What the hell was McCort talking about?

"We think there are some things you need to know. About your dad."

A vein began to pound in Ken's temple. He felt a sudden and intense need to get outside where he could breathe. He shifted in the chair. Whatever it was, whatever else his father had done, he didn't want to know about it. His emotions must have been easy to read.

"It's nothin' bad. It's just we think you should know how much help your dad was ta Bill 'n me over the years."

The constriction in Ken's chest loosened. "What do you mean?"

The sheriff got up and poured coffee into a stained earthenware mug, then raised the coffee pot in McCort's direction. McCort shook his head. "Ken?"

"No thanks." He couldn't swallow a drop.

When Tate was seated again, McCort began. "A lot of bad things can go on in the mountains. People not respectin' the environment, dumpin' trash, poachin'."

Tate jumped in. "He helped us track a killer once. Some kook grabbed his estranged wife and headed east, toward Tyron Pass. Your dad knew those mountains like the back of his hand. Led us right to them. The woman was beat up pretty bad. But at least she was alive." His face turned grim. "Which is more than could be said for her parents. The guy shot them both dead when he grabbed the wife."

It had happened when Ken was a junior in high school. People had talked about nothing else for weeks—the man stood the sheriff and his men off for nearly two days before finally surrendering. But there'd been no mention of Ken's father when the news folks talked about the dramatic rescue.

"He helped me crack a major poachin' case 'bout three years back," said McCort. "Some rich guy from Portland thought he and his friends could hunt bears whenever they wanted to. Thought they were too far back in the woods for anyone ta know 'bout it." He smiled. "They didn't know your dad."

"I guess not," mumbled Ken.

"And the people we think burned those helicopters… ELF, they call themselves… Earth Liberation Front. They been messin' around loggin' sites." There was a look of disgust on McCort's face as he spoke. "I asked your dad ta keep his eye out for me. He gave me the location of a couple of their camps. I'm hopin' we'll catch them at one."

Ken stared at one man and then the other, shaking his head. "I had no idea. Why didn't he say anything?" His father had never given a hint.

McCort cleared his throat. "I haven't told Ellen. For some reason, your father never wanted her to know what he was doin' for us. Said she'd just worry. Bill an' me thought someone in the family should be aware."

Ken wiped his eyes with the back of his hand, not wanting these two men, who'd been his father's friends, to know how much hearing their news distressed him…now, when it was too late. "I appreciate you telling me. I thought I knew everything there was to know about him. I was wrong."

McCort walked out to the truck and surprised Ken even further. "Bill an' me both knew your dad had somethin' from his past he was hidin'. An' we knew he wasn't in the States legally. But he was a good man. We respected him. I don't think there's a man or woman that knew him didn't feel the same."

Ken's throat closed. He could only nod his appreciation as Ian clasped his hand and slapped him on the shoulder. "Hope to see you again b'fore ya leave, Ken. Say hello to your mom for me. I been keeping an eye on her. Checkin' in now and then to see how she's doin'. I owe your dad that much."

Ken drove home going over Tate's and McCort's revelations. Were he and Marie the only ones who hadn't known? He breathed heavily. How many more secrets were left to unravel?

Late that afternoon an FBI agent arrived at the house to interview Ken. The man wasn't telling much—too early in the investigation to know anything. But he said Ken's description of the fire and the way the helicopters exploded into flames would be helpful.

"Sorry I can't help any more than that," Ken said. "The whole thing really pisses me off. I mean, where do these guys get off? Someone could have been seriously hurt there. Me, for one."

The agent looked at Ken for a long moment then simply said, "We'll be in touch."

A few minutes later Ken watched the agent get into his car and drive off. "Asshole," he muttered. He turned to go to his room and think more about what he'd learned that morning, but Mrs. Weitzel was standing in the doorway.

"Your mother isn't back from town with the truck. I've got everything packed for the afternoon delivery. Do you think I should take it in before she gets back?"

Ken looked at his watch. It was nearly four-thirty. "I guess you'd better. Did Mom say where she was going?"

"I think she may have stopped to see Marie. She's been worried Marie hasn't called or come out for a few days—especially with your leave being up soon."

"Better make the delivery. I'll carry it out to your car." Even though he liked Mrs. Weitzel and was becoming used to her being around the house, Ken wasn't sure he should be discussing family matters with her.

Chapter Ten

MARIE

"Ma-ma. Ma-ma."

Marie reached out a hand for Paul. The space was empty, the sheet cool. Her stomach knotted.

"Ma-ma. Ma-ma."

She pried her swollen eyes open and looked at her son, watching her from behind the rails of his crib.

"Ma-ma."

"Just a minute, bubber." Her words came out in a croak. "Mommy's getting up in just a minute."

She closed her eyes again. Oh, God, she thought. I can't stand it.

The next two days were a blur of misery and self-pity. She fed Henry Reed. Bathed him. Dressed him. She did little for herself. When Paul called, asking if he could come over and talk—we have to make some plans, he said—she put him off. She didn't want him to see her blubbering like a baby.

On the third day, when her mother knocked on her door at eleven-thirty, she was still in her nightgown, hair uncombed, face unwashed, her eyes red-rimmed and swollen.

"Marie! What's wrong? Are you sick?"

"Paul left me."

"What?"

Marie threw herself into her mother's arms and let out a wail that sounded much like Henry Reed's. Her mother held her and soothed her. "Oh, honey." Henry Reed started crying. Marie sobbed harder.

Finally, she pulled herself together enough that her mother led her by the hand to the couch. "Let me get a damp cloth. You need to wash your face." Before going into the bathroom, her mother got a cracker for Henry Reed, who stopped crying and stuffed the cracker into his mouth.

Marie lifted her face and let Ellen gently wash away the residue of a thousand tears. "I can't believe Paul would leave you and Henry Reed," her mother said.

"He says he feels like an old man with no future. He hates his job and he wishes we never got married. He wishes Henry Reed had never been born." Marie's words ended on a moan.

Ellen frowned. "Did he say that?"

"He didn't have to." Marie started to cry again.

She poured out everything to her mother—the long silences, Paul's disapproval of everything she'd done in trying to find out about her father, the arguments about Henry Reed. "When I got pregnant, Paul asked me if I wanted to get an abortion. I wouldn't hear of it. But I never even asked him what he wanted."

"That doesn't mean he didn't want you to have the baby. Maybe he was trying to be sure you wanted to."

"He never said so."

"But, honey, he's always been so good with Henry Reed. I can't believe he regrets having him."

"Maybe. It doesn't make any difference now. He's gone."

"I tell you what. I'm going to go turn the shower on. You get a shower and wash your hair while I fix a bowl of soup and a sandwich. You'll feel better when you've cleaned up and had something to eat."

Wordlessly, Marie followed her mother's instructions, though she doubted she could eat a bite. When she was toweling off, squeals of laughter came from the living room—her son playing with his grandmother. The happy sounds only seemed to emphasize the desperate, hollow feeling inside her.

"I'm going to end up like Marie-Catherine and Claudia." She was dressed and sitting at the table with her mother. Her mother had fed Henry Reed and put him down for his nap. "Like them, I'll be bringing up a child on my own." A fresh surge of tears threatened when she thought of all the lonely years ahead, years without Paul.

Ellen set her spoon down. "The way you've spoken of your aunt, she's obviously someone you admire. If it comes to bringing up Henry Reed on your own, which I doubt will happen, perhaps she should be your role model."

"You mean I should go back to school? Get a college degree? How could I do that? There's no college in Platt City."

"That's not what I was getting at, though you might eventually want to consider it since it's what you planned to do before Henry Reed came along." When Marie started to protest, Ellen held up her hand. "What I mean about using Marie-Catherine as a role model is that she didn't give in.

She didn't let herself be a victim; she did what she had to do. She carried on."

"I love him so much, though, Mom. What if he never wants me back?"

"I don't think that's likely to happen." Her mother laid a caressing hand on Marie's cheek and gazed into her eyes. "But if it does, you'll manage. Believe me."

Henry Reed woke and they took him for a walk in his stroller. "The fresh air brought roses to your cheeks, too," Ellen said, after they'd returned to the apartment. She looked at her watch. "I need to go, but think of what I said about Marie-Catherine and about being strong. No matter what happens with you and Paul, you have to be strong— for yourself and for your son."

"I'll try."

"I had to learn that lesson the hard way. I wish I'd been a better role model for you and Ken. Especially for you, Marie. I guess it was easier to just let things happen—go with the flow, as they say now. But marriage isn't about one person stepping aside to let the other person have it all his or her way. It's about caring for each other, compromising when necessary, and communication. Your father and I had the caring part in abundance, but we messed up with the communication part, and the compromising was all one-sided. That wasn't fair to me, nor was it fair to you and Ken."

Marie smiled through fresh tears. "You're a wonderful role model now, Mom."

Paul called later that evening, after she'd fed Henry Reed and gotten him into his pajamas. "Can I come over?"

"When?" She fought the feeling of panic threatening to close down her breathing. She wanted to see him, but she was afraid of how she'd feel when he left.

"Is now okay? I want to see our son before he goes to bed."

Her heart seemed to skip a beat. "I guess."

"Have you had dinner? Can I bring a pizza or something?"

"I don't think so. This isn't a celebration or anything. Just come over. Mom and I took him for a walk this afternoon, but if you want, you can take him out again. As long as you're not gone long."

"I'll be over in a few minutes."

He knocked on the door instead of using his key. Glad her mother had insisted she take a shower and clean up, she wiped her damp palms on her jeans before opening the door.

Unsure what to say, she turned and walked toward Henry Reed's playpen. Paul followed. The baby dropped the plastic car he'd been playing with, pushed upright and held out his arms to be picked up.

"How've you been?"

"Not very good." That might qualify for the understatement of the year. She leaned over the playpen and picked up her son.

Henry Reed lunged toward Paul. "Da-da. Da-da."

Paul took the baby from her. "I guess that was a stupid question."

"I'll get his jacket."

"That's okay. I don't need to take him out. I know it's near his bedtime."

"Suit yourself." She turned away, not wanting him to see how much she was hurting.

"Let's read a book, bubber. Where has Mommy put your books?"

"They're over on the coffee table. He likes the ones with the farm animals the best."

"I know."

"Look, as long as you're here, maybe I'll run to the store. I'm nearly out of milk and a couple of other things." She couldn't stand being in the same room with him any longer. She had to get away and anywhere would do. "I won't be gone long." Before he could agree or disagree, she grabbed her purse and keys.

It wasn't until she was on her way to the store in the truck that she wondered what Paul used to get back and forth to work. Or even if he was going to work. Maybe he'd already quit his job, seeing he hated it so much. Again the tears sprang. She tightened her lips and shook her head, determined not to cry. For one thing, she didn't want to go back to the apartment with red eyes.

She stayed away as long as she could. When she let herself in, Paul was on the couch with Henry Reed asleep on his chest. The look on Paul's face was one of such deep longing and regret that she couldn't help herself. She stood in the doorway, a bag of groceries in each hand, while tears ran down her cheeks.

"I didn't want to wake him."

She nodded, unable to speak. She crossed the room and put the groceries on the kitchen counter, then surreptitiously wiped the tears away on the sleeve of her jacket. "I'll get him." She gently took the sleeping baby off Paul's chest. She carried him into the bedroom, put him into his crib, and pulled the blanket over him. When she turned around, she jumped, startled at finding Paul right behind her. He leaned over the crib rail and stroked one of Henry Reed's pudgy hands.

Marie left the room.

After a moment or two, Paul followed. "Can we talk now?"

"What do you want to talk about?"

"Us."

"Is there an 'us'?"

"No matter what happens between you and me, there'll always be an 'us'." Paul nodded his head toward the bedroom. "We're his parents. Nothing will change that."

"Have you decided what you're going to do?"

"I'm still thinking about it."

"Then there's nothing for us to talk about. Not until you decide whether you want to be a full-time husband and father or just a part-time father."

"I haven't quit my job. I'm going to take care of you and Henry Reed. I just need some time on my own. Some time to think." There was pain in his voice. "I still love you."

She swallowed and lifted her chin. "What do you want from me, Paul? Permission? I can't give that to you. I don't understand how you can tell me one minute that you love me and Henry Reed and the next minute that you need time away from us. Why can't you think right here?"

"I don't know."

"Well, I don't know either. But I think you should go now. It's been a long day."

An even longer night followed.

Chapter Eleven

ELLEN

Ellen pulled into Frank Klein's driveway, admiring the neatly trimmed yard and the house's freshly painted shutters. Still unsure exactly what she was expecting to accomplish, she set the brake and turned off the engine.

Frank opened the door. "I'm glad you've come."

"What are we going to do about these kids of ours, Frank?"

"C'mon into the kitchen. I've got a fresh pot of coffee brewing and I can warm up some of your cinnamon rolls in no time."

"I'll pass on the rolls—I have to say, bread and rolls have somehow lost their appeal." Frank joined her in a chuckle. "But I'd love a cup of coffee."

Frank's kitchen was as neat and tidy as his yard. Despite the fact that he'd been a widower for over seven years, the evidence of Virginia was everywhere, from the embroidered tea towels hanging on the oven door to the floral prints on the wall, from the brightly colored braided rug on the floor in front of the sink to the plate rail that held her collection of old ironstone dinnerware.

Frank gestured toward the table, already set with woven placemats. "Make yourself comfortable." He got mugs from the cupboard and poured cream into a pitcher, setting it and a sugar bowl on the table. He filled the mugs and set them on the table, too.

Ellen sat in one of the four ladder-back chairs around the round maple table. "Paul's at work?" She reached for her mug.

Frank gave a half-smile. "I don't know what kind of job he's doing, though. I can't imagine he's keeping his mind on business."

Ellen stirred cream into her coffee. "What's going on with him, Frank?"

"Damned if I know, Ellen. I thought they were happy as a couple of bugs until Paul came to me a few weeks ago."

"Marie's devastated—can't understand what she's done. It sounds to me, though, it's not so much what she's done, but more like Paul thinks life is passing him by." Frank nodded agreement. She blew on her coffee then took a careful sip. "I know he always wanted to be an engineer. Working in a lumberyard must seem a long way from his dream."

Frank blew on his own coffee, but put it down without drinking any. "You're right. I understand him having some regrets, but at some point we all have to put our dreams aside and adjust to what life deals us."

Ellen thought about that for a few moments, wondering what Frank had given up. "Henry Reed's unanticipated arrival on the scene definitely complicated things. But I don't agree that means Paul should give up his dreams." She thought Frank was showing little understanding for his son, which seemed unlike him.

"You can't change what life hands you, Ellen."

"Not everything, no." She realized he was thinking of Virginia. "But some things you can change. And sometimes you can make things happen."

"I'm not following you."

Ellen shrugged and smiled. "I'm not sure exactly what I'm getting at, to tell the truth. Only that I don't think Paul should have to sit back and say 'that's life' and accept whatever happens. That's something I've learned since Henry's death. Paul has wanted to be an engineer since as long ago as I can remember."

"True, but—"

"And he loves Marie—has loved her almost as long as he's wanted to be an engineer."

Frank kept on nodding. "And now they're married and have a baby. Now my son needs to put the first part of that equation aside and get on with what's real."

Ellen stirred her coffee more. "My goodness, Frank. I've never heard you so pessimistic. We all need dreams. Why shouldn't Paul have his? And why shouldn't he try making his dreams come true?"

Frank stood and crossed to the window above the sink. He stared out for a moment or two before turning back to Ellen. "Are you saying you think he can still be an engineer? Be realistic. It takes years of schooling." He shook his head. "I don't see that happening."

"Why not? What's stopping him?"

"Money. Do you know how much it costs to get a degree these days? Hard enough for a young single person. A married man with a child?" He shook his head again. "Pretty tough."

Ellen sat back in her chair. She was surprised at the lack of ambition Frank seemed to be showing for his son, and even more, his lack of empathy. She knew it had nothing to do with his love for Paul, so what was he afraid of?

Frank gazed at her. "You're probably thinking I don't want my son to succeed."

"No, of course I don't think that. But, this doesn't sound like you."

Frank returned to his seat. He leaned toward Ellen, arms on the edge of the table. "I just think, as hard as it's been for the two of them here—money being tight and all—how much harder they'd have it on an even smaller budget with no family around to give them moral support. Paul would still need to earn a living. Between that and attending classes, when would he study? As Henry Reed grows, he'll require more. Then there's the expense of school itself, books, lab fees and all that."

"There would be one major difference—they'd be working together toward a goal." Ellen looked at him through narrowed eyes. "And we could help them. It could become a shared goal."

Frank leaned back in his chair, shaking his head. "I don't have that kind of money, Ellen. Do you?"

"No." Although her bread-making business was more than breaking even, she didn't need George Baker to tell her she couldn't afford the kind of outlay she and Frank were talking about. "But I think I could give them a little something each month. Maybe you could, too?"

Frank's eyes narrowed. "Maybe."

"And they're young and healthy. They can both get part-time jobs. Other students do it. Grants and loans are out there, too." Ellen wondered if Frank was afraid of being lonely if Paul and Marie moved away.

"Have you talked to Marie about this?"

Ellen shook her head. "I thought it best to let them work things out on their own. Do you think Paul wants to be married to Marie? That's my main question right now."

"He's been absolutely miserable this past week."

"Marie said he's worried she'll end up pregnant again."

"Babies do have a way of happening, don't they?" Frank's slight smile was followed by a frown. "I guess what I'm really worried about is, how hard it would be on them if they tried this college thing and it didn't work. Paul says he feels like a failure now. How much worse would he feel if he tried to go back to school and couldn't make it?"

"I can't answer that." Ellen was glad she was wrong about Frank's motivation. Still, his lack of encouragement and enthusiasm was telling. He must be nearing sixty-five— maybe it was age causing him to be so cautious.

"Well, I can answer it, because I've been there. I'd hate for him to go through that."

Ah. But Frank's fear shouldn't dictate Paul's and Marie's future. "I can understand your concern, Frank, but I think it would be harder on Paul if he never tried. And with both of us behind them, they should have a better chance at success, don't you think?"

"Maybe." Frank sighed. "You're definitely right about one thing, though. They need to work through this on their own. I guess after they've done that, if going back to school is the direction they decide to take, they'll have my help if they want it."

Ellen heaved a sigh as she got in the truck and headed back home. She'd done her best to convince Frank they should help the kids and she hoped he would remain resolved. She felt certain he would, assuming school was the course her daughter and son-in-law settled on. But feeling as he did, she worried he might influence Paul's decision.

Not intentionally, of course. Frank wouldn't do something like that knowingly. Still, his fear that Paul would fail might come through. Would that be enough to sway Paul's decision, make him lose confidence? And why had Paul let go of his dream so easily? She answered her own question: Paul was always responsible—helping his mother in the final stages of her illness, helping Frank manage his grief. When Marie got pregnant, he had undoubtedly been overwhelmed with all his newfound responsibilities.

She passed the airport and was momentarily distracted. Yellow crime-scene tape still surrounded the area where the helicopters had been.

She shook her head then straightened in her seat and frowned. Why were she and Frank focused only on Paul going to college? Marie should have a chance to continue her education, every bit as much as Paul. She turned into her lane, glad to be home. Well, the kids would work it out. If they couldn't do it together, she'd do her best to help Marie become the independent young woman she needed to be.

Marta was in the kitchen. "That FBI man was here again."

"Oh? What did he want?" There'd been another big article in the paper that morning. Ken had been right—a radical environmental group had been named as the probable suspects.

"He wanted Ken to look at some pictures."

"I hope he won't need to spend a lot of time on this." Her son had only a week before he had to go back to the Marine Corps. She didn't want him tied up answering questions he'd already answered. He should be out seeing his friends, visiting old haunts. He should be having fun.

"He needs a girlfriend," Marta said, as if reading her mind.

"Maybe he has one." Ellen wondered if it were so. "There are lots of young women in the service. Did you know they can even serve on ships now?"

"On Navy ships? That doesn't seem right," Marta said, shaking her head and tsking at the thought.

"I think it's a good thing." Ellen surprised herself with that answer. What a long way she'd come in the short span of a year.

"Want me to take the dinner delivery?" Ken asked from the doorway.

"That would be great," said Ellen.

"Did Mrs. Weitzel tell you the FBI agent was here again?"

"She did. She said he wanted you to look at some pictures. What were they?"

"Pictures of suspects. I couldn't help. It was too dark for me to recognize anyone."

"That's too bad. I still can't believe it. How can people who claim to love and want to protect the environment be so destructive? And don't they think other people have rights?" She knew it was a rhetorical question; neither Ken nor Marta had the answers she sought.

The bell on the stove rang, indicating the oven had risen to the proper temperature. She opened the door and slid in several trays of rolls.

Marta stood at the counter, rolling out pie crusts. Five finished pies were cooling on the table. "These are for tomorrow," she said to no one in particular. "They'll stay fresh in the refrigerator overnight."

"Between the two of you," said Ken. "I think I've gained ten pounds since I got home."

"Good," said Marta. "You needed some fattening up."

"It was probably so hot in Bahrain, no one wanted to eat." Ellen had noted how thin Ken was when he got home, too, but she hadn't worried about it. He wasn't skinny. He was whip-lean with his thinness. She thought he'd never looked so fit.

Ken leaned against a counter. "Not really. The mess hall was always cool—they kept the air-conditioning working in there, at least—and they served four meals a day. A lot of guys actually gained weight."

Less than two hours later, the finished rolls loaded into the truck, Ellen stood on the porch and watched Ken drive down the lane. She would miss him when he left. North Carolina was too far away.

Chapter Twelve

KEN

Ken looked in the rearview mirror and saw his mother standing on the porch, watching. He rolled the window down and waved. It would be hard on her when he left. Him, too, for that matter. It was time, though. He thought about what was going on between Paul and Marie on the drive into town, and when he pulled out of the restaurant parking lot after delivering his mother's bread order, the truck cab filled with the lingering scent of yeast, he decided to stop by the lumberyard.

Paul stood on the loading dock as a pickup loaded with sheetrock pulled away. Papers, attached to the clipboard in his hand, fluttered in a light breeze.

"Hey, Paul."

Paul jerked around, frowning. "Hi." There was caution in his voice, as though he half-expected Ken to take a swing at him.

Ken thought maybe a sock on his jaw might bring Paul to his senses. "Must be close to quitting time. Wanna go grab a beer?"

"Okay." Paul still sounded tentative.

"When can you leave?"

"In about fifteen minutes. I need to wash up and check out first. And I need a ride."

"I'll wait for you out front."

Twenty minutes later, Paul opened the passenger door and climbed into the truck. "Rose's?"

"Unless you want to crash one of the tourist joints."

Paul chuckled. "And fight off ferns all night? No thanks."

When they were seated in a booth at Rose's, Ken asked Paul what he wanted to drink.

"Whatever you're having." Paul pulled out his wallet.

"Put it away. This round's on me." Ken went to the bar and ordered two Henrys.

"Everyone is talking about Marrick-Pacific and those helicopters," Paul said when Ken returned with the beers. "Has the FBI told you anything?"

The bartender came from behind the bar and plugged coins in the jukebox. Willie Nelson started complaining about being on the road again.

"Not much." Ken slid into the booth. "I couldn't tell them much either—nothing they didn't already know. They did find some footprints and tire prints in the snow. They think they can tie them to whoever did it. I'd like to get hold of the bastard and beat the shit out of him."

"I heard the helicopters went up fast."

"They're made of magnesium and beer-can strength aluminum. With all the fuel on board, they burned like a son-of-a-bitch. After a few minutes, about the only things left were the rotors."

"Who'd want to burn up a couple of helicopters?"

"Earth Liberation Front maybe. Probably." Ken took a sip of his beer.

"Why?"

"According to the sheriff, they don't like that Merrick-Pacific has contracted to the Forest Service to take out some old-growth timber."

Paul nodded. "There's been some talk about that at work. You'd be surprised how many people, loggers, even, think the old-growth should be left alone."

"Sheriff says he thinks whoever did it used milk jugs filled with fuel, sponges saturated in fuel and joss sticks—you know, incense burners. When the sticks burned down far enough, the sponge ignites, drops into the milk jug filled with fuel and ka-boom. It's in a so-called handbook—*Arsoning Around with Auntie Alf.*"

Paul frowned. "Auntie Alf?"

"Animal Liberation Front. They were around first, before Earth Liberation Front. ELF."

Paul shook his head, still frowning. "Crazy."

Ken nodded then decided to get to the point. "What's the deal with you and Marie?" He'd been wondering all week if Paul was having an affair, if there was someone else on the side.

Paul stared at his beer mug. "I don't know, man. I love Marie. I want to be with her and the baby. But it's not enough—know what I mean?" He looked up at Ken, his expression hang-dog.

You weasel, Ken thought, his lips tightening. You'd better not be cheating on my sister.

Appearing oblivious, Paul took a pull of his beer and wiped his mouth with the back of his hand. "It's like I get up and go to the lumberyard in the morning. I work my ass off all day doing stuff any idiot could do, I go home, I play with Henry Reed for a while, we eat dinner, go to bed, and that's it. The next day I do it again. I tell myself that should be enough, but it isn't." He rubbed his forehead with the tips of his fingers. "There has to be more to life."

Ken relaxed against the seat. Maybe he was wrong. "What is it you'd rather be doing?"

"I don't know. Listening to you talk about the places you've been—the Mediterranean, Yemen, Bahrain. I'd like to see those places."

Ken didn't like the direction this was taking any better than what he'd been thinking before. He kept his voice non-committal. "They were an experience, alright."

"I always thought I'd get a degree in engineering then go to work for a company like Boeing or McDonnell-Douglass, designing planes or rockets. Or setting up my own machine shop somewhere. Maybe that's a kid's dream and I'd've ended up designing toasters. McDonald-Douglass doesn't even exist anymore." He took another swallow of beer. "Either way, there's not much chance of it happening now."

Ken was getting a little fed up with Paul's 'poor me' attitude. "Why? Just because you're married? Lots of guys go to school with a wife and kid."

"Do you have any idea how much it costs to support a wife and kid? Do you know how much we pay for that friggin' apartment? And it's already too small."

"Whatever it is, I'll bet it's too much."

"You got that right." Paul drained his glass and stood. "I'll get the next round."

"Okay."

Paul went to get their beers. Ken, with several inches of beer still in his glass, watched a couple shooting pool and thought about Paul, ready to throw everything he had away for what he thought Ken had. Freedom. He didn't really blame Paul. The idea of a wife and child, marriage…he shook his head. Still, Paul had made that decision. Walking away shouldn't be an option.

Moonlight lit their way to the truck. Paul climbed in, nearly missing his step. "Thanks for listening, man." His words lacked the crisp edge of sobriety.

Ken hunched his shoulders against the bitter cold and started the engine. "So what are you going to do?" It was the same question he'd asked at the beginning of the evening.

Paul threw his head against the seatback, his eyes closed. "I don't know. I love her. I love my kid. I told you that. I guess it'll have to be enough. I guess I'll just have to make it enough."

Ken dropped Paul off at his father's, then headed home. Paul's answer wasn't what Ken wanted for his sister. Marie deserved better than just being "enough."

Enough wasn't what he wanted for himself, either. Being home, surrounded by trees and mountains—they were a powerful draw. But Travers, Costello, the gunny, the rest of the men he'd spent the last three years with—even Sharpe—he'd miss their camaraderie if he got out. There was still a lot of world he wanted to see, too.

His mother seemed to be doing okay on her own. He'd thought she needed him, but he could see she didn't. Jeez, she didn't even need his help getting the lane cleared when it snowed. Had it all arranged. Still…God, he wished he could make up his mind. He gave a heavy sigh.

"We didn't wait dinner for you, but there's plenty of stew left. It just needs heating up," his mother said when he got home. She was in a robe and slippers.

"Sorry. I should have called. Paul and I went out for a couple of beers."

"Oh?"

"I think he's decided to move back with Marie."

"You don't sound entirely pleased with that."

"I'm not sure I am." He leaned against the table. "It's like he's settling. I don't think that's fair to Marie."

She crossed to the stove and turned the flame on under the stew.

"I'll get that, Mom. You're ready for bed."

"I'd rather talk to you. With all that's been going on, we haven't had enough time together. You'll be leaving in less than a week."

"I know. Thirty days has gone by fast."

"Has it? You haven't been bored?"

"Well, maybe now and then." It had been a little more often than that, if he were being honest.

"It's too bad so many of your friends have moved away."

"Yeah." Like him, they'd all wanted out of Platt City.

"So, when you get back to North Carolina, what will you do?"

"Same as always. Go on maneuvers. Train. Go to Morehead City on the weekends. Swoop."

"Swoop? What is that?"

Ken laughed. "It's when a bunch of us get in somebody's car on Friday night and drive for hours to Atlantic City or D.C. or some other big city—at least one bigger than Jacksonville—spend four or five hours, then turn around and drive back to Camp Lejeune."

"Why in the world would you do that? It sounds dreadful. How can you go to work the next day?"

It was dreadful. Dreadful, exhausting and also exhilarating. "Probably not well," he admitted. "Some people do it every weekend."

"Well I hope you aren't one of them."

He went to her side and put his arm around her shoulders. "Don't worry, Mom. Your little boy can take care of himself."

She gave him a playful shove. "I know that."

"Come and sit down. I need to talk to you about something." Maybe she could make some sense of his confused thoughts.

"Let me get you some of this stew first." She ladled stew into a bowl, cut two slices of rye bread and brought both, plus butter from the fridge, and set them on the table. "Anything else you'd like?"

"Mom, this is great. More than enough." He was still full from the beer he'd drunk. "Come and sit down."

His mother took a seat across from him. "What is it? You've been mulling something over ever since you came home."

"My enlistment is up in a few months. I'm trying to decide whether to re-enlist."

"Oh." Her face sagged a moment, then she swallowed and lifted her chin. "I guess I always thought you'd get it out of your system with the one time."

"It's not a bad career choice. I like it and I like the people—most of them, anyway."

"Couldn't you find something else you'd like just as well? You have so much talent. And you've been saving money for college. With what the Marine Corps has matched, you could go to college next year."

"I don't have enough for four years, but I'll get a pretty big bonus if I re-enlist."

"Enough to go to college?"

"For that or to put a down payment on some property. Maybe down along the Snake—if Simplot hasn't bought up all the land before I get a chance. Or over around Lewiston or even Spokane. Not a big place. Not at first, anyway. Just big enough for a few head of cattle—Herefords."

"I can see you've given this some thought."

"I've thought about it since I was a kid. That re-enlistment bonus could make it happen."

"It seems like you've already made up your mind what you want to do."

"Not entirely."

"I don't understand."

"I miss the family. I miss the mountains. I miss all this." He waved his hands around.

"Ah. That is a dilemma."

"And it isn't like I can't buy property without the bonus money. I'm young, healthy and I'm not afraid of hard work. I could get a job at the mill or somewhere else that pays decent, save up and then buy the property." He knew it was true, though the idea of living in Platt City and working in the lumber mill for ten years, or however long it took to save up enough money, was the last thing he wanted. But there was nothing saying where he had to live—he didn't know why he kept putting Platt City into the equation. Well, he did know why. "The thing is, for a while I thought you needed me here. But after watching you this month—I know you're okay. You're more than okay. You're great."

She smiled at him and patted his hand. "Thank you. That may be one of the nicest things anyone has ever said to me."

"Another part of me wants to put all that on hold, the ranch and all, and re-enlist no matter what. Because I think what I'm doing is important. Let me tell you about a girl in Manama." His mother's eyes quickened with interest. He grinned. "It's not what you're thinking. She's a little girl—only seven years old."

She was silent as he told her about Farida, not commenting until he came to the end of the story. "What can we do for her?"

"I'm not sure. I'm not sure there's anything we can do that her adoptive family isn't already doing." He'd sent them pictures of Idaho and its mountains—something Farida would never have seen. Might never see. "Something has to be done, though. On a broader scale, I mean. There's so much hatred for Americans—it seems to be all over the Middle East. I told you about the Cole, but I didn't tell you about one day when I was in Manama; I got lost and ran into three young Bahraini men. I can't describe the hatred on their faces when they saw me. I really feared for my safety."

She drew a sharp breath and shifted in her chair. "My goodness, what did you do?"

"I ran. I was outnumbered and in a place where there were no other Westerners. I don't mind telling you, it scared the shit out of me. Sorry." Thinking of that day—his fear, their hatred—he shuddered, opening and closing his fingers. "The thing is, all that is going to get worse. I know it."

"But what can you do? You're just one person."

"I know, Mom. But I think we, the United States, I mean, are going to have more problems in the Middle East than we've ever imagined."

Alarm and apprehension played across her face. "I don't like to think of you mixed up in something like that."

"I don't like the idea of it either. They've been fighting tribal wars over there for centuries. Religious wars, too, even before the Crusades. I don't know if we can win if it does come to a fight. But I'd feel like hell if something like that happens and I'm not there to do my share." And his buddies were.

"Oh, Ken. Don't you think you've done enough?"

His stomach tightened at seeing the distress in her eyes. "Maybe I'm wrong and it won't come to that. Outright war, I mean. But I think this terrorism thing is going to get worse. That's what really scares me. And it scares me because it's here, too. Like those environmental bastards who burned the helicopters."

"I know." She shook her head. "I can't believe something like that could happen right here in Idaho. Or anywhere else in America."

"And when I see all that, I think about Dad, and I wonder what he was thinking of when he and his brother were in that group—the FLQ. How could he have let himself get drawn into it? I've seen firsthand what happens with that kind of violence. Marie said the FLQ claimed they targeted property with their bombs, not people, but that's bullshit. People get hurt. That's all there is to it. How could Dad have had anything to do with it?"

"He didn't. Marie told you it was a ruse. You know your father wouldn't have condoned hurting people."

"I really don't know what to think. It's like he was two different people: the person who was a Quebec separatist, who'd do anything to achieve Quebec independence, and the person I knew, the man who was only happy when he was out in the woods communing with nature."

"I think he was a little more than that." A steely look appeared in her blue eyes. "He gave you all he could. He carried a burden of guilt—you've learned some of the reasons—but think of how good he was to you, to all of us. He gave what he had to give."

"When he was around," said Ken, then instantly regretted it. "I'm sorry. That was out of line." He reached across the table and took her hand. "It really was."

"I'm glad you're finally figuring that out."

He took the last bite of stew and pushed the bowl aside. "His whole other life thing really throws me for a loop, though. Doesn't it you? Jeez, Mom, how did you keep it to yourself all those years?"

344

"Like I told Marie, there was really nothing to keep silent about. I didn't know about his family. I thought they were all dead. And I didn't know anything about the journalism and politics and all. I just knew about his not being here legally and about our not being officially married. I didn't think that concerned anyone but your father and me. I forgot about it, if you want to know the truth."

He drew back, eyebrows raised in question. "Forgot about it?"

Her eyes sparkling with defiance, she lifted her chin. "Yes, forgot about it. It was a marriage in every sense but a piece of paper."

Not to mention the little matter of an existing wife and child, he thought. "I guess I see your point." He got up and took his empty bowl to the sink, came back and sat down. "But getting back to what we were talking about before, what do you think? Should I get out or re-up?"

She reached across the table and covered his hand with hers, giving his hand a squeeze. "You already know what my preference would be. But it's your decision and you're the only person who can make it."

Chapter Thirteen
MARIE

Marie was in her nightgown, brushing her teeth when she thought she heard a knock on the door. Paul? Another knock. It had to be Paul—who else at this time of night? Should she answer? Yes? No? Yes? She dropped her toothbrush in the sink and rushed to the door, now afraid he might give up and leave. He stood there, looking as though he wasn't going to move until she let him in.

"I wasn't expecting you." That was pointless—he knew she wasn't expecting him. She stood back to let him in, suddenly feeling uncomfortable wearing only her nightgown. "Just a minute, I'll be right back." She darted into the bedroom and got her robe out of the closet. This was ridiculous. Paul has seen her a million times in less. Still, she felt better, more in control, belting her robe.

In the living room, Paul sat on the sofa, a cold Coke on the coffee table in front of him.

"Good, you've got something to drink." She pulled the belt of her robe tighter. Why did she feel as though Paul was a visitor she needed to entertain?

"Sorry, I didn't know if you wanted one."

"I just brushed my teeth." Marie lowered herself to the other end of the sofa. Filled with unspoken questions, she glanced at Paul's profile then down at her hands. She squirmed in her seat, growing more uncomfortable as the seconds ticked by.

Finally, Paul broke the silence. "You're probably wondering why I'm here. Especially without calling first."

She nodded. "Why didn't you? Call, I mean."

"I've been thinking."

"About what?"

He took a deep breath. "Us. I miss you and Henry Reed a whole lot."

The muscles in her shoulders and back relaxed, but only a little. "We miss you." What was he saying?

He blurted it out. "Can I come home?"

She was stunned. She wanted to yell and scream, yes, yes, yes, yes. But something kept those words in check. "Well…"

"I mean it, Marie. I've just missed you so much. My life isn't anything without you."

"Oh God, Paul. I've been miserable, too. This has been the worst ten days of my life."

"So, it's okay? I can come back?"

"I don't know." What was the matter with her? What was she saying? Wasn't this exactly what she wanted? She stood and took a few steps away. "I just don't know, Paul."

Paul frowned. "What do you mean? Do you want me to come back or not?"

She turned and faced him. "I do, but I'm confused." She'd been thinking, non-stop since he'd left, once she'd managed to stop feeling sorry for herself, and was being as honest as she could be. "I still don't understand why you left. And now, well, now I don't understand what's changed. If it's just that you miss us, well…what about next week, next month?" She held out her hands, palms facing upward. "What about when we're together again and nothing's changed, you still hate your job?"

"I don't know."

She pressed her lips together, shaking her head. "I don't know, either. And I'm scared, Paul. I'm scared to take the chance you'll leave us again."

"Your brother told me I should go to school. He said I shouldn't give up my dream of wanting to be an engineer."

Marie sat on the couch again, a little closer to Paul than before. "He did?"

"He said lots of men go to college with a wife and child. I suppose he's right. I guess I just thought, well, when you got pregnant, that was the end—I'd have to forget it. Both of us had to forget it—you wanted to go, too."

"Oh, Paul."

"I think I've been holding it against you for quite a while. And then you went off to Montreal, like what I wanted or thought about that just didn't count. It felt like I was doing all the giving in or giving up. I wanted to say, 'what about me, don't I count?' I know that wasn't very mature, but…I guess I just got to resenting it."

"I'm sorry. I'm glad you've finally told me."

"Can I hold you?" She went into his arms, eagerly opening her lips to his, his tongue probing, her heart beating wildly. His hand slid inside her robe, cupping her breast, his thumb rubbing her nipple into instant erectness. "Let's go to bed."

His whispered words against her neck sent shivers down Marie's spine. She burned with wanting him. She drew a shaky breath and pushed him away. "No, Paul. We can't."

He tried to pull her to him again. "Sure we can. We're still married and we love each other."

She resisted. It was the hardest thing she'd ever done. "No. Paul, please." Her voice shook. "We can't. We need to figure things out first. Sex would just confuse things." He didn't protest though she could see by his frown that he wanted to. "I think we should stay separated for a while longer."

"How much longer? A day? A week? I want to come home."

"I don't know—as long as it takes to figure things out, I guess."

Paul's eyes narrowed, but he finally gave a curt nod.

Before he left, after going into the bedroom to see Henry Reed, she invited him to dinner the next night. "I'll make us something special. This time I won't overcook everything." She gave a weak smile.

It was still early when Marie drove up the lane toward her mother's house, but smoke coming from the chimney assured her that Ellen was awake. She laughed to herself. Why had she worried? Her mother and Mrs. Weitzel had probably been up for hours.

"What a nice surprise," her mother said as Marie carried Henry Reed into the kitchen and set him on the floor. "Marta and I were just about to have breakfast. Want some?"

"No thanks. I've eaten, but Henry Reed is always ready for a piece of toast." She pulled his jacket off and hung it with hers on one of several hooks by the door. He pushed to his feet and headed directly for his grandmother, who gathered him up.

"Is that right, sweetie? Would you like a piece of toast?"

"Cookie," he said.

"Not this early, my friend."

When they were seated at the table, Henry Reed in Marie's old high chair, Marie wasn't sure where to begin, though she'd lain awake thinking the entire night. She also wasn't sure how much she wanted to say in front of Mrs. Weitzel.

Her mother must have sensed her reluctance. "You and Paul have been talking?"

Marie nodded. "He came by last night."

"And he wants to come back home."

"How did you know?"

"He and Ken went out a couple of nights ago. Ken was pretty sure that's what he was going to do. What did you tell him?"

Mrs. Weitzel didn't interrupt, but like a curious bird, her eyes darted from Marie to Ellen.

"I told him I thought we should stay separated until we figured things out." Marie took a sip of coffee while she thought how to explain. "I guess I'm confused. I know a lot of what I did was wrong. I should have considered Paul more when I found out I was pregnant. We always had big plans—you know that. He wanted to design airplanes for

350

Boeing. I was going to teach. But I thought we could be happy with him working at the lumberyard, getting promoted, maybe go to work myself when Henry Reed started school, buy a house. That sort of thing. I mean, isn't that what everyone wants?"

Neither her mother nor Mrs. Weitzel disagreed.

"I should have listened to him about going to Montreal, too. I don't mean I think I shouldn't have gone, but I should have listened to his concerns more."

"How did he take your decision not to get back together right away?"

"I'm worried he might think I'm being petty and spiteful." Marie broke off another piece of toast for Henry Reed.

Her mother's head tilted to one side. "He knows you better than that."

Marie shrugged. "He said he talked to Ken about going back to school. I think that's what he wants to do. I called Pearl Whitebear this morning—woke her up, in fact. Anyway, she's going to have the university's Admissions Office send a packet of information to Paul. She said with his high school grades, he was sure to qualify for some scholarship money. And she told me about financial aid—student loans and even grants we wouldn't have to pay back."

Her mother nodded. "And what about you? Where do you fit into this scheme of things?"

"That's the part I'm not so sure of. I'm wondering if Henry Reed and I shouldn't just stay here. Moscow isn't that far away. Paul could see us on weekends. If he wants." A lump formed in her throat. She swallowed.

"Is that what you want? Is there any reason you and Henry Reed shouldn't go to Moscow, too?"

"I'm not sure I want to, Mom. I mean, I do want to. I love Paul, unconditionally, totally. But...I don't want him to think we're holding him back from what he wants to be. We've been together so long, maybe we need to take this time to find out who we are. As individuals, I mean. Does that make sense?" Would anyone ever know how much it cost her to say that?

Eyebrows raised, her mother looked askance. "But you seem to be willing to give up your own dreams to ensure Paul's dreams come true. Is that fair to you?"

"If, in the end, we're both happier, then yes, it would be." She looked away, unable to meet her mother's questioning eyes. Henry Reed had finished all the toast and was ready to get down. She wiped his hands and released the tray. "Okay, bubber. Go get 'em." He slithered out of the chair and immediately went to his grandmother to be picked up.

Ellen stood and carried Henry Reed to a box of toys she kept in the corner of the kitchen. "Here you go, sweetie. Here's a nice truck for you to play with. See. Look at it go." She sent the truck rolling along the floor and the baby clambered after it. She returned to the table. "If you do decide to stay in Platt City while Paul is in school, what would you do? I can't see you staying in that apartment all day long, taking care of Henry Reed."

"You're right. It would be too expensive, even if that were what I wanted to do. We couldn't afford an apartment here and a place for Paul in Moscow." She paused, her voice growing shaky. "But, supposing Henry Reed and I were to move back here—after Ken leaves—what would you think of that?"

Her mother stared at her.

"I could help—with deliveries, with the baking. To help pay for our room and board. Or I could get a job in town, maybe at the restaurant. I'd need to hire a babysitter." Grow up, she told herself. You're not a child. Her mother would want her there...want to be with her even if Paul didn't. She clamped her teeth together, determined not to start crying again.

"Well, honey, I hardly know what to say. Of course you can come and live here while Paul's in school—if you're absolutely sure it's what you really, really want to do. But I think you should go home and think about it some more. I'm wondering if you're not feeling guilty about what you think you've done to thwart Paul's dreams, and now you're trying to atone by giving up your own."

Marie frowned. "It's not like that."

"I think it's a lot like that. And no matter what you're feeling now, you're likely to regret it and resent it later." Marie started to interrupt but her mother held up a hand to stop her. "You and Paul need to talk about all your options. He loves you and Henry Reed very much. Frank does, too. I know you probably think this is a decision that affects only the two of you, but we're your family and it affects all of us."

Chapter Fourteen

ELLEN

Marie helped Henry Reed into his jacket. He was too young to help, but kept repeating "bye-bye." After Marie zipped his jacket, he wiggled free of her grip and reached his arms to Ellen.

Marie scooped him up. "No you don't, bubber. We're going home. Wave to Gramma and Mrs. Weitzel."

From the porch, Ellen watched Marie buckle the baby into his car seat before getting into the truck and starting the engine. As they drove off, emotion built in Ellen's chest. Marie was such a good mother. So patient—just like her father.

Shivering, she went back into the house and closed the door. She turned to Marta, who'd remained silent the whole time Marie was there. "Well. What do you think of that?"

"If she moves in, I think I should find another apartment. Henry Reed will need his own bedroom."

"You will do no such thing. You are family, too, and this is where you belong. We'll work out something for Henry Reed, if that's what it comes to. I just can't imagine it will though. Paul is and always has been the love of Marie's life. And vice versa."

"People change."

"Sometimes they have to." Like when someone dies and you suddenly need to make a new life for yourself. She sighed. "I can't see that happening with those two. I think this is just a bump in the road. They'll figure it out."

While the afternoon batch of bread was rising, Ellen put on jacket and boots. "I'm going for a walk."

Marta nodded. "Don't worry about the delivery. I'll make it if Ken's not back in time."

Ken had gone into town to see if there was anything else he needed to do about the helicopter fires before he left. Even though he'd be going back to the Marine Corps in two days, he'd apparently still not decided whether to re-enlist. Well, it was a big decision. She couldn't blame him for wanting to give it a lot of consideration. Just as she didn't blame Paul or Marie for the problems they were going through. She thought about what it would be like if Marie and Henry Reed were to live with her—how wonderful it would be to see her grandson every day.

She didn't want to go down that road. Once Marie considered it from all angles, she'd move to Moscow with Paul. Assuming going back to school was what Paul decided to do. Ellen was happy she didn't have to make those kinds of decisions any more. She'd made hers when she was their age. She didn't regret them then and she didn't regret them now. She hoped her children would be able to say the same when they were her age.

Four or five inches of new snow covered the ground, though it was clear under some of the trees. She found the deer path and followed it. The doe and her fawns—how big had they grown? A few birds darted from branch to branch. She threw out bread crumbs for them.

When she finally returned to the house, Ken met her at the door with a sandwich in his hand. "Hey, Mom."

She stomped snow off her boots before going inside. "How did your meeting go?"

"Good. They're pretty sure they know who did it. Some guy named William Dern. He's wanted for some other stuff, too."

"Good. I hope they catch him and put him in jail for a long time."

"Before someone gets killed. But that may be the hard part. Catching him, I mean. These guys can really go to ground. And there's a lot of places up in the mountains where someone can hide."

She nodded. From someone or something.

"Ian McCort told me they have the location of a couple of their camps though, so maybe they'll catch them." Ken slid a chair from the table and sat. "Sorry I didn't get back sooner. Mrs. Weitzel had her car loaded and was just leaving when I got home."

"She likes to help."

"I like her. At first it was kind of hard having her around all the time, but I got used to it. Do you want part of this sandwich? It's bigger than I thought."

Ellen shook her head. "I had a late breakfast." She joined him at the table. "I'm glad you like her. She thinks a lot of you, too. You and Marie. We've become her surrogate family; I'm her younger sister and you two are the children she never had."

"I guess a person can never have too much family," Ken said and gave her a sidelong look.

She'd wondered when he was going to bring that up again. "You and Marie have no doubt talked a lot about your Canadian relatives."

"They sound interesting. I guess I wonder how you feel about them."

"Me? I don't feel anything about them." She shrugged at his surprised look. "I only knew about Claudia and I wouldn't let myself think about her. When I was young, it would have been easy to try and compare myself to her, if I'd known what she was like. But I didn't. And then, I just didn't think about her anymore. Perhaps that's strange to you, but it's the way it was."

Ken nodded and swallowed a bite of sandwich. "Marie says she's pretty lonely now her daughter's grown up and married."

"Your half-sister, you mean." There, she'd said it.

"What do you think about that?"

"I should be asking you that question. What do you think of having a sister you never knew existed?"

He gazed at her a moment, then shrugged. "I don't know. I guess I'm not as consumed with curiosity as Marie."

"You never are."

"True. But you have to admit, it's pretty wild to think about. I can't help wondering what she's like, what she looks like. I guess I'd like to get to know her."

Ellen watched the emotions play across his face. She knew he was trying not to hurt her feelings.

He studied her as well. "What about Marie-Catherine and our grandfather? What do you think about them?"

"I wouldn't mind meeting them someday." Her words

surprised them both. "Maybe we could even be friends. We're certainly not enemies."

"And Jeannine?"

"I'm going to write and invite her to visit. She deserves to meet and get to know us, you and Marie, especially. Maybe she and her little girls can come the next time you're home on leave."

"I think that would be good, Mom. I think Dad would like that."

"I think he would, too."

Chapter Fifteen
MARIE

Marie lay in bed, listening to the near soundless breathing of Henry Reed, asleep in his crib, and the heavier breathing of Paul, lying next to her. Maybe she should pinch herself, make sure she wasn't dreaming. It seemed too perfect to be true; after all the tears, all the anguish, everything between her and Paul was going to be okay. He would be starting classes at the beginning of the next semester and with any luck, she would start in the fall. She was eager to see the apartment near the university Pearl Whitebear had told her about. It sounded perfect, especially after Paul said his father promised to help with the rent and other expenses. Her mother, too. Maybe they'd drive over to Moscow this weekend, after Ken left, to take a look at it.

The sky was beginning to lighten. It would be time to get up and fix breakfast before long. She slid her hand across the sheet to feel the reassuring warmth of Paul's body. What had she been thinking when she'd suggested to her mom and Mrs. Weitzel that she might stay in Platt City and let Paul go to Moscow on his own?

"Are you crazy?" he'd said when, her stomach twisted in knots, she brought it up to him the evening before. "You must be, to think I'd go and leave you here."

"But Paul. It might be for the best. You could concentrate on your studies better without us. And staying in a dorm would be cheaper."

"Marie," he said, taking her into his arms and stroking her cheek. "If I'm going to school for the next four or five years, I want you beside me. You and Henry Reed." He gazed into her eyes. "Besides, you'll be in school, too. We're going to do this together or we won't do it at all."

With that, she'd dissolved into tears. "This time you're going to have a real partner, I promise."

"I just want you."

She rolled onto her side, facing him in the bed. He opened his eyes, smiled and reached for her. Henry Reed slept on.

Chapter Sixteen

KEN

Ken headed back home from the restaurant after making the afternoon bread delivery, thinking about the rest of the gear he needed to pack and what was sure to be a long flight back to the East Coast the next morning. He came to the logging truck road and, on impulse, he turned onto it. Ignoring the No Trespassing sign, just as he and his friends had so often done in the past. He drove down the paved road until he came to a worn track just before the bridge. He turned and followed the track to clearing at the river's edge.

There were lingering signs of summer: a thick rope hanging from a bare tree branch; a pair of high-top red tennis shoes, tied together by the laces, dangling from another branch; some soda and beer cans sticking out of the snow. He turned off the engine, but didn't get out of the truck.

The laughter of his friends echoed all around him as he remembered summers past—the wild splashing, the horseplay, the crazy dares. Many times he'd come alone and sat on the rocks under the bridge, throwing stones at empty tin cans while a logging truck roared above his head. Sometimes, out of frustration or boredom, he'd recklessly swam to exhaustion, barely having strength to fight the current back to shore.

The last time he'd been there—when his anger at his father had erupted and his father had followed him to the river, when he'd told his father he was leaving, joining the Marine Corps—that was the memory closest to his heart.

He tried to recall what had sparked that particular fight, or rather, which particular hunting or fishing trip had started it, but it escaped him. Instead, the image of his mother crying at the sink came to mind. He'd been four or five. It was the image that had fueled his childhood and teenage anger. As he sat, though, another memory emerged. It must have happened about the same time. Maybe even the same hunting or fishing trip.

Ken, his mother and Marie were finishing dinner when they heard the familiar sound of his father's truck driving down the lane and pulling to a stop.

He didn't know how long his father had been gone. Most likely a week or two. Ken watched the stillness on his mother's face as his father's footsteps sounded on the porch. When the door opened and shut, a gust of wind sent sparks shooting up the chimney. Without a word, his father walked across the room to the table, then dropped down beside Marie's highchair, leaned over and retrieved her spoon from the floor. Ken saw again the loving look in his mother's eyes and the warm and welcoming smile that played across her lips as she reached out and rested a hand on his father's cheek.

Why had that memory remained submerged while the memory of his mother's tears stayed front and center? Had he been jealous all those years of his mother's love for his father? God, what a jerk he'd been.

He thought of the things Marie had found out about

their father beginning with the first visit from Pearl Whitebear, when Pearl Whitebear told Marie about their father's involvement with the FLQ. Even then, Ken knew in his heart his father could never have taken part in the things the FLQ was accused of doing. Yes, he'd written articles and made speeches and maybe they'd riled some folks. But his father hadn't been responsible for what other people did with their anger. That was on them.

And look what he'd done after coming to Idaho. Despite all Ken's accusations to the contrary, he had provided for his wife and family. For one thing, his mother would never have been able to start her business had his father not made those secret monthly additions to the insurance money left by her parents. And look at what he'd done for Ian McCort and Bill Tate—all with no fanfare and no thanks. Especially, no thanks from his son.

After Ken made his announcement, told his father he was joining the Marine Corps, his father had accepted his decision. They'd stayed on the riverbank, sitting shoulder-to-shoulder, listening to the river and talked about some of the hunting and fishing trips they'd taken, including the last one, up on the Imnaha River. "That's when you promised to teach me to drive. I wanted to impress Julie Frazier," Ken had said, adding with a laugh, "Too bad she moved away before I could learn and show off my skills."

A breeze had rustled the long, sweeping branches of the trees lining the far bank of the river, making their shadows toss and dance as they skipped across the water and climbed the bank to where Ken and his father sat. "It's time to go home," his father had finally said. "Your mother's waiting."

Ken stared across the river. The same trees lined the bank, their branches, now bare, whipped by the wind. *Oh, God, Dad. I know I said I hated you, but I didn't. I loved you. Why did you have to go and die before I could tell you?*

He made no effort to wipe away the tears spilling from his eyes and coursing down his cheeks. He thought again how his father had said he'd honor whatever path Ken chose.

All at once Ken's doubts and questions seemed to fall away. The Marine Corps was the path he'd chosen then and he knew, now, it was still the right path for him. Maybe, in a way, he was repeating what his father had done—running away. But he didn't think so. It wasn't that he was running away from anything—he'd miss home and everyone here, the mountains and rivers, too. It was more like he was running toward something. What that something was hadn't come into focus yet, but he knew it was out there, waiting for him.

The cold creeping into the truck's cab finally forced him to reach out and start the engine. It's time to go, he thought, almost echoing his father's words. He put the truck in gear. It shot forward.

About the Author
TONI MORGAN

Born in Alaska, raised in Oregon, where she studied history at Portland State University, and married in Hawaii, Toni Morgan has lived all over the United States, from California to Washington, D.C., and the world, from Denmark to Japan. She now makes her home in southwestern Idaho. She is the author of six novels: TWO-HEARTED CROSSING (2017) and PATRIMONY (2018) published by Adelaide Books; ECHOES FROM A FALLING BRIDGE, HARVEST THE WIND, LOTUS BLOSSOM UNFURLING, and QUEENIE'S PLACE in the pre-press process. Toni's articles and short stories have been published in various newspapers, literary magazines, and other publications (authortonimorgan.com)

www.ingramcontent.com/pod-product-compliance
Lightning Source LLC
Chambersburg PA
CBHW051115120726
47905CB00005B/1290